Transnational Families in Africa

Transnational Families in Africa

Migrants and the role of Information Communication Technologies

Edited by Maria C. Marchetti-Mercer, Leslie Swartz and Loretta Baldassar

WITS UNIVERSITY PRESS

Published in South Africa by:
Wits University Press
1 Jan Smuts Avenue
Johannesburg 2001

www.witspress.co.za

First published 2023

http://dx.doi.org.10.18772/22023128646

978-1-77614-864-6 (Paperback)
978-1-77614-865-3 (Hardback)
978-1-77614-878-3 (Web PDF)
978-1-77614-867-7 (EPUB)

This publication is peer reviewed following international best practice standards for academic and scholarly books.

This book will be made open access within three years of publication thanks to Path to Open, a program developed in partnership between JSTOR, the American Council of Learned Societies (ACLS), University of Michigan Press, and The University of North Carolina Press to bring about equitable access and impact for the entire scholarly community, including authors, researchers, libraries, and university presses around the world. Learn more at https://about.jstor.org/path-to-open/.

Project manager: Alison Lockhart
Copyeditor: Russell Martin
Proofreader: Alison Lockhart
Indexer: Sanet le Roux
Cover design: Hothouse
Typeset in 11 point Minion Pro

CONTENTS

FOREWORD

As someone who has lived in three countries, and has two adult children living in the northern hemisphere, to which I 'telecommute' while I rebuild my life back in my country of origin in the southern hemisphere, I, like the authors, can relate personally and intimately to the rich observations contained in this book. My research and clinical practice with transnational families and intercultural couples also informed my reading. My Basque grandparents could never have imagined that their economic exile in Chile when the Spanish Civil War started would set a path that several of my family relatives have also followed, because of a lack of job opportunities, because we wanted to pursue graduate studies abroad, or because we became political exiles. In some cases, as often happens to migrants, we long to go back, like my grandmother, who was never able to go back to Spain where her distant relatives and friends – as I found out while doing research in the Basque country – had missed her for decades. In speaking about this, I always wonder how her grief and longing would have been reshaped if Skype had been available to her.

Some of us have had the privilege of being part of a circular form of migration, going back to our countries of origin, some even living in the country where our grandparents began their adult lives.

Paradoxically, in the process, some of us returning to Spain found out that our ancestors had migrated from Italy, and there are other stories like this. My own children each hold three passports, a valuable inheritance for those of us who had to migrate because we lacked opportunities or because a dictatorship made our lives miserable. I can share many stories about the circular way in which millions live challenging lives, or are challenged by geopolitical borders that are actually fragile boundaries, epitomising how humanity has always been moving, albeit not always voluntarily or with outcomes that lead to a better life. I share these stories because this book is deeply personal, as much as it is the result of high-quality research with families from many countries. I feel privileged to have had the opportunity to be part of a cohort of transnational fellow world citizens, and also to have encountered one of the authors of this book in a meeting where dozens of researchers shared their work with transnational families all over the world.

Understanding migrations and their psychosocial and cultural impact is impossible without thinking about the impact of information communication technologies (ICTs), or social technologies, as I now call them. The research in this book adds to the evidence of the use of ICTs that has steadily developed in the last two decades, in parallel with the development of video conferencing and texting platforms, social platforms, and the spread of cell-phone usage. Some of the technologies have changed in these decades, too. Two to three decades ago, before cell phones became popular, for instance, we saw the rapid rise of shops in neighbourhoods with a high concentration of recent migrants that offered phone services and the first computers connected to the internet.

In this edited collection, the researchers highlight current conditions, and they invite readers to think about how structural inequities and the politics of migration require us to consider these social technologies as part of the intersectional distribution of power and wealth. ICTs per se can determine certain relationships, but access to them and levels of literacy determine which and how many of these tools are available to transnational families to connect and care across distance. The research in these chapters also provides evidence of another theoretical idea: distance is a social construction. Crossing two hundred kilometres can be as hard as crossing an ocean, depending on what tools are available to connect or to make possible face-to-face visits. The narratives in each of the chapters are based on ethnographic and in-depth interviews in several territories and with a variety of families in Africa.

Migrations are constitutive of our identities, and this research brings to the fore how this happens in several countries in Africa. This is the only book so far that analyses the mediating impact of social technologies on migration patterns across and within countries on the African continent. This research not only attends to those who leave Africa to find refuge in other continents but it also engages with the stories of migrants and refugees who have crossed national borders, as well as those who move from rural places to large cities. Distance is not so much a physical thing, as we learn in this research; distance can be more of an obstacle to family support and connection when relatives are only a hundred or two hundred kilometres away than when distance means taking an expensive flight. In the end, it is about the resources available.

The variety of migration patterns and the diverse set of technologies that are or can be adopted make comparative analysis of technology usage, adoption and impact difficult. Technologies are also evolving at a rapid pace. However, some patterns do emerge in the analysis, and the data in their complexity and nuance provide us with some compelling directions to take if we wish to create practices and policies to support these migrants. Probably one of the lessons for which this research provides good evidence is that technology use is not only multidimensional, but can also intensify and reproduce various forms of inequality. The pathos of immigration, with its associated suffering and pain, as well as its opportunities, is unequally distributed. ICTs in themselves do not overcome the structural inequities that the carriers of vulnerability have to deal with.

If you are new to this research topic, the book not only explains the basics of the role of ICTs in supporting migrants' connection and well-being, but also points out the naivety of simplistic conclusions. ICTs may mitigate separation and create seemingly co-present relationships between family members across physical distance. In the research you are about to read, however, the authors question the often optimistic and technocratic assessment of how positive ICT use has been for the well-being of trans-national families, a phenomenon that is increasingly common in a world that seems more interconnected. The challenges that transnational families confront in keeping family members connected across distance are not new, but while our ability to connect virtually may seem revolutionary to our generation, ICT use is also a challenge for many families. For instance, virtual communications require negotiating silence and what is told to the other and when. This is not something that can be taken for granted. Most social media are about performativity, so connecting virtually leads to questions about how and what to perform. Our public and private selves are in a continuous dialogue that can be tested when they are on display in synchronous and asynchronous forms of communication. The immediacy of the connection may preclude the thoughtfulness and delayed response implied when in the past a letter may have been written, or presents were sent at some expense and trouble through the post, or a prohibitively expensive phone call was made. This book provides us with a framework to address these questions without simplifying the answers. It always contextualises not only the world of intersubjectivity, but also the intersectional social, cultural and political dimensions that determine how this subjectivity is played out.

For those learning research methodology, this book also sheds light on the particularities of conducting transnational qualitative research; you will find great lessons not only on how to situate our empathetic listening to the participants in our interviews, but also on how to embed the analysis in our own experiences as transnational researchers. Qualitative data analysis is always influenced by the context, as much as by the subject of study. In this case, we are studying the impact of a tool that we also use.

The similarities between the methodology and the research question are addressed up front. In sum, the research narrative reflects well the practice of fruitful reflexivity. This attention to reflexivity is explicit, as the authors set out to compare the findings that emerge in different contexts and from immigrants defined by different determinants and immigration pathways. In that sense, comparing, and questioning the comparisons, form a refreshing exercise. It is helpful to recognise the parallels that may exist between rural–urban migration and inter-country migration: it is not distance as an objective variable that matters, but how distance is constructed and defined by social and political determinants. True, all immigrants need to adapt to difficult circumstances, but this adaptation is not a psychological construct that is devoid of its contextual determinants. Learning about the migration from and to other countries (Zimbabwe, Malawi, Kenya and the Democratic Republic of Congo) and within South Africa, as well as the out-migration to non-African countries, is a lesson about how technology mediates all forms of psychosocial processes, including how we manage intimacy, secrets and boundaries. Some of these psychosocial processes may be associated with adolescence, but that developmental task seems to be ongoing in our lives as we adopt a digital-platform-driven world where everyone has to intentionally define how to perform the self. Similar processes occur among transnational individuals who are working through family cut-offs, trauma and abuse and, overall, managing the suffering and silences that are required as they build a new life elsewhere.

Despite these parallels, and despite the high hopes around the death of distance, we cannot assume, as this research shows, that this negotiation is devoid of limitations and burdens. We do not all share access to the same tools or have the same ability to use them. Inequality is rampant. As reported in this book, less-resourced migrants may use cell phones, but they may not be able to access applications that lower the cost of communicating. If distance is a social construction, 'mobility capital' is a currency that may impact most on how that distance is perceived, since the resources to travel determine the characteristics of virtual communication and how it develops. As the evidence here suggests, virtual communication changes and intensifies from the pre- to the post-travel period. In a similar fashion, 'bodies considered normal' are also more able to interact virtually and to travel. Those bodies that need more care and support are affected more severely by the limitations of virtual communications in satisfying the need for care.

On a different note, one that is also related to the way economic determinants contextualise the psychology of migration, the book investigates how families construe the rationale for leaving their country of origin. Remittances are key for many – it provides proof of why the costs of distance are bearable – but that is not always the reason for leaving. As we read in Chapter 9: 'in the final analysis, all the migrants and their families in our samples relied heavily on technology to maintain relationships with their loved ones, but their access to technology, suitable devices and adequate infrastructure, as well as the financial means to maintain ICT use, differed greatly'.

The researchers are to be commended for staying the course, even in the context of a pandemic. This book is respectful and cares for those who shared their stories. It is a privilege to have been one of the first to read this manuscript, to be part of the journey. I wholeheartedly invite you to read the stories with the same empathetic ear, as they add to the knowledge we need to understand the families that construct closeness through distance.

Gonzalo Bacigalupe, EdD, MPH
Professor of Counselling Psychology
University of Massachusetts, Boston

ACKNOWLEDGEMENTS

This book is the product of the work of a very dedicated team of individuals whose passion and hard work we have to acknowledge. First of all, we thank the original team members, who often worked under very difficult and challenging circumstances, especially during the Covid-19 pandemic. Thank you also to the colleagues who joined us from other parts of Africa as the project unfolded: Ms Glory Kabaghe from the MAC-Communicable Diseases Action Centre at the College of Medicine in Blantyre, Malawi, and Professor Josephine Arasa, from the School of Humanities and Social Sciences at the United States International University in Nairobi, Kenya, who assisted us with data collection in those countries.

This book is based on research supported wholly by the National Research Foundation (NRF) of South Africa, Grant Number: 118578. The financial assistance of the NRF towards this research is hereby acknowledged. Opinions expressed and conclusions arrived at are those of the authors and are not necessarily to be attributed to the NRF.

We are very grateful that the NRF saw potential in this project and was prepared to support it financially. We are especially proud of the postgraduate students Lactricia, Thembelihle, Risuna, Siko and Sonto, who were funded by the NRF and who made vital contributions to this book. We know that their careers will soar.

We also owe a great debt of gratitude to the staff at Wits University Press, especially Roshan Cader, for supporting us through the complexities of the publishing process. We would also like to thank the two anonymous reviewers for giving up their time to go through the initial manuscript and for the very helpful and constructive feedback – we believe that the quality of this book has been much enhanced by their insights and knowledge of the field, and by the expert editing of Russell Martin.

Thank you also to Dr Idette Noomé from the Department of English, University of Pretoria, who assisted with the process of language editing, for her invaluable insights and meticulous work.

Last, but never least, we also would like to thank our families for their support throughout this whole process.

Maria C. Marchetti-Mercer, Leslie Swartz and Loretta Baldassar
Johannesburg, Stellenbosch and Perth
March 2023

PART 1

THEORETICAL CONTEXT

1

Setting the Scene

Maria C. Marchetti-Mercer, Leslie Swartz and Loretta Baldassar

HOW THE PROJECT CAME ABOUT

We often assume that for people to take care of each other, geographical closeness is essential – the traditional understanding of care between family members presupposes physical proximity between these individuals. This applies particularly to the hands-on tasks involved in looking after children or caring for elderly relatives or people with disabilities. But is this always true? What options are open to family members who have been separated by migration?

The issue of proximity and care has received attention in the literature exploring the experiences of migrant and transnational families (see, for example, Brandhorst, Baldassar and Wilding 2020; Baldassar et al. 2016; Kilkey and Merla 2014; Merla, Kilkey and Baldassar 2020; Mazzucato and Schans 2011; Schmalzbauer 2004). It is clear that today new forms of communication can play a central role in maintaining family relationships across distance, as several studies have confirmed, though some have also questioned this (see, for example, Baldassar 2007b, 2008, 2016b; Horst 2006; Madianou 2012, 2016; Madianou and Miller 2013;

Marchetti-Mercer 2012a, 2012b, 2016, 2017; Marchetti-Mercer and Swartz 2020; Nedelcu and Wyss 2016; Wilding 2006). The value of information communication technologies (ICTs) in maintaining relationships despite geographical distance has become even more prominent in the last few years, when lockdowns were implemented in many countries and across borders to counter the Covid-19 pandemic. These lockdowns forced families into physical separation even if they lived in the same city, sometimes even in the same house; hence, people came to rely heavily on technology to stay in contact and support each other across a distance (Brandhorst, Baldassar and Wilding 2020; Merla, Kilkey and Baldassar 2020). The importance of ICTs in maintaining and supporting family relationships is now no longer a strategy of migrant and transnational families only, but a global experience.

In this complex global context, this book explores experiences of migration and proximity with specific reference to South Africa, a country historically defined and characterised by various highly diverse migratory trends, including outward, inward and internal mobility.

Internal African migration began in the colonial period and apartheid years (1948 to 1994) when mostly black men moved to urban areas to seek employment, while their families stayed behind in the rural areas (Posel 2004; Reed 2013; Von Fintel and Moses 2017). Families were split up, and there were few means of communication to maintain relationships. Visits back home were difficult because of the distance and travelling costs, and were often confined to specific times of the year. Despite the demise of apartheid in 1994, this 'circular' migratory trend is still evident today (Bennett et al. 2015; Posel 2004), as black people still move to urban areas, where more economic possibilities are available to them. As we show in Chapter 3, internal migration in South Africa – even across what may appear rather short distances – remains an important feature of South African migration. Older people and children still stay behind in the rural areas, and family relationships continue to be affected by this distance (Mlambo 2018), despite the increased ability to stay connected by means of new ICTs.

South Africa has high mobile-phone penetration – it was estimated in 2017 that 18.48 million people had access to a smartphone; this figure was expected to exceed 25 million by 2022 (Statista 2018).[1] More recent data point to the fact that there was an increase in both mobile cellular subscriptions (nine million) and smartphone subscriptions (five million) between 2020 and 2021 (ICASA 2022). However, sub-Saharan Africa in general still does not match the level of connectivity in other parts of the world, with smartphones accounting for less than half of the total mobile connections (GSMA 2021). Our research indicates that most local migrants and their families in rural areas have limited financial resources. This constrains their access to technology, and makes data costs difficult to afford.

Another migratory trend in South Africa is emigration to other parts of the world (see Marchetti-Mercer 2012a, 2012b; Myburgh 2004). This trend increased during the apartheid years, when several emigration waves were linked to moments of political crisis or rapid change. After the coming of the new democratic dispensation in 1994, outward migration, particularly of educated, highly qualified and skilled South Africans, has continued, a trend which has been described as a 'brain drain' (Hagopian et al. 2004). Although thus far most of these migrants seem to be white people, other South Africans are increasingly joining this trend (Crush 2002; Gwaradzimba and Shumba 2010; Marchetti-Mercer 2012a). One result is that a large number of elderly people are 'left behind', while their children and grandchildren live abroad.

A third migratory phenomenon is the increasing influx to South Africa of migrants from other parts of Africa (Adepoju 2003; Gordon 2015; Wentzel and Tlabela 2006). There is a historical precedent for this, but this inward movement has escalated enormously since 1994, following the opening up of South Africa's borders. These migrants are a diverse group, ranging from refugees fleeing unstable political or economic situations to economic migrants attracted by possibilities of employment. They come from other countries in the Southern African Development Community (SADC) or other parts of Africa. A vast number of them enter the country undocumented (Segatti 2011): approximately ten per cent of the people living in South Africa may be undocumented migrants (Owusu-Sekyere and Willis 2022).

Each type of migration has its own specificities, so those involved report significantly different life experiences. But they have one experience in common – and that is the focus of this book: the inevitable creation of transnational families whose members are separated by geographical distance, requiring them to make an effort to stay connected despite what at times may feel like insurmountable challenges.

The chapters in this book are based on the findings of two research projects exploring the impact of different South African migration patterns on families separated by distance. The first of these projects, led by Maria C. Marchetti-Mercer and Leslie Swartz, focused on outward migration from South Africa to other (mainly non-African) countries, especially the United Kingdom, the United States, Australia, Canada, New Zealand and the United Arab Emirates. The second project, described at length in this book, was led by Maria C. Marchetti-Mercer, Leslie Swartz and Loretta Baldassar, and widened the focus to include African migrants moving to South Africa, as well as the local internal migration of rural and urban families, which is closely linked to South Africa's history of forced migration (Wentzel and Tlabela 2006). We consider internal African migration, as well as migration into South Africa from other African countries, as there is still only limited research on this topic. The first project focused on the impact of international migration to non-African countries on elderly family members left behind; the second had a specific focus on the use of ICTs in maintaining family relationships, and looked more specifically at migration in Africa.

An important part of our investigation was to examine issues of access to ICTs and possible differences in this regard between the diverse groups under discussion. At the start of the project, we assumed that economic hardship might inhibit poorer communities' access to technology, given the high cost of data in South Africa, and this assumption was proved correct. We found that ICTs are essential to maintaining relationships of care across large distances, but there are inequities in access to ICTs: these findings support Baldassar's argument that the 'freedom to connect to the internet today is also about the right to access care and support networks' (2016a, 160). Limited access to technology as a means of communication therefore not only constrains access to knowledge and information – which is recognised by the United Nations as a human right (La Rue 2011) – but also constrains migrant families' capacity to care for each other when they are separated. Such inequities require us to advocate for a form of 'digital justice', which may be of particular relevance to developing African countries such as South Africa (Eko 2013).

WHO ARE THE RESEARCHERS?

The ICT project involved collaboration between 13 researchers at different stages of their careers. Most of us can draw on our own experiences of being separated from our families through migration. The ways in which our own stories are linked provide some important context for how this book was born and how we came to write it.

The three principal authors and editors share personal, professional and cultural links, and all have their own experiences of migration. *Maria C. Marchetti-Mercer* is an Italian-born clinical psychologist and family therapist who emigrated to South Africa as a child. She is now working as a professor of psychology at the University of the Witwatersrand, in Johannesburg, South Africa. Much of her research in the last 15 years has focused on the impact of emigration on South African families. *Leslie Swartz* is a fellow clinical psychologist and professor of psychology at Stellenbosch University. He has published widely in the field of disability studies. His family migrated to South Africa from Zimbabwe (then Rhodesia) when he was a child. Leslie and Maria have worked together on both projects referred to in this book. *Loretta Baldassar* is a professor of anthropology and sociology and director of the Social Ageing (SAGE) Futures Lab at Edith Cowan University, Perth, Western Australia. Loretta has published extensively in the field of migration, focusing especially on the role of ICTs in maintaining relationships of care in transnational families. Maria connected with Loretta after reading Loretta's book *Visits Home: Migration Experiences between Italy and Australia* (2001). Loretta's mother and her family migrated to Australia from Sondrio, Italy, in the early 1900s; her father arrived in Australia from the Veneto region during the massive influx of southern Europeans after the Second World War. Maria's family of origin also comes from Veneto. They thus share similar family histories and experiences around migration and growing up as second-generation Italian migrants in countries where English is the lingua franca. Maria visited Loretta in Perth in 2017; this was the start of the relationship that would form the basis for the book. Leslie and Loretta have never met in person but have used ICTs to connect and discuss the project. Despite the distance, we have published an article together (Marchetti-Mercer, Swartz and Baldassar 2021) and have managed the second research project that forms a large part of this book.

The background of the rest of the team also reflects many of the themes/areas that were investigated in the project. *Ajwang' Warria* was a senior lecturer in the Department of Social Work at the University of the Witwatersrand at the time of the second research project but moved to the University of Calgary, in Canada, at the end of 2022. She is originally from Kenya and moved to South Africa in 2002. Her research has focused mainly on migration, child protection and intervention research. *Esther Price* was a clinical psychologist and lecturer at the University of the Witwatersrand at the time of the study, but she lived in Malawi for several years prior to that. She too has recently moved to Canada and is working with FVB Psychologists in Mississauga, Ontario. Her work includes research on bullying and peer victimisation, as well as trauma and post-traumatic stress. *Daniella Rafaely* is a lecturer in the Department of Psychology at the University of the Witwatersrand. She studies social interaction, social categories and common-sense knowledge, using a range of discursive methodologies.

A number of postgraduate students also formed part of the team. *Sonto Madonsela* acted as manager of this research project and book as part of her National Research Foundation (NRF) internship in the Department of Psychology at the University of the Witwatersrand. *Lactricia Maja* completed her Master's degree in social and psychological research at the University of the Witwatersrand in 2021. She originally comes from Lebowakgomo, Limpopo Province, but came to Johannesburg in 2004 to pursue her Master's studies. *Thembelihle Coka* completed a Master's degree in research psychology at the University of the Witwatersrand in 2021, although her family lives in Dundee, KwaZulu-Natal Province. *Siko Moyo* is originally from Bulawayo in Zimbabwe, where he still has family. He came to the University of the Witwatersrand to pursue his studies and completed his Master's degree in community-based counselling psychology there. *Risuna Mathebula* completed her Master's degree in community-based counselling psychology at the University of the Witwatersrand in 2022. She is originally from Giyani in Limpopo and came to Soweto as a young child.

Lastly, we were fortunate to connect with two colleagues in two of the African countries that we included in our data collection: Malawi and Kenya. *Glory Kabaghe* works at the MAC-Communicable Diseases Action Centre at the College of Medicine in Blantyre, Malawi. Her professional background is in community-based nursing. We were also joined by Professor *Josephine Arasa*, who works in the School of Humanities and Social Sciences at the United States International University in Nairobi, Kenya, and who assisted with the data collection in Kenya.

WHAT WILL YOU FIND IN THIS BOOK?

This book is the product of the work of different people, mostly from a professional social sciences background. None of us would necessarily see ourselves as experts in migration studies (except for Loretta Baldassar) or demography, so you will find that our angles in writing the various chapters reflect a focus on family relationships and a quasi-therapeutic interest in the experiences of our participants, as that is the overwhelming focus of most of our professional work. This is not a book about 'hard facts' and statistics but about the stories of people who have experienced the highs and lows of family separation as a result of migration. It is about how they have engaged with the technologies available to them (despite the limitations of accessing and using these technologies) to stay connected with their much-longed-for distant families. Some of those we spoke to are people who have had to face the challenges of moving to a new country or a strange new city that is often neither welcoming nor supportive of strangers, but who still want to care for those they have left behind. Some of them shared their stories as family members left behind – several were elderly people who see their children and grandchildren leave to go to unfamiliar places, with all the fears and anxieties of loss, but also with all the hopefulness that such a departure can bring. We explore the challenges and opportunities presented by one tool available to them to prevent a loss of connection and emotional ties: the mobile phone. In many cases, this is not a smartphone but often an old 'brick' with outdated features and large buttons. This tool with its different applications – apps for short (often very few apps) – has become the main enduring link that they have with their distant loved ones, other than rare visits. Our study also highlights the complexities related to visits, as well as how distance is experienced differently, depending on people's socio-economic status. Something we could not initially have envisaged, the impact of the Covid-19 pandemic, also became an important focus of the research as we witnessed the negative impact of the pandemic on families' opportunities to see each other and to recharge and revitalise family relationships.

The stories of our participants vary: some of them have more access to advanced technology, either because of financial access to better-quality mobile phones, or because of their youth and digital literacy. Other stories reflect the sad reality that when you face financial constraints every day of your life, spending money on sophisticated mobile phones or even the data to use the different apps may not be a priority or a possibility. In these situations, people may have to forgo the opportunity to stay connected to their loved ones, or may have to share phones with friends and neighbours when they are desperate to be in touch. Elderly people who struggle with new technologies also encounter challenges related to physical deterioration, such as loss of sight or hearing, and increasing difficulty with fine motor skills. These are some of the stories we share in this book.

As the title suggests, we want to offer an African perspective on the phenomenon of transnational families, their experiences of migration and caring across distance, and their use of ICTs. You might ask what distinguishes African transnational families based in Africa from other families researched elsewhere. While there are many similarities between them, the vast majority of the literature focuses on transnational families who have members living in the Global North (such as those described in the recent volume edited by Javiera Cienfuegos, Rosa Brandhorst and Deborah Fahy Bryceson 2023). Our book is distinctive in its focus on transnational families whose members live in different countries in Africa, all of which form part of the Global South. The stories we heard foregrounded kinship, the importance of the extended family, and the centrality of obligations towards one's family of origin as important factors. All these dimensions play a role in the type of relationships maintained even after individual family members migrate from their place of origin. Not surprisingly, they are also often the main areas of concern and care that feature in ICT use.

INTERNATIONAL BACKGROUND TO THIS RESEARCH

Prior work on the role of ICTs in maintaining family relationships despite geographical separation has centred around the experiences of 'transnational' families, defined as families in which some members have migrated but still maintain strong links with family in their country of origin. The concept of the transnational migrant was developed in the work of Nina Glick Schiller, Linda G. Basch and Cristina Blanc-Szanton (1992), who described a new type of migrating population that has at its disposal networks, activities and ways of life that reflect both their host countries and their countries of origin. Their work heralded a 'transnational turn' in migration studies that foregrounds the shared 'social field' of ongoing connections between home and host communities – Alexis Silver points out that 'once migrants travel across the border, their families do not cease to be active influences in their lives' (2011, 213).

Several researchers emphasise the crucial role of ICTs in this process. An early example is Raelene Wilding, who comments: 'The use of ICTs is important for some transnational families in constructing or imagining a "connected relationship", and enabling them to overlook their physical separation by time and space – even if only temporarily' (2006, 132). Gonzalo Bacigalupe and Susan Lambe report that ICTs now link 'millions for the purpose of sharing information and memories, exchanging wealth and products, organizing events, and much more. They are a splendid opportunity to maintain legacies, create new memories, and establish a coherent identity and continuity for family members' (2011, 22).

Opportunities and constraints on our capacity for family and social connection across distance provided by the ever-increasing digital technologies available are captured by Mirca Madianou and Daniel Miller's (2013) reflections on 'polymedia' environments, in which the ability to choose between different types of ICTs (see also Baldassar and Merla 2014) affords a variety of experiences of different kinds of co-presence across distance. For example, access to an 'always on' device can provide a sense of constant ambient co-presence with distant loved ones, even when no messages or calls are actually exchanged (Madianou 2016). New communication technologies and advances in modes of travel can enable transnational emotional interaction (Baldassar 2007a, 2007b), including 'virtual', 'imaged' and 'proxy' forms of co-presence (Baldassar 2008, 252). Loretta Baldassar, Raelene Wilding and Cora Baldock (2007) have examined how these kinds of interaction through technology allow for relationships that are mutually supportive, despite distance.

Increasing access to ever-expanding polymedia environments may mean that distance will in future no longer be a key defining issue in maintaining transnational family relations. However, there is a caveat: the potential of ICTs to be the 'death of distance' is limited by the very real inequalities of differential access. The importance of physical contact in maintaining relationships must also be considered, particularly forms of physical contact that cannot easily be replaced by technology, including hands-on caregiving, especially for people who are ill, are dependent on others for physical care, or have physical impairments (Marchetti-Mercer 2012b, 2016; Marchetti-Mercer and Swartz 2020; Mulder and Cooke 2009), or for young children. The question then is under what conditions technology is most likely to deliver an adequate sense of co-presence across distance. We need to recognise the full spectrum of ICT-mediated relationships across distance, including instances where the technology delivers a mere 'illusion of intimacy' (Marchetti-Mercer 2012b; Wilding 2006). What are the intersectional factors at play, including the degree of internet access, the kind of digital tools and the level of digital literacy required? What is the impact of factors such as age and physical capacity, the stage in the migration and family life cycle, the density of support networks, gender, birth order, regional background, class, and ethnicity? Is some degree of physical presence and interaction always needed to meet our human need for interaction (Marchetti-Mercer 2017)? In this regard, Baldassar (2016a, 2016b) argues that it is not helpful to oppose the notions of virtual and physical co-presence or even attempt to assess whether virtual co-presence can approximate physical forms of being together. Rather, we should consider how different forms of co-presence in transnational family relations are co-constitutive and inter-relational (Baldassar 2016b), for example, by exploring how physical forms of co-presence during visits and virtual forms of co-presence online together contribute to building family relationships across distance.

A common theme in all the stories from our South African data suggests that leaving one's family and region or country of origin, even if it offers several gains, has a price. When migrants decide to leave, they report experiencing strong feelings of guilt unless they are given a 'licence to leave' by their families (Baldassar 2015, 87). This permission by those left behind is often necessary to maintain positive relationships beyond the moment of migration. Distance may also evoke guilt at not being present for each other to provide support and care to meet perceived family obligations (Baldassar 2007b). Baldock (2003) uses Janet V. Finch's (1989) work to explore the concept of family obligations that are negotiated over time in the context of a specific family and are often linked to cultural understandings and practices. Obligations may also reflect the particularistic identities of individuals and their acceptable roles in the family (Finch and Mason 1993). Furthermore, Baldassar (2015) argues that the very act of migration, because of the physical separation it causes, places a migrant in a potential moral bind, especially in respect of the obligation to care for ageing parents. Providing mutual emotional and practical support is often an important aspect of the child–parent relationship, but these tasks may be more challenging to negotiate for families that are separated.

We conducted the research for this book mindful that prior studies in this area have focused mostly on the experiences of more resourced communities and societies in wealthier nations. Although there is a growing literature on African transnational families, the migrant members of these families investigated in the literature are mostly located in the Global North (see Caarls et al. 2018; Cebotari, Mazzucato and Appiah 2018; Coe 2008; Mazzucato and Cebotari 2017; Mazzucato et al. 2015; Stulgaitis 2015; Sutton 2004; Yount-André 2018). The bulk of recent work on the impact on family lives in the South African context has focused on middle-class individuals leaving the country (for example, Jithoo, Marchetti-Mercer and Swartz 2020; Marchetti-Mercer 2012a, 2012b, 2016, 2017; Marchetti-Mercer et al. 2020), and it does not yet address a very large part of the migratory experience in South Africa. There is thus an urgent need for a book that reflects experiences relating specifically to the Global South.

SOUTH AFRICAN MIGRATORY BEHAVIOUR AND THE USE OF ICTs

South African society has been profoundly shaped by migration, notably by colonial settlement and land dispossession, mainly in the nineteenth to mid-twentieth centuries. Preben Kaarsholm (2019) argues that, in order to maintain order and power, like the preceding colonial governments, the apartheid state in the twentieth century controlled the movement of populations and residential spaces through extensive identification, registration, monitoring and classification technologies (see also Bonnet 2021). The resulting class, race and gender structures still mark South African society (Marchetti-Mercer 2017). The migration of especially men from across the subcontinent to urban areas for low-paid work continues. It is therefore not surprising that migratory movements and behaviour still characterise the very fabric of South African society.

Migrant Labourers

During the colonial and apartheid eras, black South Africans were dispossessed of much of their land and confined to 'native reserves', which became known as 'homelands' or Bantustans, where living conditions were unsustainable. To earn a living, black African men and often women left these areas in search of employment in urban centres, leaving their families behind (Casale 2004; Posel and Casale 2003; Reed 2013). Many men sought employment in the mines on the Witwatersrand and elsewhere in the country (Ramphele 1993), while women took up employment as domestic workers in white urban homes (Phillips and James 2014). Children were often left in the care of grandparents and extended family members. This migrant labour had a profound impact on black South Africans and their family lives. Families were often separated, with limited means of communication and opportunities to visit loved ones (Murray 1981; Ramphele 1993; Van Onselen 2021).

Despite the advent of democracy, this pattern of migration remains evident, because the legacy of apartheid's economic inequalities continues to be reflected in the vast economic disparity between the white and new upper- and middle-class black population, on the one hand, and the majority of the black population, on the other. Many black people from the poorer and under-resourced rural areas still move to urban areas such as Johannesburg and Pretoria in order to look for jobs or self-employment opportunities, leaving older people and children behind.

This national political economy of migrant labour is also reflected in the more recent global domestic migrant-worker care chains characterised by the movement of poor women from the Global South to take up care-worker jobs in the Global North, leaving behind their children, often in the care of grandmothers (Yeates 2012).

What has changed, however, is the possibility of contact between separated family members, which has been greatly increased by the introduction of mobile phone communication. Most people in South Africa possess mobile phones. According to Statistics South Africa's general household survey conducted in 2018, a massive 89.5% of South African households exclusively use cellular phones. However, according to the same survey, only 10.4% of households have internet at home, though 64.7% of South African households surveyed reported at least one member who had access to or used the internet whether at home, at work, in their place of study or at internet cafes. Household access to the internet at home was highest in the Western Cape (25.8%) and Gauteng (16.7%) and lowest in Limpopo (1.7%), from where the rural participants in our study came. These figures highlight the fact that the advent of mobile access to the internet has made such access much more possible for households in rural areas, which is more common than internet access at home. Although the use of mobile internet access devices in rural areas (45%) still lags behind their use in metro (67.5%) and urban areas (63.7%), it is much more common in rural areas than any of the alternative ICTs (Statistics South Africa 2018a, 58). However, the cost of data remains very expensive compared with that in First World countries and even some other African countries, making this kind of communication difficult to afford.

Contemporary 'Brain Drain' from South Africa

Marchetti-Mercer (2012a, 2012b, 2016, 2017) has described the phenomenon of South African out-migration to non-African countries in a number of works. During the apartheid era (1948–1994), South Africa experienced migration waves mostly linked to political moments such as the Soweto uprising in 1976 and its aftermath, and the states of emergency and political persecution and bannings under apartheid. However, emigration from post-apartheid South Africa continues (Marchetti-Mercer 2012a, 2012b, 2016), mainly to English-speaking countries, especially Australia, New Zealand, Canada, the United Kingdom and the United States (Crush 2000). Recently, the United Arab Emirates (UAE) has also become a popular destination, especially Dubai and Abu Dhabi (Höppli 2014). The official statistical data and the estimates collected by Thomas Höppli (2014) indicate that the total number of South African-born immigrants in 23 destination countries reached about 750 000 in 2013. The unofficial figures may be considerably higher. This phenomenon has been described as a 'brain drain' by Jonathan Crush (2002), because many who leave the country have very specialised skills. There is a widespread perception that this migration is restricted to the white segment of the population, but in fact it seems that black professionals have recently begun to outnumber white emigrants as they join the global skills market (RSA 2017). Their leaving has consequently had a widespread social and economic impact.

One salient aspect of this migratory phenomenon is the increasing number of elderly people left behind, with a reduced support system, when their children migrate (Antman 2010; Horowitz and Kaplan 2001; Marchetti-Mercer 2009, 2012a, 2012b, 2016; Marchetti-Mercer et al. 2020). There is a broader literature on the impact of migration on older people left behind (see, for example, Vullnetari and King 2008). Their well-being may become the responsibility of siblings or other family members left behind, who then have to take on the burden of care for these ageing parents. This is also likely to affect family relationships and dynamics (Marchetti-Mercer 2016; Marchetti-Mercer et al. 2020).

African Migration into South Africa

In her overview of the phenomenon of African migration into South Africa, Alida Bonnet (2021) explains that the apartheid state created extensive migration systems. The aim of this was to supply the workforce in the agricultural and mining sectors (Gordon 2015). As a result, migrants were often recruited from neighbouring countries to work as cheap labour in South African mining, industry and agriculture (Gordon 2015). Aderanti Adepoju (2003) lists Botswana, Lesotho, Malawi, Mozambique and Eswatini (then known as Swaziland) as countries from which labour was commonly recruited. The migrant labourers were housed in single-sex hostels and were segregated from their families in the same way as black South African labourers (Adepoju 2003; Kaarsholm 2019).

Following the election of a democratic government in 1994, the numbers of migrants and refugees into South Africa have grown enormously (Gordon 2015; Kalitanyi and Visser 2010; Posel 2004; Rutherford 2008), making South Africa one of the key destinations in Africa today for economic immigrants and asylum seekers (Gordon 2015; Mosselson 2010). Bonnet (2021) agrees with Loren B. Landau (2005a) that the increased access afforded to foreign nationals may be an attempt by post-apartheid South Africa to become more integrated into the global community.

Africa Check (2016) released a report outlining the most salient trends in this migration phenomenon, showing the status quo up to 2016. This report used figures from the last census in 2011 (Statistics South Africa 2015) and Statistics South Africa's (2016) *Community Survey*. This survey showed that about three-quarters of South Africa's international inward migrants come from other African countries, mainly from other SADC countries, notably South Africa's landlocked neighbours, Lesotho and Eswatini; Zimbabwe and Mozambique in the north-east; and Namibia in the west, as well as further afield, including Malawi, a historical source of labour in South Africa. Only 7.3% of these migrants came from non-SADC countries (Africa Check 2016). Other African sources of migrants are the Democratic Republic of Congo (DRC), Nigeria and Kenya (Africa Check 2016). Many DRC immigrants are refugees. Kenyan migrants also differ from the other groups as they tend to be highly skilled, travel with valid visas, and come to South Africa for professional and study purposes (Marchand, Reinold and Dias e Silva 2017). Some non-African sources include the United Kingdom and China, India and Pakistan (Africa Check 2016).

Statistics South Africa has conducted three censuses since the advent of democracy, in 1996, 2001 and 2011, and the 2022 census was in progress at the time of writing this book. We have consulted a number of mid-year population estimates to reflect on recent migration trends (see, for example, Statistics South Africa 2018b, 2021).

Statistics South Africa's (2015) report on migration dynamics points out that the pattern of international inward migration has changed since 1994 to include a greater variety of migrants, ranging from skilled to low-skilled people, and from documented to undocumented migrants. This is in contrast to apartheid-era regional labour migrants, who traditionally came from countries such as Lesotho and Eswatini, Malawi, Mozambique and Zimbabwe, and who were mostly employed in the mining industry (Statistics South Africa 2015, 129). South Africa is an important migration destination because of a number of 'pull' factors, including better socio-economic or educational opportunities, better social infrastructure than in their home countries, and a relatively stable political situation (Statistics South Africa 2015). Conversely, 'push' factors leading to migration to South Africa include political unrest in many African countries, together with economic crises and even environmental degradation; these have led to a rise in the number of displaced persons on the continent (Statistics South Africa 2015, 123). Zimbabwe is a case in point: as a result of that country's political instability, roughly 45% of all immigrants to South Africa in 2011 were Zimbabwean.

Once in South Africa, most foreign migrants settle in Gauteng, because it is regarded as the economic centre of South Africa (Landau 2005a, 2005b). The largest population of migrants of foreign birth live in Gauteng, followed by the Western Cape (Statistics South Africa 2015), which had the second-highest percentage (12%) of foreign migrants in the 2011 census. Next came KwaZulu-Natal, followed by Limpopo, North West and Mpumalanga. The Northern Cape, one of South Africa's poorest provinces, attracted the lowest number. Anecdotal evidence suggests that African migrants from Mozambique or Zimbabwe are more likely than migrants from other areas to settle in Limpopo, North West and Mpumalanga in the north, because of similarities in cultural background and language and proximity to their countries of birth (Statistics South Africa 2015, 39; see also Africa Check 2016), or because they can work in low-skilled positions, for example, as labourers on farms (Statistics South Africa 2015, 139). The more recent, 2018 mid-year population estimates predicted that a net immigration of 1.02 million people could be expected between 2016 and 2021 (Statistics South Africa 2018b). Most migrants from other African countries continue to settle in Gauteng (47.5%), but the province also attracts domestic migrants from rural provinces such as Limpopo, KwaZulu-Natal and the Eastern Cape.

At a social level, foreign migrants living in South Africa face many difficulties. A number of studies have shown that many South Africans have a negative attitude towards immigrants from other African countries, associating them with increased crime, the spread of HIV, and a threat to their culture and work opportunities (Crush 2001; Gordon 2015; Landau 2006). Loren B. Landau and Iriann Freemantle (2010) point out that despite South Africa's attempts to overcome the exclusionary patterns of the apartheid era, it has failed to prevent everyday discriminatory practices and policies against foreign nationals. These negative attitudes have often translated into actual violent xenophobic attacks such as those seen in informal settlements in 2008 and in March 2019 (Bonnet 2021).

The 2021 mid-year population report showed that especially international migration (inward and outward) was deeply affected by the Covid-19 pandemic and travel bans. Moreover, the countries outside Africa that were South Africans' preferred emigration destinations all displayed an overall decline in the proportions of immigrants entering them (Statistics South Africa 2021).

WHY DO WE NEED THIS BOOK AND WHAT GAPS ARE WE HOPING TO ADDRESS?

So far, there has been little research on the transnational family experiences of South African and other African migrants, especially one with an African focus. One of the leading South African researchers in the field of migration studies, Ingrid Palmary, pointed out in an article published in the *South African Journal of Psychology* exploring the relationship of psychology with migration studies that there is 'very little work within migration studies that can directly be identified as psychology – with the exception of the trauma interventions with refugee communities' (2018, 4). Indeed, prominent work on the experiences of migrants and refugees seems to fall into the broader remit of the social sciences, and specifically migration studies, with a relative lack of emphasis on our primary area of concern – the issue of family relationships, which interfaces with psychology. Migration as a phenomenon has long been studied from the perspectives of various disciplines (Brettell and Hollifield 2014; Cohen 1996) such as anthropology, geography, sociology, history, economics and demography (Van Dalen 2018; see also Pisarevskaya et al. 2020). Some examples are the Southern African Migration Project led by Jonathan Crush, and the work of the African Centre for Migration and Society at the University of the Witwatersrand, led for a considerable time by Loren B. Landau and Ingrid Palmary.

In the field of psychology, and specifically family therapy, only a few researchers have explored the experiences and challenges that migrants and their families face as they move into foreign countries. Noteworthy examples are the research by Ricardo C. Ainslie (1998), John W. Berry (1992, 2001), Celia J. Falicov (2005, 2007), Leon Grinberg and Rebeca Grinberg (1989) and Carlos E. Sluzki (1979). The most recent work in the field has looked at experiences relating to transnationalism, which has become a prominent concept, as we discussed earlier.

Recent studies on South Africa by Sulette Ferreira (2015), Ferreira and Charlene Carbonatto (2020), Nthopele Tselane Mabandla (2019), Marchetti-Mercer (2012a, 2012b, 2016, 2017), Marchetti-Mercer and Swartz (2020), Marchetti-Mercer et al. (2020), and Swartz and Marchetti-Mercer (2019) have attempted to shed light on mostly middle-class migrants to non-African countries and their families, often with a specific focus on elderly parents left behind. However, a noticeable limitation of these studies is their middle-class family focus, which tends to include more white migrants, with the exception of Mabandla's (2019) work.

Palmary argues that the field of transnationalism offers new possibilities for psychology, especially as it relates to understanding how 'access (or lack thereof) to technology, shape the possibilities for … frequent family contact … This represents a rather new area of focus for migration studies and one where the impact of psychology is not yet being felt. It is, however, a topic of obvious concern to psychologists and one where psychology is in a position to contribute well-developed bodies of theoretical and empirical work' (2018, 8). Palmary also emphasises the disparities in access to technology, especially in rural areas, which may impact on the emotional labour required by families: 'In this sense, understanding evolving family structures remains an important area where psychology can contribute' (2018, 11). We have therefore chosen to pursue the importance of family relationships and dynamics in this project, as it underlies much of our work. The study of families and family relationships is not a sub-field of psychology alone, however, and is of great interest to other fields such as social work and sociology; hence, we locate our own work in the cross-cutting field of the study of family relationships rather than in any single discipline.

In the light of this theoretical context, the focus of the larger project on which this book is based is a study of the impact and use of ICTs among three specific types of migrants. Two of these are African migrant population groups, involved in internal South African migration and in African migration to South Africa. The third is South Africans migrating outward to other countries. We looked at family relationships of care between those who have migrated and those left behind, and their experiences linked to the use of ICTs.

Our research focuses on several groups of migrants and their families:

- We spoke to migrants moving from some of the rural areas of South Africa to the urban Gauteng region, and to family members left behind in the rural areas.
- We interviewed migrants to South Africa from Zimbabwe, Malawi and Kenya, as well as family members who remained in their home countries in Africa. Zimbabwe and Malawi were chosen as examples

of two of the major African countries of origin. Kenya was of interest to us because, although fewer migrants come from there, it offers an interesting example of a different type of migrant – some Kenyan migrants are highly skilled people who come to South Africa because of educational or professional opportunities.

- We also identified a group of refugees from the DRC and explored their patterns of family-making.
- We describe the experiences of middle-class families across the race spectrum whose members have emigrated to non-African countries.

Here are some key questions we ask in this book:

- What technologies do families use when migration has occurred to keep in touch and maintain ties?
- What are the enablers of and barriers to the use of these technologies, and to what extent is technology use linked to poverty and access to other resources?
- Do families budget for using technologies to maintain contact? If so, where in the hierarchy of priorities for these families is expenditure on technology to keep families in touch?
- How do families use ICTs to stay in touch and to perform caring roles? Are there differences across contexts? What roles do variables such as age, gender or disability play?
- For families in which there have been migration patterns for some time (especially South African families with a history of rural-to-urban migration), have they experienced any changes contingent on changes in technology and access to technology?
- How does technology use interact with, change or become changed by access to physical visits? What does a combined or blended pattern of care involving both technology-mediated and in-person care aspects look like, and how does this change and develop over time?
- How do technology use and access interact with broader social and kinship networks? For example, how (if at all) do groups of people

from the same rural village use technology to maintain networks and to care for vulnerable people across the usual family lines?

- To what extent do migrant families consider contact through technology to be inferior to, superior to, interlinked with or distinct from patterns of face-to-face care?
- Are there times when contact through technology is experienced as intrusive on care, or as a distraction from or a barrier to care?

Apart from addressing these questions, this book raises issues of migration and proximity, the politics of intimacy across large distances, questions of care and social roles in the context of migration, and possible consequences for conceptualisations of personhood and family relationships mediated by technology. What we discuss forms part of a global trend – all over the world, people are on the move. We try to understand the meaning and implications of this trend for individual lives as we make sense of how this phenomenon affects individuals and families, primarily in South Africa, but also in other African countries.

OVERVIEW OF THE BOOK

In the first part of the book, 'Theoretical Context', we introduce the theoretical context and research on which the book is based. We begin this in the current chapter, 'Setting the Scene', where we discuss how the book came about and the relevance of the research on which it is based. We then move on to explore methodological considerations and challenges that we faced during our research in Chapter 2, 'Methodological Challenges and Opportunities: Our Work, Our Selves'. There we describe the qualitative research approach that informs our work, as well as the thematic analysis used to identify the overarching themes that emerged throughout the interviews, as accurately as possible.

The second part of the book, 'Participants' Stories of African Migration, Family Relations and ICTs', presents the various types of migrant population we researched. We begin by looking at rural–urban migration, which has played such a significant role in the history of South Africa, in Chapter 3, '"Ah! Do I Know What Data Is, My Child?" Rural–Urban Migration and the Struggle to Stay in Touch'. This chapter explores the role of ICTs in sustaining and maintaining family relationships between those who migrate and family members left behind in rural South Africa. We not only look at how technology is used to bridge the distance and maintain healthy family relationships, but we also consider the digital divide in South Africa between impoverished, disadvantaged communities and middle-class communities.

We then shift to African migration to South Africa, to specific examples of cross-border migration within the continent, starting with migration to South Africa from Zimbabwe in Chapter 4, '"They Will Be Yearning": Zimbabwean Migration to South Africa and Keeping the Family Connected'. In recent decades, South Africa has become the preferred destination for people leaving Zimbabwe. Migrants leave behind families with whom they wish to maintain ties, as well as continue to support, through networks of care, facilitated through their use of ICTs. The stories of another group of African migrants to South Africa, those from Malawi, are described in Chapter 5, '"You Do Not Finish All Stories": Malawian Families and the Struggle to Stay Connected'. The continued threat of living below the poverty line still forces many Malawians to come to South Africa to seek work or trade in the informal sector to sustain their families. This chapter explores how migrant workers navigate the initial disconnectedness often caused by migration to maintain connections with their families left behind, as well as the role of ICTs as an important medium for this continued connection. In Chapter 6, '(Dis)connections: The Paradox of Intergenerational WhatsApp Communication in Transnational Kenyan Families', we look at migrants to South Africa from Kenya as well as those still living in Kenya with family members who moved to South Africa. We consider how family WhatsApp groups are used to maintain and sustain family relationships. The last African sample is a group of DRC refugees living in the inner city of Johannesburg. Their unique experiences are described in Chapter 7, 'Making a World of Care: DRC Refugees' Barber Shop Stories'. These stories express a strong longing for their families back home, and reveal the usefulness of technology to maintain some kind of connection. In many instances, mobile phones are the only tool available for migrants to stay connected despite long absences, and to maintain a presence in their families' lives.

Our final set of stories focuses on out-migration from South Africa to other countries. Chapter 8, 'The Luxury of Longing: Experiences of ICTs by South African Emigrants to Non-African Countries and Their Families', looks at the experiences of South African families across the racial divide in which at least one family member has emigrated to a non-African country. It focuses specifically on participants' use of ICTs and how it relates to the obligations of care by and of elderly parents who stay behind.

In the last part of the book, 'Final Considerations', we discuss the theoretical implications of our work. Firstly, in Chapter 9, 'Analysis of Important Data Emerging from the Study', we examine the most important themes that emerged from the data, especially regarding the potential of ICTs in maintaining family relationships for South African migrants, internal, inward and outward, as well as factors that inhibit communication and care relationships. In the last chapter, Chapter 10, 'Looking Ahead: Paradox, Criticality and a Way Forward', we reflect on some overarching themes in this book about African migrants and the use of ICTs to support family care in transnational kinship arrangements. We also turn a critical lens on our findings and on the methodologies we used to arrive at our findings in order to chart some new directions for future research.

NOTE

1   We use several statistical sources in this chapter. We are cognisant of the fact that different datasets and collection methods are used to gather this type of demographic information. Other sources may therefore present different information.

REFERENCES

Adepoju, Aderanti. 2003. 'Continuity and Changing Configurations of Migration to and from the Republic of South Africa'. *International Migration* 41, no. 1: 3–28. https://doi.org/10.1111/1468-2435.00228.

Africa Check. 2016. 'Factsheet: Where Do South Africa's International Migrants Come From?' https://africacheck.org/fact-checks/factsheets/factsheet-where-do-south-africas-international-migrants-come.

Ainslie, Ricardo C. 1998. 'Cultural Mourning, Immigration, and Engagement: Vignettes from the Mexican Experience'. In *Crossings: Mexican Immigration in Interdisciplinary Perspectives*, edited by Marcelo M. Suárez-Orozco, 285–300. Cambridge, MA: Harvard University Press.

Antman, Francisca M. 2010. 'Adult Child Migration and the Health of Elderly Parents Left Behind in Mexico'. *American Economic Review* 100, no. 2: 205–208. https://doi.org/10.1257/aer.100.2.205.

Bacigalupe, Gonzalo and Susan Lambe. 2011. 'Virtualizing Intimacy: Information Communication Technologies and Transnational Families in Therapy'. *Family Process* 50, no. 1: 12–26. https://doi.org/10.1111/j.1545-5300.2010.01343.x.

Baldassar, Loretta. 2001. *Visits Home: Migration Experiences between Italy and Australia*. Melbourne: Melbourne University Press.

Baldassar, Loretta. 2007a. 'Transnational Families and Aged Care: The Mobility of Care and the Migrancy of Ageing'. *Journal of Ethnic and Migration Studies* 33, no. 2: 275–297. https://doi.org/10.1080/13691830601154252.

Baldassar, Loretta. 2007b. 'Transnational Families and the Provision of Moral and Emotional Support: The Relationship between Truth and Distance'. *Identities* 14, no. 4: 385–409. https://doi.org/10.1080/10702890701578423.

Baldassar, Loretta. 2008. 'Missing Kin and Longing to Be Together: Emotions and the Construction of Co-presence in Transnational Relationships'. *Journal of Intercultural Studies* 29, no. 3 (Special Issue: Transnational Families – Emotions and Belonging): 247–266. https://doi.org/10.1080/07256860802169196.

Baldassar, Loretta. 2015. 'Guilty Feelings and the Guilt Trip: Emotions and Motivation in Migration and Transnational Caregiving'. *Emotion, Space and Society* 16: 81–89. https://doi.org/10.1016/j.emospa.2014.09.003.

Baldassar, Loretta. 2016a. 'De-demonizing Distance in Mobile Family Lives: Co-presence, Care Circulation and Polymedia as Vibrant Matter'. *Global Networks* 16, no. 2: 145–163. https://doi.org/10.1111/glob.12109.

Baldassar, Loretta. 2016b. 'Mobilities and Communication Technologies: Transforming Care in Family Life'. In *Family Life in an Age of Migration and Mobility: Global Perspectives through the Life Course*, edited by Majella Kilkey and Ewa Palenga-Möllenbeck, 19–42. Migration, Diasporas and Citizenship Series. London: Palgrave Macmillan.

Baldassar, Loretta and Laura Merla. 2014. 'Locating Transnational Care Circulation in Migration and Family Studies'. In *Transnational Families, Migration and the Circulation of Care: Understanding Mobility and Absence in Family Life*, edited by Loretta Baldassar and Laura Merla, 25–58. New York: Routledge.

Baldassar, Loretta, Mihaela Nedelcu, Laura Merla and Raelene Wilding. 2016. 'ICT-Based Co-presence in Transnational Families and Communities: Challenging the Premise of Face-to-Face Proximity in Sustaining Relationships'. *Global Networks* 16, no. 2 (Special Issue): 133–144. https://doi.org/10.1111/glob.12108.

Baldassar, Loretta, Raelene Wilding and Cora Baldock. 2007. 'Long-Distance Care-Giving, Transnational Families and the Provision of Aged Care'. In *Family Caregiving for Older Disabled People: Relational and Institutional Issues*, edited by Isabella Paoletti, 201–228. New York: Nova Science.

Baldock, Cora Vellekoop. 2003. 'Long-Distance Migrants and Family Support: A Dutch Case Study'. *Health Sociology Review* 12, no. 1: 45–54. https://doi.org/10.5172/hesr.12.1.45.

Bennett, Rachel, Victoria Hosegood, Marie-Louise Newell and Nuala McGrath. 2015. 'Understanding Family Migration in Rural South Africa: Exploring Children's Inclusion in the Destination Households of Migrant Parents'. *Population, Space and Place* 21, no. 4: 310–321. https://doi.org/10.1002/psp.1842.

Berry, John W. 1992. 'Acculturation and Adaptation in a New Society'. *International Migration* 30, no. 1: 69–85. https://doi.org/10.1111/j.1468-2435.1992.tb00776.x.

Berry, John W. 2001. 'A Psychology of Immigration'. *Journal of Social Issues* 57, no. 3: 615–631. https://doi.org/10.1111/0022-4537.00231.

Bonnet, Alida. 2021. 'Belonging and Family Relationships: The Experiences of Immigrants in Olievenhoutbosch'. Master's thesis, University of the Witwatersrand, Johannesburg.

Brandhorst, Rosa, Loretta Baldassar and Raelene Wilding. 2020. 'Introduction to the Special Issue: "Transnational Family Care 'On Hold'? Intergenerational Relationships and Obligations in the Context of Immobility Regimes"'. *Journal of Intergenerational Relationships* 18, no. 3: 261–280. https://doi.org/10.1080/15350770.2020.1787035.

Brettell, Caroline B. and James Frank Hollifield, eds. 2014. *Migration Theory: Talking across Disciplines*. Oxford: Routledge. https://doi.org/10.4324/9781315814933.

Caarls, Kim, Karlijn Haagsman, Elisabeth K. Kraus and Valentina Mazzucato. 2018. 'African Transnational Families: Cross-country and Gendered Comparisons'. *Population, Space and Place* 24, no. 7: e2162. https://doi.org/10.1002/psp.2162.

Casale, Daniela. 2004. 'What Has the Feminisation of the Labour Market "Bought" Women in South Africa? Trends in Labour Force Participation, Employment and Earnings, 1995–2001'. *Journal of Interdisciplinary Economics* 15, nos. 3–4: 251–275. https://doi.org/10.1177/02601079X04001500302.

Cebotari, Victor, Valentina Mazzucato and Ernest Appiah. 2018. 'A Longitudinal Analysis of Well-Being of Ghanaian Children in Transnational Families'. *Child Development* 89, no. 5: 1768–1785. https://doi.org/10.1111/cdev.12879.

Cienfuegos, Javiera, Rosa Brandhorst and Deborah Fahy Bryceson, eds. 2023. *Handbook of Transnational Families around the World*. Handbooks of Sociology and Social Research Series. Cham: Springer. https://doi.org/10.1007/978-3-031-15278-8_12.

Coe, Cati. 2008. 'The Structuring of Feeling in Ghanaian Transnational Families'. *City and Society* 20, no. 2: 222–250. https://doi.org/10.1111/j.1548-744X.2008.00018.x.

Cohen, Robin. 1996. *Theories of Migration*. Cheltenham: Edward Elgar.

Crush, Jonathan. 2000. *Losing Our Minds: Skills Migration and the South African Brain Drain*. Migration Policy Series no. 18. Southern African Migration Project, Cape Town, South Africa: IDASA. http://samponline.org/wp-content/uploads/2016/10/Acrobat18.pdf.

Crush, Jonathan. 2001. 'The Dark Side of Democracy: Migration, Xenophobia and Human Rights in South Africa'. *International Migration* 38, no. 6: 103–133. https://doi.org/10.1111/1468-2435.00145.

Crush, Jonathan. 2002. 'The Global Raiders: Nationalism, Globalization and the South African Brain Drain'. *Journal of International Affairs* 56, no. 1: 147–172.

Eko, Lyombe. 2013. 'Putting African Accents in United Nations Internet for Development Policies'. *Journal of Information Technology and Politics* 10, no. 3: 341–356. https://doi.org/10.1080/19331681.2013.794119.

Falicov, Celia J. 2005. 'Emotional Transnationalism and Family Identities'. *Family Process* 44, no. 4: 399–406. https://doi.org/10.1111/j.1545-5300.2005.00068.x.

Falicov, Celia J. 2007. 'Working with Transnational Immigrants: Expanding Meanings of Family, Community, and Culture'. *Family Process* 46, no. 2: 157–171. https://doi.org/10.1111/j.1545-5300.2007.00201.x.

Ferreira, Sulette. 2015. 'Parents Left Behind in South Africa after the Emigration of Their Adult Children: An Experiential Journey'. DPhil dissertation, University of Pretoria, Pretoria.

Ferreira, Sulette and Charlene Carbonatto. 2020. ' "A License to Leave South Africa": A Qualitative Study of South African Parents' Narratives of Their Children's Reasons for Emigration'. *Social Work* 56, no. 3: 310–327. http://dx.doi.org/10.15270/52-4-860.

Finch, Janet V. 1989. *Family Obligations and Social Change*. Cambridge: Polity.

Finch, Janet V. and Jennifer Mason. 1993. *Negotiating Family Responsibilities*. London: Routledge.

Gordon, Steven L. 2015. 'Xenophobia across the Class Divide: South African Attitudes towards Foreigners 2003–2012'. *Journal of Contemporary African Studies* 33, no. 4: 494–509. https://doi.org/10.1080/02589001.2015.1122870.

Grinberg, Leon and Rebeca Grinberg. 1989. *Psychoanalytic Perspectives on Migration and Exile*. London: Yale University Press.

GSMA (Groupe Speciale Mobile Association). 2021. *The State of Mobile Internet Connectivity 2021*. https://www.gsma.com/r/wp-content/uploads/2021/09/The-State-of-Mobile-Internet-Connectivity-Report-2021.pdf.

Gwaradzimba, Ellen and Almon Shumba. 2010. 'The Nature, Extent and Impact of the Brain Drain in Zimbabwe and South Africa'. *Acta Academica* 42, no. 1: 209–241. https://hdl.handle.net/10520/EJC15473.

Hagopian, Amy, Matthew J. Thompson, Meredith Fordyce, Karin E. Johnson and L. Gary Hart. 2004. 'The Migration of Physicians from Sub-Saharan Africa to the United States of America: Measures of the African Brain Drain'. *Human Resources for Health* 2, no. 7: 1–10. https://doi.org/10.1186/1478-4491-2-17.

Höppli, Thomas. 2014. *Is the Brain Drain Really Reversing? New Evidence*. Policy Research on International Services and Manufacturing Working Paper 1. Cape Town: PRISM, University of Cape Town.

Horowitz, Shale and Dana Evan Kaplan. 2001. 'The Jewish Exodus from the New South Africa: Realities and Implications'. *International Migration* 39, no. 3: 3–32. https://doi.org/10.1111/1468-2435.00154.

Horst, Heather A. 2006. 'The Blessings and Burdens of Communication: Cell Phones in Jamaican Transnational Social Fields'. *Global Networks* 6, no. 2: 143–159. https://doi.org/10.1111/j.1471-0374.2006.00138.x.

ICASA (Independent Communications Authority of South Africa). 2022. *State of ICT Sector Report March 2022*. https://www.icasa.org.za/legislation-and-regulations/state-of-the-ict-sector-in-south-africa-2022-report.

Jithoo, Vinitha, Maria C. Marchetti-Mercer and Leslie Swartz. 2020. 'The Search for Significance: Meaning Making in Elderly South Africans Following the Emigration of Their Adult Children'. *South African Journal of Psychology* 50, no. 4: 469–479. https://doi.org/10.1177/0081246320907029.

Kaarsholm, Preben. 2019. 'Aspiration, Exclusion and Belonging in South Africa and Kenya'. *African Studies* 78, no. 1: 1–5. https://doi.org/10.1080/00020184.2018.1540512.

Kalitanyi, Vivence and Kobus Visser. 2010. 'African Immigrants in South Africa: Job Takers or Job Creators?' *South African Journal of Economic and Management Sciences* 13, no. 4: 376–390. https://doi.org/10.4102/sajems.v13i4.91.

Kilkey, Majella and Laura Merla. 2014. 'Situating Transnational Families' Care-Giving Arrangements: The Role of Institutional Contexts'. *Global Networks* 14, no. 2: 210–229. https://doi.org/10.1111/glob.12034.

Landau, Loren B. 2005a. *Migration, Urbanisation and Sustainable Livelihoods in South Africa*. Migration Policy Brief no. 15; Policy Briefs Series. Southern African Migration Project.

Landau, Loren B. 2005b. 'Urbanisation, Nativism, and the Rule of Law in South Africa's "Forbidden" Cities'. *Third World Quarterly* 26, no. 7: 1115–1134. https://doi.org/10.1080/01436590500235710.

Landau, Loren B. 2006. 'Transplants and Transients: Idioms of Belonging and Dislocation in Inner-City Johannesburg'. *African Studies Review* 49, no. 2: 125–145. https://doi.org/10.1353/arw.2006.0109.

Landau, Loren B. and Iriann Freemantle. 2010. 'Tactical Cosmopolitanism and Idioms of Belonging: Insertion and Self-Exclusion in Johannesburg'. *Journal of Ethnic and Migration Studies* 36, no. 3: 375–390. https://doi.org/10.1080/13691830903494901.

La Rue, Frank. 2011. *Report of the Special Rapporteur on the Promotion and Protection of the Right to Freedom of Opinion and Expression*. United Nations. https://www2.ohchr.org/english/bodies/hrcouncil/docs/17session/a.hrc.17.27_en.pdf.

Mabandla, Nthopele Tselane. 2019. 'The Impact of International Migration on Black South African Families'. Master's dissertation, University of the Witwatersrand, Johannesburg.

Madianou, Mirca. 2012. 'Migration and the Accentuated Ambivalence of Motherhood: The Role of ICTs in Filipino Transnational Families'. *Global Networks* 12, no. 3: 277–295. https://doi.org/10.1111/j.1471-0374.2012.00352.x.

Madianou, Mirca. 2016. 'Ambient Co-presence: Transnational Family Practices in Polymedia Environments'. *Global Networks* 16, no. 2: 183–201. https://doi.org/10.1111/glob.12105.

Madianou, Mirca and Daniel Miller. 2013. 'Polymedia: Towards a New Theory of Digital Media in Interpersonal Communication'. *International Journal of Cultural Studies* 16, no. 2: 169–187. https://doi.org/10.1177/1367877912452486.

Marchand, Katrin, Julia Reinold and Raphael Dias e Silva. 2017. *Study on Migration Routes in the East and Horn of Africa*. Maastricht: Maastricht Graduate School of Governance.

Marchetti-Mercer, Maria. 2009. 'South Africans in Flux: Exploring the Mental Health Impact of Migration on Family Life'. *African Journal of Psychiatry* 12, no. 2: 129–134. https://hdl.handle.net/10520/EJC72734.

Marchetti-Mercer, Maria C. 2012a. 'Is It Just about the Crime? A Psychological Perspective on South African Emigration'. *South African Journal of Psychology* 42: 243–254. http://hdl.handle.net/2263/19278.

Marchetti-Mercer, Maria C. 2012b. 'Those Easily Forgotten: The Impact of Emigration on Those Left Behind'. *Family Process* 51, no. 3: 373–383. https://doi.org/10.1111/j.1545-5300.2012.01407.x.

Marchetti-Mercer, Maria C. 2016. '"If You Uproot a Tree You Leave a Big Hole Behind": Systemic Interconnectedness in Emigration and Family Life'. *Contemporary Family Therapy* 38, no. 3: 339–352. https://doi.org/10.1007/s10591-016-9386-6.

Marchetti-Mercer, Maria C. 2017. '"The Screen Has Such Sharp Edges to Hug": The Relational Consequences of Emigration in Transnational South African Emigrant Families'. *Transnational Social Work* 7, no. 1: 73–89. https://doi.org/ 10.1080/21931674.2016.1277650.

Marchetti-Mercer, Maria C. and Leslie Swartz. 2020. 'Familiarity and Separation in the Use of Communication Technologies in South African Migrant Families'. *Journal of Family Issues* 41, no. 10: 1859–1884. https://doi.org/10.1177/0192513X19894367.

Marchetti-Mercer, Maria C., Leslie Swartz and Loretta Baldassar. 2021. '"Is Granny Going Back into the Computer?" Visits and the Familial Politics of Seeing and Being Seen in South African Transnational Families'. *Journal of Intercultural Studies* 42, no. 4: 423–439. https://doi.org/10.1080/07256868.2021.1939280.

Marchetti-Mercer, Maria C., Leslie Swartz, Vinitha Jithoo, Nthopele Mabandla, Alessandro Briguglio and Maxine Wolfe. 2020. 'South African International Migration and Its Impact on Older Family Members'. *Family Process* 59, no. 4: 1737–1754. https://doi. org/10.1111/famp.12493.

Mazzucato, Valentina and Victor Cebotari. 2017. 'Psychological Well-Being of Ghanaian Children in Transnational Families'. *Population, Space and Place* 23, no. 3: e2004. https://doi.org/10.1002/psp.2004.

Mazzucato, Valentina and Djamila Schans. 2011. 'Transnational Families and the Well-Being of Children: Conceptual and Methodological Challenges'. *Journal of Marriage and the Family* 73, no. 4: 704–712. https://doi.org/10.1111/j.1741-3737.2011.00840.x.

Mazzucato, Valentina, Djamila Schans, Kim Caarls and Cris Beauchemin. 2015. 'Transnational Families between Africa and Europe'. *International Migration Review* 49, no. 1: 142–172. https://doi.org/10.1111/imre.12153.

Merla, Laura, Majella Kilkey and Loretta Baldassar. 2020. 'Introduction'. *Journal of Family Research* 32, no. 3 (Special Issue: Transnational Care – Families Confronting Borders): 393–414. https://doi.org/10.20377/jfr-420.

Mlambo, Victor. 2018. 'An Overview of Rural–Urban Migration in South Africa: Its Causes and Implications'. *Archives of Business Research* 6, no. 4: 63–70. https://doi. org/10.14738/abr.64.4407.

Mosselson, Aidan. 2010. '"There Is No Difference between Citizens and Non-citizens Anymore": Violent Xenophobia, Citizenship and the Politics of Belonging in Post-apartheid South Africa'. *Journal of Southern African Studies* 36, no. 3: 641–655. https://doi.org/10.1080/03057070.2010.507570.

Mulder, Clara H. and Thomas J. Cooke. 2009. 'Family Ties and Residential Locations'. *Population, Space and Place* 15, no. 4 (Special Issue): 299–304. https://doi. org/10.1002/psp.556.

Murray, Colin. 1981. *Families Divided: The Impact of Migrant Labour in Lesotho*. African Studies Series, vol. 29. Cambridge: Cambridge University Press.

Myburgh, Andrew. 2004. 'Explaining Emigration from South Africa'. *South African Journal of Economics* 72, no. 1: 125–151. https://doi.org/10.1111/j.1813-6982.2004. tb00107.x.

Nedelcu, Mihaela and Malik Wyss. 2016. '"Doing Family" through ICT-Mediated Ordinary Co-presence: Transnational Communication Practices of Romanian Migrants in Switzerland'. *Global Networks* 16, no. 2: 202–218. https://doi.org/10.1111/ glob.12110.

Owusu-Sekyere, Emmanuel and Alexandra Willis. 2022. 'Undocumented Migrants: The Myths, Realities, and What We Know and Don't Know'. *Daily Maverick*, 23 March.

https://www.dailymaverick.co.za/article/2022-03-23-undocumented-migrants-the-myths-realities-and-what-we-know-and-dont-know/.

Palmary, Ingrid. 2018. 'Psychology, Migration Studies, and Their Disconnections: A Review of Existing Research and Future Possibilities'. *South African Journal of Psychology* 48, no. 1: 3–14. https://doi.org/10.1177/0081246317751276.

Phillips, Laura and Deborah James. 2014. 'Labour, Lodging and Linkages: Migrant Women's Experience in South Africa'. *African Studies* 73, no. 3: 410–431. https://doi.org/10.1080/00020184.2014.962875.

Pisarevskaya, Asja, Nathan Levy, Peter Scholten and Joost Jansen. 2020. 'Mapping Migration Studies: An Empirical Analysis of the Coming of Age of a Research Field'. *Migration Studies* 8, no. 3 (September): 455–481. https://doi.org/10.1093/migration/mnz031.

Posel, Dorrit. 2004. 'Have Migration Patterns in Post-apartheid South Africa Changed?' *Journal of Interdisciplinary Economics* 15, nos 3–4: 277–292. https://doi.org/10.1177/02601079X04001500303.

Posel, Dorrit and Daniela Casale. 2003. 'What Has Been Happening to Internal Labour Migration in South Africa, 1993–1999?' *South African Journal of Economics* 71, no. 3 (September): 455–479. https://doi.org/10.1111/j.1813-6982.2003.tb00081.x.

Ramphele, Mamphela. 1993. *A Bed Called Home: Life in the Migrant Labour Hostels of Cape Town*. Athens, OH: Ohio University Press.

Reed, Holly E. 2013. 'Moving across Boundaries: Migration in South Africa, 1950–2000'. *Demography* 50, no. 1: 71–95. https://doi.org/10.1007/s13524-012-0140-x.

RSA (Republic of South Africa). 2017. *White Paper on International Migration for South Africa*. Department of Home Affairs, July 2017. http://www.dha.gov.za/WhitePaperonInternationalMigration-20170602.pdf.

Rutherford, Blair. 2008. 'An Unsettled Belonging: Zimbabwean Farm Workers in Limpopo Province, South Africa'. *Journal of Contemporary African Studies* 26, no. 4: 401–415. https://doi.org/10.1080/02589000802481973.

Schiller, Nina Glick, Linda G. Basch and Cristina Blanc-Szanton. 1992. 'Towards a Definition of Transnationalism'. *Annals of the New York Academy of Sciences* 645, no. 1: ix–xiv. https://doi.org/10.1111/j.1749-6632.1992.tb33482.x.

Schmalzbauer, Leah. 2004. 'Searching for Wages and Mothering from Afar: The Case of Honduran Transnational Families'. *Journal of Marriage and Family* 66, no. 5: 1317–1331. https://doi.org/10.1111/j.0022-2445.2004.000095.x.

Segatti, Aurelia. 2011. 'Reforming South African Immigration Policy in the Postapartheid Period'. In *Contemporary Migration to South Africa: A Regional Development Issue*, edited by Aurelia Segatti and Loren B. Landau, 9–30. Washington, DC: World Bank Publications.

Silver, Alexis. 2011. 'Families across Borders'. *International Migration* 52, no. 3: 192–220. https://doi.org/10.1111/j.1468-2435.2010.00672.x.

Sluzki, Carlos E. 1979. 'Migration and Family Conflict'. *Family Process* 18, no. 4: 379–390. https://doi.org/10.1111/j.1545-5300.1979.00379.x.

Statista. 2018. 'Number of Smartphone Users in South Africa from 2014 to 2022 (in Millions)'. https://www.statista.com/statistics/488376/forecast-of-smartphone-users-in-south-africa/.

Statistics South Africa. 2015. *Census 2011: Migration Dynamics in South Africa*. Report no. 03-01-79. Pretoria: Statistics South Africa. https://www.statssa.gov.za/publications/Report-03-01-79/Report-03-01-792011.pdf.

Statistics South Africa. 2016. *Statistics South Africa Community Survey in 2016*. Statistical Release P0301. Pretoria: Statistics South Africa.

Statistics South Africa. 2018a. *General Household Survey*. Statistical Release P0318. Pretoria: Statistics South Africa.

Statistics South Africa. 2018b. *Mid-year Population Estimates*. Statistical Release P0302. Pretoria: Statistics South Africa. https://www.statssa.gov.za/publications/P0302/P03022018.pdf.

Statistics South Africa. 2021. *Mid-year Population Estimates*. Statistical Release P032. Pretoria: Statistics South Africa. http://www.statssa.gov.za/publications/P0302/P03022021.pdf.

Stulgaitis, Manal. 2015. *A Transnational Family-Friendly State? The Position of Transnational Families in the Context of South African Law and Society*. CSSR Working Paper no. 367. Centre for Social Science Research, University of Cape Town. http://hdl.handle.net/11427/21572.

Sutton, Constance R. 2004. 'Celebrating Ourselves: The Family Reunion Rituals of African-Caribbean Transnational Families'. *Global Networks* 4, no. 3: 243–257. https://doi.org/10.1111/j.1471-0374.2004.00091.x.

Swartz, Leslie and Maria C. Marchetti-Mercer. 2019. 'Migration, Technology and Care: What Happens to the Body?' *Disability and Society* 34, no. 3: 407–420. https://doi.org/10.1080/09687599.2018.1519409.

Van Dalen, Harry. 2018. 'Is Migration Still Demography's Stepchild?' *Demos: Bulletin over Bevolking en Samenleving* 34, no. 5: 8. https://pure.uvt.nl/ws/portalfiles/portal/25905116/demos_34_05_epc_vandalen.pdf.

Van Onselen, Charles. 2021. *The Night Trains: Moving Mozambican Miners to and from the Witwatersrand Mines, 1902–1955*. New York: Oxford University Press. https://academic.oup.com/book/39309.

Von Fintel, Dieter and Eldridge Moses. 2017. 'Migration and Gender in South Africa: Following Bright Lights and the Fortunes of Others?' *Regional Science Policy and Practice* 9, no. 4: 251–268. https://doi.org/10.1111/rsp3.12106.

Vullnetari, Julie and Russell King. 2008. '"Does Your Granny Eat Grass?" On Mass Migration, Care Drain and the Fate of Older People in Rural Albania'. *Global Networks* 8, no. 2: 139–171. https://doi.org/10.1111/j.1471-0374.2008.00189.x.

Wentzel, Marie and Kholadi Tlabela. 2006. 'Historical Background to South African Migration'. In *Migration in South and Southern Africa: Dynamics and Determinants*, edited by John Oucho, Pieter Kok, Derik Gelderblom and Johan van Zyl, 71–96. Cape Town: HSRC Press. https://www.hsrcpress.ac.za/books/migration-in-south-and-southern-africa.

Wilding, Raelene. 2006. '"Virtual" Intimacies? Families Communicating across Transnational Contexts'. *Global Networks* 6, no. 2: 125–142. https://doi.org/10.1111/j.1471-0374.2006.00137.x.

Yeates, N. 2012. 'Global Care Chains: A State-of-the-Art Review and Future Directions in Care Transnationalization Research'. *Global Networks* 12, no. 2: 135–154. http://lekuvam.se/wp-content/uploads/2020/03/5.-YEATES-2012-Global_Networks.pdf.

Yount-André, Chelsie. 2018. 'New African Frontiers: Transnational Families in Neoliberal Capitalism; Introduction'. *Africa: The Journal of the International African Institute* 88, no. 4 (November): 641–644. https://doi.org/10.1017/S0001972018000396.

2

Methodological Challenges and Opportunities: Our Work, Our Selves

Daniella Rafaely, Loretta Baldassar, Leslie Swartz and Maria C. Marchetti-Mercer

In this chapter we provide an overview of the methodological choices and processes that guided our data collection and analysis. We began with an abiding interest in migration experiences and in how families negotiate the meaning and impact of these experiences in their relational practices and narratives. We were particularly curious about how technological advances may have altered these relationships and how people use technology in the intimate spaces in which relationships are enacted and shared across distances. Our research was guided by these broad issues and by the various questions set out in Chapter 1.

As mentioned in the previous chapter, the decisions that led to this book reflect the personal and professional stories that brought the different researchers together. In 2008, Maria began investigating the stories of families leaving South Africa. She soon became interested in the effect of emigration on those 'left behind' and how migrants and their families used technology, especially information communication technologies

(ICTs), to maintain relationships of care with their migrant children and grandchildren. This led to a joint project with Leslie that explored the care of older adults whose children had migrated, and again the use of ICTs emerged as a significant theme. During this research process, Leslie and Maria realised that there was a gap in the current literature on the use of ICTs among migrants in South Africa and on the rest of the continent. This gap reflected a trend in the literature, which has focused on migrant experiences in the Global North, albeit sometimes on migrants who come from the Global South. This suggested an as-yet-unexplored area of study, which offered an opportunity for investigation, especially in South Africa as a country that has been defined by a range of migratory patterns involving migrants from all over the continent. Such research would provide an important contribution to migration studies and the role of technology in relationships and patterns of care, especially in developing contexts. Maria and Leslie then invited Loretta Baldassar, an international expert on transnational migration and caregiving, to begin conceptualising what such a project might entail. After receiving a National Research Foundation (NRF) Human and Social Dynamics in Development Grant, which confirmed the importance of this topic of study, Maria began to assemble a research team that could do justice to the vast scope of the project. The funding provided a significant opportunity to bring together emerging and established scholars and to develop the academic skills of a number of graduate students. We built the team to include members who have an interest in families and migration, and who also have connections with the different geographical and social locations on which we focused.

Our journey, like that of so many others at this time, was greatly affected by the outbreak of the Covid-19 pandemic. As a result, a large part of our research process, including a portion of the data collection, analysis, writing, workshops, meetings and seminars, was accomplished online, using the very same technological practices that we were interrogating as our topic. This coincidence encouraged us as a team to reflect in profound ways on the opportunities offered by technology, as well as its fundamental limitations, in creating, shaping and sustaining different types of relationships and in the joint navigation of various tasks. Hien Thi Nguyen et al. (2021) discuss this phenomenon in their chapter 'Researching Older Vietnam-Born Migrants at a Distance: The Role of Digital Kinning' in *Qualitative and Digital Research in Times of Crisis: Methods, Reflexivity, and Ethics*. They note that 'researchers, too, are incorporated into the practices and processes of digital kinning with participants' (185). This point re-emphasises the relationships between researchers and participants, and 'highlights the continuum and situated relatedness of the researcher' (185). Nguyen et al. eloquently describe the phenomenon that emerged for us as researchers during the writing of this book, and we hope that the conceptual extension of 'digital kinning' to the researcher–participant relationship (and relationships within the research team) is useful for future research on the effects of Covid-19 on society and online data-collection processes.

As mentioned in Chapter 1, our principal investigator, Maria, is an Italian-born scholar who moved to South Africa as a child. Her interest in home, locality, language, culture and relationships was born of her own struggle with a dual identity and nationality. At its heart, migration is a story of identities – the identity that you are born with, the new identity that you cultivate as a stranger in a new country, and the tension between these identities when engaging with family back home or with new family in the destination country. ICTs constitute one platform, an increasingly common one, on which we perform and negotiate identity and social and family relationships. It is thus a rich site for examining the co-construction of relationships of care between migrants and their families.

RESEARCH DESIGN

Our interest in our participants' experiences guided us towards a qualitative research approach. Although qualitative research includes a broad and diverse range of methodologies, it is epitomised by the search for in-depth

understanding and description of interpersonal or intra-personal phe-
nomena and by the use of various analytic methods that can foreground
the experiential, narrative or phenomenological elements of the data.

We used a thematic analysis approach (Braun and Clarke 2006, 2023) to
analyse our data. There were a number of reasons for this methodological
choice. First, and most important, thematic analysis is well suited to an analysis of the interview data that formed the basis for this study. It provided
a mechanism for the faithful reporting of participants' lived realities, while
encouraging inductive observations, which have been collated into larger
thematics. Second, thematic analysis is used throughout the humanities and
social sciences and is thus a useful method for interdisciplinary collaboration. It is also a method that can be used by researchers at all levels in varying
forms of complexity. This aspect was important for our project, which
involved collaboration between experienced academics and postgraduate
students. Thematic analysis is at once a rigorous and extremely broad
methodology that can be applied to the analysis of narratives, experiences
and even discourses. Its accessibility, derived from Virginia Braun and
Victoria Clarke's (2006, 2023) detailed and easy-to-follow instructions,
made it appropriate for members of our group who were early or inexperi-
enced researchers. At the same time, its broad framework allowed the more
established researchers and editors to develop the complexity of the thematic findings. Finally, the use of thematic analysis enabled the authors
to engage in collaborative sessions of data analysis. These sessions were an
integral part of the creation of this book, since they allowed for the identification of themes across the different datasets. Furthermore, our collaboration and discussion generated some important and exciting observations
that informed many of our overall findings.

REFLEXIVE INTERDEPENDENCE

In almost all our data collection, our access to participants and their communities would not have been possible without our research team. We learned
the meaning of research interdependence, the co-constitution of researchers,

participants and data, during this time. For example, many of the young researchers were Maria's students, who would not typically have had access to this type of publication opportunity without their supervisor's support. On the other hand, Maria would not have acquired the type of data necessary for this book unless the students had come on board. They were the ones who gained entry into their communities of origin to conduct the research. The participants recruited by our researchers connected us with their families back home, families that we would have never met or been able to interview had our researchers and migrant participants not been as willing and engaged as they were. These families, and their willingness to speak intimately about their experiences of loss and sacrifice, hope and aspirations, were crucial to the richness of the book that we have written. The international researchers that we had to recruit on a post-hoc basis because of the Covid-driven border closures made it possible for us to gain access to participants in other African countries. It also opened up the possibility of some of the matched pair interviews that provide such tension, intersection and contrast in the findings. We found ourselves constantly re-evaluating the extent of the interdependent network that was created, and that took on a life of its own during the writing of this book. Reflexivity is a key feature of many approaches to qualitative research (Braun and Clarke 2019); and working in a diverse group helped us all to think more carefully about our own positioning.

COVID-19

Triangulation of data is typically a process that requires close and consistent engagement if data have been collected by two or more individuals. A further reflexive lens on the analytical process was provided by undertaking a study about ICTs and their ability to deliver care and create connection and closeness among families, while simultaneously using ICTs to achieve connectedness among the research team in the process of analysis and writing. It required us to to look more closely at our topic, our role, our method, our expectations and assumptions, and our own experience of inevitable reliance on the very resources and processes we were studying.

Many of our initial plans were derailed by the outbreak of Covid-19 in 2020. Our schedule for conducting interviews was delayed, in-person team meetings and workshops were cancelled, and it took us a while to work out how to move our project online. Throughout, our team members were willing to engage, whether over the telephone, via email or on Zoom. They were also instrumental in providing us with an entry point for data collection in the communities that we could not access on our own – families in rural areas or other African countries.

As the research process unfolded during the pandemic, we became ever more reliant on the very technology we were researching. Our participants, too, were becoming more reliant on this technology at the same time as we had to fall back on it. There was an extremely powerful learning curve for both the researchers and the participants (in fact, for millions of people worldwide) in digital literacy, access and understanding. This increasing reliance on digital connectivity profoundly altered the hierarchical relationship between researchers and research subjects, and between research students and principal investigators, and among other power dynamics often inherent in the research process. For example, those members of the team with greater digital literacy were not always those with the most research knowledge or expertise. The relative values attached to different kinds of knowledge were problematised in this time, as postgraduate students with high digital fluency often surpassed more experienced senior academics who were more technologically challenged. This rupture in the typical (and often invisible) power dynamics led us to reflect more profoundly on our own role in reproducing and reinforcing the normative relations that are often in fact deeply problematic. It also offered us a first-person experience of struggling with diverse capacities to use and access ICTs, evoking profound empathy with our research participants who face ICT challenges. Accessibility issues around the availability of data, connectivity, power, devices, Wi-Fi and technological knowledge came up over and over again; when they surfaced in research interviews, we were intimately familiar with these nuances and the type of impact they had on the integrity of relationships and communication. Furthermore, the reliance on ICTs to complete the research successfully helped to make researchers more aware of their preconceived assumptions about both the limitations and potential of ICTs in delivering care and intimacy across distance, thereby forcing the team to review our own biases. Shared notions about the potential of ICTs to overcome distance and deliver strong and supportive transnational networks needed to be interpreted and analysed in the context of the very practical constraints of differential access and inequity that deeply characterised our samples.

TRANSLATION

Many of our interviewees speak English as a second or foreign language, which required them to be their own interpreters as they spoke. In some cases, participants spoke in their first language (not English), and those of our researchers fluent in the language concerned took on the role of translator or interpreter as well as researcher.

The topic of translation is complex in qualitative research, which assumes the primacy of language and its ability both to construct and to reflect our reality. In contrast to research paradigms in which accuracy is the ultimate goal of translation, and reality (and identity) is thought to be stable, objective and transferable across language, our qualitative research methods and frameworks assert the co-construction of meaning, reality and identity in discourse, and the significant role of the translator in this process. Since many of our researchers are multilingual, they were able to take on the role of researcher and translator simultaneously. However, the assumption that the translation of a lived reality can map unproblematically onto another language is deeply flawed, because it may erase the labour of translation and the translator as a co-constructor and analyst in the process of sense-making and meaning-making. As Ingrid Palmary (2011) notes, translation is a political and colonial act that (at least on the surface) makes the 'other' intelligible and creates the illusion of a shareable reality. Since language and culture are profoundly interconnected, the frequent invisibility of the translation process also serves to erase the differences in culture that are so difficult to research, understand and analyse. Therefore, by

41

making invisible the process of translation or interpretation, we implicitly smooth over the complexities and negations that are present in this type of research, and risk producing a hegemonic and colonial interpretation of an unknowable other. It is important that we acknowledge that issues of language and (mis)interpretation are at the heart of many refugee or migrant experiences, and that smoothing over the challenges of language and communication does not do full justice to the issues at stake (Schouten et al. 2020; Swartz and Kilian 2014).

We ensured as far as possible that in the research process, interview transcripts were produced in their original language, with translations beneath them. We also mobilised the young researchers who conducted these interviews to perform the data analysis, which, we hope, will allow them to find a way to communicate to our audience (who either speak English frequently or adopt it as a lingua franca) the complexity of the lived realities of the participants. We have made the editorial decision to write this book in English, but we are aware that our act of translation has the potential to erase and transform the original. We also recognise that strict fidelity to an original may itself be considered a patriarchal gesture (Palmary 2011) and that a more fruitful approach is to view the process of data collection, translation and analysis as co-constructed and inevitably subjective but still an ultimately worthwhile endeavour.

We hope that the simultaneity of the researcher–translator process achieves some accuracy in terms of the data that have been collected and the analysis that follows. We also recognise that accuracy in itself is insufficient, and that the political, economic, relational, cultural and gendered experiences of our participants, expressed and produced in language, can never be adequately grasped or conveyed.

MATCHED AND UNMATCHED INTERVIEWS

As noted above, we attempted in many cases to hear the experiences of our participants (many of whom were migrants living in Johannesburg) and then to follow this thread by interviewing their family members back home (in rural South Africa) or at least to interview 'families left behind' in the countries of origin, to gain a fuller picture of migration as experienced from both sides. In many cases, our participants made this possible for us, and we were able to gather data from multiple sources in order to enhance and deepen our understanding of the complexities of the migration experience. We did not collect matched pairs for statistical purposes, and so ruptures or contradictions in the narratives were not a cause for concern but rather a resource for careful analysis. These fissures led to findings that reflected the tensions and contestations of migrant experience, and mirrored the experience of separate worlds described by many of our migrant participants. The presence of sometimes totally dissimilar experiences between migrants and families highlighted for us the alienation inherent in the act of leaving home and inhabiting multiple worlds, here and there, past and present.

That said, we became keenly aware of the strengths and limitations of matched sampling methods (Bilecen 2020; Mazzucato and Schans 2011). In gaining access to non-migrant family members back home directly through their family in South Africa, researchers were sensitive to the understandable tendency of participants to direct us to the more positive relationships in their families. Participants acted as 'gatekeepers', enabling access to certain people, but also potentially blocking our access to or even awareness of others, as they selected interviewees 'back home' whose experiences and perspectives might most closely align with their own.

CREDIBILITY AND TRUSTWORTHINESS

The process of analysing data of this scope – spanning five countries, nine interviewers and more than eighty participants for the research on local migration and migration from African countries alone – was daunting, to say the least. Much of the preliminary analysis was done at a group level, with all the researchers attending data-analysis workshops in order to guide an iterative process of reading the transcribed interviews and finding points of thematic convergence. As each researcher was an expert on the data that he or she had collected, this collaborative process allowed for the formation of unique insights and exciting findings. Researchers shared their emerging analyses, which were supported or contested by those of other researchers in an interactive and iterative process that refined, honed and shaped the thematic findings and the intricate details with which they are woven.

A data-analysis expert, Daniella Rafaely, who is also the first author of this chapter, was brought on board on a consultative basis to support and assist with the analytic process. At the second workshop, we had a group data session, which included all the researchers. Each researcher shared what they considered their most important research findings. Collaborating on a whiteboard, we traced these findings and their expression across various settings, noting how overarching themes were uniquely substantiated in different contexts. The use of ICTs is intimately related to larger thematics, including family dynamics, age, migration behaviour, socio-economic status, digital literacy, rurality, gender, and more; this book is a reflection of these many intersecting and pervasive details that shape the ways in which individuals engage with technology, and the way in which technology shapes relationships.

As the principal investigator, Maria was deeply involved with all aspects of the data-analysis process, engaging individually with each researcher and, together with Leslie, assisting in structuring each chapter. Maria's encompassing view of the totality of the project was an important point of contact for the researchers, and was crucial in the recognition of themes and patterns emerging from the data. Loretta was able to provide us with her insights in the latter part of the project by offering a meta-perspective on the data-analysis process, which helped us place the data in the context of the larger international research that has been done on the topic.

The various interactions and collaborations, between co-authors of chapters, between researchers writing independent chapters, between researchers and editors and the external data analyst, and between the editors themselves, generated an emerging co-construction of meaning that each individual would not have produced on his or her own. This was powerful testimony to the value of collaboration and peer review – a hallmark of rigorous research.

ETHICAL CONSIDERATIONS

Prior to commencing the data-collection process, we received ethical approval for this project from the University of the Witwatersrand Human Research Ethics Committee (Non-Medical). In addition to applying for and gaining formal ethics approval, we reflected individually and as a group on some of the ethical challenges of undertaking a project of this magnitude. For example, for some of the elderly participants in the rural areas, there was little familiarity with what the research process involved. Among the sample in Modimolle village, one of the researchers, Lactricia Maja, was initially mistaken for a government official. In many instances younger family members sat in during interviews, potentially affecting issues of confidentiality. A number of interviews were conducted online, and ethics forms could not be emailed or faxed beforehand, which meant that consent forms had to be read to participants and consent was obtained verbally and recorded. There were instances where participants needed money for data, which we were able to provide through our NRF project funding, and which we hope was of value to the participants beyond their participation in the project. However, in instances where people refused to be interviewed unless they were compensated for their time, we did not include them as participants. With the refugees from the Democratic Republic of Congo, we were dealing with an extremely vulnerable population, and they shared very traumatic events with Thembelihle Coka. This placed her in a difficult position, where she had to negotiate between gathering the necessary information from her participants and being an empathetic listener to the difficult stories they shared. It must also be noted that foreign migrants in South Africa are often the target of xenophobic attacks, so where interviews were conducted face to face in public spaces, researchers had to be cognisant of the fact that participants might be reluctant to be identified as foreigners.

It was important to keep in mind that the data held benefits for us as academics in terms of the publishing possibilities, yet we could not guarantee any benefit to our participants in the long run. We struggled with the ethical dilemma of exploiting our participants' time and experiences for academic purposes that were unlikely to have an impact on, or to ease, their living circumstances. Ultimately, there was no direct benefit to the participants themselves, beyond the often-affirming personal experience of sharing their life stories. We acknowledge that the benefit of this research lies in our understanding of the larger migrant population, although it may hold implications for policy development that might address their plight.

In interviewing participants, the power disparity between researchers and participants became increasingly evident and was magnified by our status as academics or university representatives. This created an enormous gap that may have left participants feeling alienated and even, at times, intimidated. It was thus important that participants felt heard and respected, and this was a key value that we practised throughout the data-collection process.

OVERARCHING THEMES AND CONCLUDING REMARKS

In the latter part of the book, in Chapter 9, we present overarching themes that we identified throughout our analysis of the interviews conducted. Overarching themes are a common phenomenon in qualitative research, highlighting the commonality of human experience, or, more critically, the normativity of certain discourses and ways of speaking. We present these themes cautiously, noting to ourselves and our readers the subjectivity inherent in any thematic analysis, the naturalisation of (often problematic) discourses, which are disguised and reproduced in thematic findings, and the erasure of nuance and difference, which may be the price for thematised findings. Nevertheless, we believe these themes are valuable in a number of ways. Firstly, as a comment on normative discourses of migration, relationship, culture and technology, they offer insight into the organisation of our social world and into the deeply held and sustained assumptions and beliefs by which we live. Secondly, they provide a narrative structure for presenting complex and unique findings that are, nevertheless, empirically grounded and based on participant experiences and orientations. Finally, although thematising – essentially categorising – is implicitly ethical work that elides the processes and assumptions that drive it, it is in the process of categorisation that more and more nuanced differences are able to emerge and be made visible, thus allowing our analysis to demonstrate and reflect the depth of the uniqueness, subjectivity, dissimilarity and unknowability at the heart of our participants' experiences. It is in the nature of all research that we cannot do full justice to everything that was told to us; we hope we show in this book that we have tried our best to understand, and convey, the importance of our participants' stories.

REFERENCES

Bilecen, Başak. 2020. 'Asymmetries in Transnational Social Protection: Perspectives of Migrants and Nonmigrants'. *Annals of the American Academy of Political and Social Science* 689, no. 1: 168–191. https://doi.org/10.1177/0002716220922521.

Braun, Virginia and Victoria Clarke. 2006. 'Using Thematic Analysis in Psychology'. *Qualitative Research in Psychology* 3, no. 2: 77–101. https://doi.org/10.1191/1478088706qp063oa.

Braun, Virginia and Victoria Clarke. 2019. 'Reflecting on Reflexive Thematic Analysis'. *Qualitative Research in Sport, Exercise and Health* 11, no. 4: 589–597. https://doi.org/10.1080/2159676X.2019.1628806.

Braun, Virginia and Victoria Clarke. 2023. 'Is Thematic Analysis Used Well in Health Psychology? A Critical Review of Published Research, with Recommendations for Quality Practice and Reporting'. *Health Psychology Review* (19 January): 1–24. https://doi.org/10.1080/17437199.2022.2161594.

Mazzucato, Valentina and Djamila Schans. 2011. 'Transnational Families and the Well-Being of Children: Conceptual and Methodological Challenges'. *Journal of Marriage and Family* 73, no. 4: 704–712. https://doi.org/10.1111/j.1741-3737.2011.00840.x.

Nguyen, Hien Thi, Loretta Baldassar, Raelene Wilding and Lukasz Krzyzowski. 2021. 'Researching Older Vietnam-Born Migrants at a Distance: The Role of Digital Kinning'. In *Qualitative and Digital Research in Times of Crisis: Methods, Reflexivity, and Ethics*, edited by Helen Kara and Su-ming Khoo, 172–188. Bristol: Policy Press.

Palmary, Ingrid. 2011. '"In Your Experience": Research as Gendered Cultural Translation'. *Gender, Place and Culture* 18, no. 1: 99–113. https://doi.org/10.1080/0966369X.2011.535300.

Schouten, Barbara C., Antoon Cox, Gözde Duran, Koen Kerremans, Leyla Köseoğlu Banning, Ali Lahdidioui, Maria van den Muijsenbergh, Sanne Schinkel, Hande Sungur, Jeanine Suurmond et al. 2020. 'Mitigating Language and Cultural Barriers in Healthcare Communication: Toward a Holistic Approach'. *Patient Education and Counseling* 103, no. 12: 2604–2608. https://doi.org/10.1016/j.pec.2020.05.001.

Swartz, Leslie and Sanja Kilian. 2014. 'The Invisibility of Informal Interpreting in Mental Health Care in South Africa: Notes towards a Contextual Understanding'. *Culture, Medicine and Psychiatry* 38: 700–711. https://doi.org/10.1007/s11013-014-9394-7.

PART 2

PARTICIPANTS' STORIES OF AFRICAN MIGRATION, FAMILY RELATIONS AND ICTs

3

'Ah! Do I Know What Data Is, My Child?' Rural–Urban Migration and the Struggle to Stay in Touch

Lactricia Maja, Risuna Mathebula, Sonto Madonsela and Maria C. Marchetti-Mercer

Urbanisation and its effects have long been a topic of concern for social scientists, and there is continuing interest globally in this phenomenon, including in the Global South (Sridhar and Mavrotas 2021). The great interest worldwide in international migration and refugee issues holds the risk that internal migration – movements within countries – may sometimes be overlooked, despite the fact that colonial (and post-colonial) economies have a long history of dependence on rural–urban migration. Moreover, circular migration continues to inform population flows in countries such as South Africa (Zaami 2022). In Africa, a classic early study of the topic was produced by Philip Mayer (1961). Rural–urban migration issues continue to form the focus of analysis in various health, economic, welfare and political science studies (Démurger 2015; Harington, McGlashan and Chelkowska 2004; Kok et al. 2003; Mlambo 2018; Posel 2004; Posel and Casale 2003; Reed 2013; Stapleton 2015). Given that rural–urban migration is a common experience for many South Africans, it is fitting to include this phenomenon in this book.

The two rural sites for our research in Limpopo province were Giyani and Modimolle. These towns in Limpopo are located in South Africa, but their reality is in many crucial respects different from that experienced by people who live in the country's urban hubs. These rural towns are remote and, in many ways, utterly disconnected from many of the privileges associated with urban living. The most extreme of South Africa's deep and sustained inequalities are reflected in such rural communities, where the pressing concerns of shelter, food, water and heat often outweigh the less immediate need for electricity, telecommunications and other luxuries. When it comes to moving to large urban areas such as Johannesburg (the economic heart of the Gauteng Province and of the country as a whole), even when distances may appear relatively short, as was the case for the participants in our study, migration still comes with challenges.

From this group of participants we heard no stories of long journeys across multiple countries, such as were told by the immigrants from the Democratic Republic of Congo in Chapter 7. But although rural–urban migration may appear to be easier than international migration, rural–urban migrants may still undergo a process of alienation and acculturation similar to that of migrants entering a new country. Most of our migrant participants travelled to Johannesburg from Giyani in the least expensive way – by taxi, bus or train, 'which takes over eight hours (depending partly on whether the interface between the different legs of the journey can be managed), with the cost being over R1000' (Rome2rio n.d.; approximately US$55). The median household income in the greater Giyani district was about R14 600 (approximately US$799) per year in 2016, with almost a quarter of households reporting no income at all, according to Statistics South Africa (2016). If one owns a car, travelling from Giyani to Johannesburg is not too difficult, with reasonably good roads the whole way; but if one has little or no income, the trip is much more arduous and uncertain, and costs a substantial proportion of a household's annual income.

In this chapter, we discuss the experience of migration when people migrate for the purpose of studying, and to find work, as well as what people shared about communication between the rural areas at home and the city where the migrants now live.

METHODOLOGICAL REFLECTIONS

The research team investigating the internal rural–urban migration from Limpopo consisted of Lactricia Maja, Risuna Mathebula, Sonto Madonsela and Maria C. Marchetti-Mercer. Two members of our research team, postgraduate students Lactricia and Risuna, both from Limpopo, explored the impact of rural–urban migration on both migrants and the families they left behind. Many of the participants were recruited through the informal process of acquaintanceship, known in qualitative methodology as the snowballing technique (see Biernacki and Waldorf 1981; Sadler et al. 2010). Lactricia interviewed ten participants in person who had at least one adult child who had migrated to Gauteng. Sonto and Lactricia then interviewed online two adult children and one adult grandchild from this sample living in Johannesburg. Risuna interviewed seven participants in Giyani village and seven of their family members living in Gauteng. Families were often eager to be interviewed and to share their experiences, but, in many cases, those interviewed were the parents or grandparents of the migrants, which often meant that their age and lack of digital literacy precluded them from engaging deeply with many of the information communication technologies (ICTs) that we were investigating.

The link between advanced age, geographical location and lack of digital literacy has been established in the literature in other areas in the world (Doerr et al. 2022). Nevertheless, its confirmation in our local research was a striking, recurrent and thought-provoking finding. We learned that the older generation in a rural setting are often intimidated by and distrustful of technology. Many are unable to use it in the same way that younger people do. We learned that the value of access to mobile data, the lifeblood of ICT use, is in fact relative: data access has different values in urban and rural spaces, partly because, in many cases, the main obstacle to communication was not access to data, but the availability of a digital device, or the right kind of device, to use the data available.

As is often the case in fieldwork of this kind, Lactricia was treated with extreme wariness when she went to Modimolle to conduct her interviews. Many of her participants believed her to be a government employee, because of her clothing, which was read by participants as 'urban' and as 'foreign' in the local context. Lactricia reports that in one case a participant's daughter 'mistook [her] for a government employee trying to take advantage of her mother by robbing her of her pension money'.

Lactricia's reflections on this experience critically informed how she managed the remaining interviews. For example, she had initially endeavoured to dress in a manner respectful of her participants, but since her clothing was interpreted as evidence that she was a government employee, in a country where many citizens are deeply disillusioned with the ruling party, she had to rethink this decision. Moreover, as a young black woman studying towards a postgraduate degree, she may have been experienced as threatening, which meant that participants may have limited the amount of information they were willing to share. Lactricia also reflected on the interview process itself, reporting that all the responses did not come from participants alone. Invariably, at some point, the participants' children and grandchildren helped them to answer some of the questions asked during the interview process. This communal way of responding was something we should probably have anticipated, given how close together people live and the intergenerational family structure characteristic of many South African families. The phenomenon may also be understandable in the context of social values of relatedness and, in particular, *ubuntu*, an important Afrocentric principle that encapsulates the relationality of the self and the way in which the self and the community are co-constitutive of one another (Chisale 2020).

Sonto was involved in contacting the family members of Lactricia's participants in Johannesburg. Like Lactricia, Sonto encountered a number of challenges in this process, but these were different. Participants struggled to make the time, or requested access to internet data in order to be part of the project. All these interviews were carried out online prior to Covid-19, but, with hindsight, we can see that the logistics of arranging them already demonstrated many of the themes that would emerge regarding the use of ICTs, such as lack of data and difficulties with synchronous interactions. Even with urban participants, easy access to technology was not a given, showing that the digital divide in South Africa is not a matter of simple geography, but rather an issue of access largely dependent on socio-economic status.

For Risuna, her own experiences of travelling between rural Giyani and urban Johannesburg mirror the experiences of migrants themselves. This movement between urban and rural life proved to be profoundly disorienting, and this is something she saw reflected in the experiences of the people she interviewed. She herself felt, and observed in others, a sense of inhabiting disparate realities. Risuna was able to immerse herself in this lived experience during her data collection, and her own experience of rural–urban circular migration lent an important dimension to her analysis of the data.

MOVING TO THE CITY

One of the participants we interviewed was Sontaha, a 23-year-old tertiary student from a rural village in Limpopo. She has six siblings. All of them have been raised by their grandmother. She always wanted to further her studies after school, but, like many young South Africans, she was worried about how she would afford this, as her grandmother survived on an old age pension of around R1 500 per month (approximately US$84.28). There was a lack of information and limited resources in her village, so she could not access information on how to apply for financial aid. Luckily, she met a friend who was able to obtain the information needed, and she applied successfully for financial aid to study. At the time of our meeting, she was in her first year of study. Even though this was Sontaha's dream, leaving home was not an easy decision. She worried a great deal about who would take care of her ageing grandmother. All her siblings had moved to the cities in search of jobs, and if she left, her grandmother would be alone. The decision to leave was very difficult, but her faith played a significant role in her decision – she believed that with the assistance of prayer, she could rely on God to care for her grandmother. Summarising her decision to migrate to the city, Sontaha said: 'I love school and I like to study. So, it was not easy for me to study at home with my granny, doing nothing, when other people outside are fighting for their future. So, I decided that I'll also go to school and continue my study … At [home, there are few] schools, they are just secondary but there's no college or varsities near around.'

Sontaha would like to use technology to be in more regular contact with her grandmother, but the latter has never learned to use a smartphone or social media platforms such as WhatsApp. As a result, they communicate mainly through direct phone calls. As a result of poor eyesight, Sontaha's grandmother cannot read text messages. In addition, there are connectivity problems, and it is often impossible to get in touch with the village. In-person visits are also limited: Sontaha's grandmother is unable to visit Johannesburg because of her old age, and Sontaha cannot visit as often as she would like because of the demands of the educational institution where she studies and the costs involved. Since visits are not possible, they rely heavily on phone calls to stay in touch. Every morning before attending class, Sontaha calls her grandmother to ask how she is feeling and if she has had anything to eat. As part of reciprocal care, Sontaha sometimes receives groceries from her siblings through the mail, and every month her grandmother sends her what money she can.

Other people who spoke to us in our research have similar stories. Khumo explained: 'We lacked resources in our area and I thought I should move out of home to come … Firstly, it was Joburg. I went to Joburg where I started working, I started with my studies.' Similarly, Blessing told us: 'Oh, my decision to migrate [from] my home Limpopo to Pretoria? It's because of academic purposes. I'm a third-year student in Faculty of Education, doing Bachelor of Education I and FET (Senior Phase and Further Education and Training Teaching).' This finding confirms the work of Carren Ginsburg et al. (2016), who report that the desire to obtain an education is the primary determinant of internal migration, particularly in the rural-to-urban direction.

Mmabatho is an example of someone who left to find work: 'I said, "Mommy, it is better to leave, maybe I will find employment somewhere else." ' Peter, a parent who lives in the rural area, commented: 'There is no work here, apart from when a person leaves and goes to Gauteng. If you choose to reside here in our village, you will be jobless, as there are no jobs around here … All my children who left, left for work reasons and so that they could also improve the situation for their families left behind.'

The stories we heard were of migration undertaken out of necessity, into a different world, and into the struggles of staying in touch. Families left behind also struggled to stay in touch, especially because of challenges with the technology. Josephine, an elderly participant in the rural area, noted: 'We have poor vision and also we struggle with regard to how to dial the numbers [on a smartphone].' Mmabatho had a similar problem: 'I cannot read the names on my contact list. When the names of the people who are on my contact list appear on the screen, I cannot read them. There are certain letters I cannot read.'

Another grandmother's comment was striking – she said: 'Ah! Do I know what data is my child? I am using a cellular phone that does not have any features … Yes! the one that is used to receive calls only' (Merriam).

Coming from a generation who were brought up with traditional learning and communication methods such as using textbooks and writing letters, elderly relatives may struggle to learn to use new digital technologies (Blažič and Blažič 2020). Despite the availability of cheaper alternatives, it seems from the people we spoke to that their preferred method of communication is phone calls using conventional telephone networks, which is probably the most expensive way to keep in touch. Those who have migrated to urban areas cannot make use of the benefits of advanced technological platforms to maintain connectedness with those left behind, because the latter are not technologically literate and are not familiar with advanced digital platforms such as video calling or social networking sites, so they do not use them. Khumo said sadly: 'My parents are old-school. It's just the cell phone, a phone call. I tried, but then ... We bought them a smartphone. We bought my mother a smartphone, but then she's refusing ... if they were also modernised I was going to even do the video calling ... So the only difficult part – it's airtime it's so expensive.' Sontaha, who calls regularly, commented: 'My granny can't use social media, so if I want to talk to her about something, I have to call and talk ... to her.'

KEEPING IN CONTACT AND THE CHALLENGES OF CITY LIFE

All these issues interweave with the complex challenges rural–urban migrants face when moving to the city. For many, the process is potentially aided by the use of ICTs, a resource that is familiar to rural dwellers in better-resourced countries or to people from more privileged groups in unequal societies, such as South Africa. The child of a better-resourced farmer, even one living in a deep rural area of South Africa, much further away geographically than Giyani is to Johannesburg or Pretoria, is likely to be able to use WhatsApp to video-call relatives back home with little difficulty. This is in stark contrast to the experiences of even young adults among our participants, and therefore the ameliorating effect of being able to be in easy contact with those at home is absent.

One of the people we spoke to was Blessing, the fifth child in a family of seven. She was born in Giyani, and was raised by a single parent who is self-employed. She was determined to receive a higher education, but this necessitated moving to Pretoria, where she was in the third year of her studies at the time of her interview. Although she was proud to be the first in her family to receive higher education, Blessing found the lack of communal life and emphasis on individualism in the city alienating and difficult to adapt to. Furthermore, because of the technology gaps we have described, she was enormously frustrated by the fact that she could not keep in optimal contact with her family. She herself struggled with technology when she first went to university. She can now use a computer and other devices, but she lamented the lack of similar access for her family left behind. It appears that migrants had to learn how to use these advanced technologies, particularly smartphones and laptops, because ICTs played such an important role in their process of adaptation and acculturation, especially as it related to work and education.

Similary, Vutomi, who came to Gauteng to find work, described the stark differences between his home village and Pretoria in terms of access to ICTs. The digital access gap between the two places is enormous. Vutomi's father, for example, had never been to school and cannot read or write. Despite this, he did learn to use a basic mobile phone as he was good at memorising numbers. However, even when Vutomi tried to stay in touch with his father, they had to contend with poor signal and network outages.

The process of migration inevitably includes a loss of the social networks and social support from one's home community. According to Douglas D. Perkins, Neil A. Palmer and Manuel García-Ramírez (2011), migrants' well-being is linked to social support from their social networks, which most of them lose as a result of the distance. Robert E.B. Lucas (2016) explains that engaging with a group of people from one's home village offers more familiar surroundings, removing the feeling of alienation in a new setting. The absence of these social networks can certainly make the experience more difficult for the migrant. As Blessing put it:

> At home, the difference is, is like I'm always surrounded with people who are closer to me, my relatives and friends, people who[m] we grew up together [with], I know them better. Like they know me very well in a way that if they can look at me, they can tell like you are angry, okay today, et cetera, et cetera … At home, our neighbours can give us, we share, so here there's no one who can share with, because people who are here, I don't know them.

Mmabatho spoke about the other side of this experience; she feels as though she has lost the opportunity to share with others, to give to them: 'When I cook, I do not share the food with anyone. Is eating alone on your own without any company nice?'

Blessing, Mmabatho and others like them face a process of cultural and social adaptation without easy access to those left behind. Migrating even a short distance in South Africa can mean entering a different language community. Mbali described this experience: 'There's a difference because around here they don't speak my language and I don't know their language. I don't even like going out because of that. I don't speak other languages. So, I option to stay inside.' Easy virtual contact with those back home could potentially ease the pain of not having others to converse with. Mbali's social retreat in the city, captured in the poignant comment 'I option to stay inside', was not offset by regular home-language chats with those left behind. The challenge of learning a new language to acculturate comes with feelings of solitude and isolation, as Mbali's words show. Significantly, language is not only a form of expression but also a way to experience connectedness, roots and belonging, which migrants do not get to express or experience in some host communities (Jaspal 2015).

For these migrants, being in an environment where ICT access is easy and common does not mean that they do not experience difficulties using and accessing technology. Cost – of devices and data – is one obvious limiting factor, but core adaptation and identity issues also play a role. At first, many migrants lack digital literacy, the ability to integrate the knowledges and skills required to use hardware and devices such as laptops, phones and other ICTs, as well as the ability to participate in information-sharing (Bawden 2008). Recalling her earlier days in the city, Blessing said: 'From an earlier time, it was difficult because it was ... some of the stuff like computer I've been using it for the first time of my life. So I was scared. Like, even using the mouse.' For these migrants, there is also fear of what life may bring in South Africa's high-crime city areas, where they do not know others and may not speak the language. In such a situation, even the very technologies that are generally used to help people feel more settled and connected – like a computer mouse – may feel like part of this frightening new world.

Once this sense of fear and unfamiliarity is overcome and literacy skills develop, things may improve. As Vutomi put it: 'Let's say a person that is living in an urban area and a person that is living in a rural area … there's so much gap in terms of the access that they have in terms of infrastructure and things like … simple things such as accessing information or those kinds of things to having access … Here we have access to free Wi-Fi.' What is interesting here is that, although Vutomi is expressing frustration about the difference between ICT access in rural and in urban settings, in his simple and factual statement 'here we have access to free Wi-Fi', he is telling a story of his own adaptation, learning about the technology, having the skill to log on to free Wi-Fi hotspots (which are certainly not yet ubiquitous even in urban South Africa), and taking ownership of this resource ('we have …') in a manner that demonstrates how much he has internalised some of the skills of a digital citizen.

THOSE LEFT BEHIND: PHYSICAL AND VIRTUAL DISTANCE

Parents and grandparents are often called upon to make peace with their children's migration because of the benefits it may hold for the latter (Marchetti-Mercer et al. 2020) and, in the case of remittances, for the family in the place of origin. In our interviews, it was evident that parents generally supported the move by their children, because it was beneficial for the household left behind: 'I was very happy and asked God to be with them and wished them to find employment … You console yourself and comfort yourself … because you yourself cannot offer them anything' (Merriam). But the gain was ambiguous, because the loss was also challenging: 'I felt sad at the same time because it was far' (Portia). This aligns with the notion of ambiguous loss identified by Pauline Boss (1991).

These challenges are alleviated to some extent through staying in touch. Communicating more immediately does help, even if it is expensive. Important events can be shared, as Mavis pointed out: 'You notify the person about funerals and weddings.' Care can also be provided when necessary: 'When I am having problems or when I am sick, I just make a phone call to inform the other person' (Mmabatho). Struggles to use the technology still create barriers, but social connections at home do help: 'When making a phone call, I would ask for assistance so that they search for him [her son] on my phone' (Josephine).

Despite all the difficulties noted by those who have migrated, those left behind observe that today's technology, more specifically the mobile phone (Vertovec 2004), has made communication much easier, as it allows families to maintain communication despite geographical distance, in comparison with old methods of communication that were used decades ago (Francisco 2015): 'Back then when we were communicating ... we were supposed to write a letter. The letter will take long period of time to get delivered to its destination. So now in this very moment in time, you can be able to talk to someone in Gauteng with this phone' (Peter).

Cost remains a determining factor. Peter commented: 'When we have money, we use it for other things because they are the priorities and that is better.' This suggests that communication can sometimes be regarded as less important than immediate survival, which takes priority, a point also made by some of the Malawian participants discussed in Chapter 5. Sarah explained: 'The difficult thing is that sometimes you find yourself not having money to buy airtime ... it is difficult because sometimes, I don't have airtime ... I end up making decisions on my own without his input ... we do need money but unfortunately we do not have it.'

BRIDGING THE GAP OF DIGITAL ILLITERACY AMONG THOSE LEFT BEHIND: 'SOCIAL REMITTANCES'?

In some instances, unfamiliarity with more advanced digital platforms such as WhatsApp and Skype seemed to be a barrier that hindered those left behind in maintaining connectedness with those who had migrated to the urban areas. But there was some evidence of digital literacy know-ledge transfer from migrants to their families back home, supported by the strong motivation that family members feel to bridge the geographical divide and stay in touch. Younger people 'at home' also facilitated access to ICTs for their older kin, suggesting that ICTs have the potential to be a more supportive dimension of transnational family relations. This exchange of information can be seen as a form of 'social remittance', which, like financial remittances, or the writing remittances identified by Kate E. Vieira (2016) in Brazil, helps to improve the standard of living in the areas of origin (Capstick 2020; Millard, Baldassar and Wilding 2018). Nsovoo, in the rural area, recalled: 'Yes, for example, when he was usually here at home before he migrated, he had to do a lot of things regarding ICTs for me. However, with him being gone, my experience went from an observer to someone who participated in it because it was up to me now to learn how to be part of ICTs.' Precious made a similar point, commenting on how she taught her mother, whom she had to leave behind, to use technology in order to take advantage of more advanced technological platforms such as WhatsApp and Skype to maintain connectedness across distance: 'My mom, I'm teaching her how to Skype, how to video-call, but she … does have WhatsApp but she is not a WhatsApp person, so I must … every time when I send her something I must still call her and let her know.'

CONCLUSION

The stories we heard in this part of our research are perhaps less dramatic than those, for example, of travelling across borders, fleeing political violence, or living with xenophobia. Instead, they reflect the ordinary everyday struggles that have long formed part of the history of South Africa and are still part of its current fabric. The process of migration from rural to urban areas, even across relatively short distances, involves both social and psychological adaptation. The stories of those who migrated revealed the alienation of the migrant, particularly in the early period of being away from home, and the experience of 'two worlds', which have to be constantly navigated. On the other hand, those left behind spoke of absence and the occasional, often unsatisfying opportunity for connection via technological platforms. The migrants who had left described the alienating and often disorienting experience of entering a new world while they were still embedded in the old, straddling these two realities and moving between them with difficulty. What we consequently observed was also a process of 'technological migration' for both those who migrated and those who stayed behind. This highlights the immense digital divide that exists between disadvantaged and impoverished communities in South Africa, on the one hand, and more affluent communities, on the other. Much has been written about inequality in South Africa, but this digital inequality perhaps remains more hidden – but is no less important – than other forms of inequality. Admittedly, since the Covid pandemic, more has been written about the digital divide in South Africa, and especially its impact on education (Lembani et al. 2020; Mkhize and Davids 2021; Woldegiorgis 2022). Kehinde Oluwaseun Omotoso, Jimi Adesina and Ololade G. Adewole (2020) have noted a gender dimension to this divide. Our data confirm that the dynamics within families and social groups across rural–urban migratory pathways warrant further exploration, especially regarding the digital divide.

In terms of how South Africa presents itself to the world, as a country of innovators and leaders (often justifiably), this story of inequality must not be lost and may not be ignored. The underlying problems are economic, but support for older people in poorly resourced communities where there has been and will continue to be out-migration may be helpful (Kabbar and Crump 2007). The need for those left behind to keep in touch with those who have left is not a trivial matter, and it must be attended to. There is already some evidence of digital literacy knowledge transfer from migrants to their families back home, supported by the strong motivation all family members feel to bridge the geographical divide and stay in touch. This is a form of 'social remittance', which, like financial remittances, may ultimately offer one kind of capital to improve the standard of living of older non-migrants in their areas of origin (Millard, Baldassar and Wilding 2018).

REFERENCES

Bawden, David. 2008. 'Origins and Concepts of Digital Literacy'. In *Digital Literacies: Concepts, Policies and Practices*, edited by Colin Lankshear and Michele Knobel, 17–32. Lausanne: Peter Lang.

Biernacki, Patrick and Dan Waldorf. 1981. 'Snowball Sampling: Problems and Techniques of Chain Referral Sampling'. *Sociological Methods and Research* 10, no. 2: 141–163. https://doi.org/10.1177/004912418101000205.

Blažič, Borka Jerman and Andrej Jerman Blažič. 2020. 'Overcoming the Digital Divide with a Modern Approach to Learning Digital Skills for the Elderly Adults'. *Education and Information Technologies* 25, no. 1: 259–279. https://doi.org/10.1007/s10639-019-09961-9.

Boss, Pauline. 1991. 'Ambiguous Loss'. In *Living beyond Loss: Death in the Family*, edited by Froma Walsh and Monica McGoldrick, 164–175. New York: W.W. Norton.

Capstick, Tony. 2020. 'Transnational Literacies as Social Remittances: The Role of Language Ideologies in Shaping Migrants' Online Literacies'. *Applied Linguistics* 41, no. 2: 301–319. https://doi.org/10.1093/applin/amz009.

Chisale, Sinenhlanhla S. 2020. 'Politics of the Body, Fear and Ubuntu: Proposing an African Women's Theology of Disability'. *HTS Teologiese Studies/Theological Studies* 76, no. 3: a5871. https://doi.org/10.4102/hts.v76i3.5871.

Démurger, Sylvie. 2015. 'Migration and Families Left Behind'. *IZA World of Labor* 2015: 144. https://doi.org/10.15185/izawol.144.

Doerr, Sebastian, Jon Frost, Leonardo Gambacorta and Han Qiu. 2022. 'Population Ageing and the Digital Divide'. SUERF Policy Brief, 270. https://www.suerf.org/suer-policy-brief/40251/population-ageing-and-the-digital-divide.

Francisco, Valerie. 2015. '"The Internet Is Magic": Technology, Intimacy and Transnational Families'. *Critical Sociology* 41, no. 1: 173–190. https://doi.org/10.1177/0896920513484602.

Ginsburg, Carren, Philippe Bocquier, Donatien Béguy, Sulaimon Afolabi, Orvalho Augusto, Karim Derra, Frank Odhiambo, Mark Otiende, Abdramane B. Soura, Pascal Zabre et al. 2016. 'Human Capital on the Move: Education as a Determinant of Internal Migration in Selected INDEPTH Surveillance Populations in Africa'. *Demographic Research* 34: 845–884. https://doi.org/10.4054%2FDemRes.2016.34.30.

Harington, John S., Neil D. McGlashan and Elzbieta Z. Chelkowska. 2004. 'A Century of Migrant Labour in the Gold Mines of South Africa'. *Journal of the South African Institute of Mining and Metallurgy* 104, no. 2: 65–71.

Jaspal, Rusi. 2015. 'Migration and Identity Processes among First-Generation British South Asians'. *South Asian Diaspora* 7, no. 2: 79–96. https://doi.org/10.1080/19438 192.2015.1007634.

Kabbar, Eltahir Fadul and Barbara J. Crump. 2007. 'Promoting ICTs Uptake among the Refugee Immigrant Community in New Zealand'. *Proceedings of the International Association for Development of the Information Society (IADIS) International Conference e-Society, 3–6 July 2007, Lisbon*, edited by Piet Kommers, 55–62. Lisbon: IADIS Press.

Kok, Pieter, Oumar Bouare, Michael O'Donovan and Johan van Zyl. 2003. *Post-apartheid Patterns of Internal Migration in South Africa*. Pretoria: HSRC Press.

Lembani, Reuben, Ashley Gunter, Markus Breines and Mwazvita Tapiwa Beatrice Dalu. 2020. 'The Same Course, Different Access: The Digital Divide between Urban and Rural Distance Education Students in South Africa'. *Journal of Geography in Higher Education* 44, no. 1: 70–84. https://doi.org/10.1080/03098265.2019.1694876.

Lucas, Robert E.B. 2016. 'Internal Migration in Developing Economies: An Overview of Recent Evidence'. *Geopolitics, History, and International Relations* 8, no. 2: 159–191. https://doi.org/10.22381/GHIR8220168.

Marchetti-Mercer, Maria C., Leslie Swartz, Vinitha Jithoo, Nthopele Mabandla, Alessandro Briguglio and Maxine Wolfe. 2020. 'South African International Migration and Its Impact on Older Family Members'. *Family Process* 59, no. 4: 1737–1754. https://doi.org/10.1111/famp.12493.

Mayer, Philip. 1961. *Townsmen or Tribesmen: Conservatism and the Process of Urbanization in a South African City*. Xhosa in Town Series, 2. Cape Town: Oxford University Press.

Millard, Adele, Loretta Baldassar and Raelene Wilding. 2018. 'The Significance of Digital Citizenship in the Well-Being of Older Migrants'. *Public Health* 158: 144–148. https://doi.org/10.1016/j.puhe.2018.03.005.

Mkhize, Themba Ralph and Mogamat Noor Davids. 2021. 'Towards a Digital Resource Mobilisation Approach for Digital Inclusion during Covid-19 and Beyond: A Case of a Township School in South Africa'. *Educational Research for Social Change* 10, no. 2: 18–32. http://dx.doi.org/10.17159/2221-4070/2021/v10i2a2.

Mlambo, Victor. 2018. 'An Overview of Rural–Urban Migration in South Africa: Its Causes and Implications'. *Archives of Business Research* 6, no. 4: 63–70. https://doi.org/10.14738/abr.64.4407.

Omotoso, Kehinde Oluwaseun, Jimi Adesina and Ololade G. Adewole. 2020. 'Exploring Gender Digital Divide and Its Effect on Women's Labour Market Outcomes in South Africa'. *African Journal of Gender, Society and Development* 9, no. 4: 85–108. https://hdl.handle.net/10520/ejc-aa_jgida1-v9-n4-a5.

Perkins, Douglas D., Neil A. Palmer and Manuel García-Ramírez. 2011. 'Psychosocial Studies of Migration and Community: Introduction to the Special Issue'. *Psychosocial Intervention* 20, no. 3: 237–242. https://doi.org/10.5093/in2011v20n3a1.

Posel, Dorrit. 2004. 'Have Migration Patterns in Post-apartheid South Africa Changed?' *Journal of Interdisciplinary Economics* 15, nos 3–4: 277–292. https://doi.org/10.1177/02601079X04001500303.

Posel, Dorrit and Daniela Casale. 2003. 'What Has Been Happening to Internal Labour Migration in South Africa, 1993–1999?' *South African Journal of Economics* 71, no. 3 (February): 455–479. https://doi.org/10.1111/j.1813-6982.2003.tb00081.x.

Reed, Holly E. 2013. 'Moving across Boundaries: Migration in South Africa, 1950–2000'. *Demography* 50, no. 1: 71–95. https://doi.org/10.1007/s13524-012-0140-x.

Rome2rio. N.d. https://www.rome2rio.com/map/Giyani/Johannesburg-Park-Station.

Sadler, Georgia Robins, Hau-Chen Lee, Rod Seung-Hwan Lim and Judith Fullerton. 2010. 'Recruitment of Hard-to-Reach Population Subgroups via Adaptations of the Snowball Sampling Strategy'. *Nursing and Health Sciences* 12, no. 3: 369–374. https://doi.org/10.1111/j.1442-2018.2010.00541.x.

Sridhar, Kala S. and George Mavrotas, eds. 2021. *Urbanization in the Global South: Perspectives and Challenges*. London: Routledge. https://www.taylorfrancis.com/books/edit/10.4324/9781003093282/urbanization-global-south-kala-sridhar-george-mavrotas.

Stapleton, Timothy J. 2015. *Warfare and Tracking in Africa, 1952–1990*. London: Routledge. https://doi.org/10.4324/9781315653716.

Statistics South Africa. 2016. *Statistics South Africa Community Survey in 2016*. Statistical Release P0301. Pretoria: Statistics South Africa.

Vertovec, Steven. 2004. 'Cheap Calls: The Social Glue of Migrant Transnationalism'. *Global Networks* 4, no. 2: 219–224. https://doi.org/10.1111/j.1471-0374.2004.00088.x.

Vieira, Kate E. 2016. 'Writing Remittances: Migration-Driven Literacy Learning in a Brazilian Homeland'. *Research in the Teaching of English* 50, no. 4: 422–449. https://www.jstor.org/stable/24889943.

Woldegiorgis, Emnet Tadesse. 2022. 'Mitigating the Digital Divide in the South African Higher Education System in the Face of the Covid-19 Pandemic'. *Perspectives in Education* 40, no. 3: 197–211. https://doi.org/10.18820/2519593X/pie.v40.i3.13.

Zaami, Mariama. 2022. 'Conceptualising Migration and Livelihoods: Perspectives from the Global South'. In *The Routledge Handbook on Livelihoods in the Global South*, edited by Fiona Nunan, Clare Barnes and Sukanya Krishnamurthy, 359–367. Oxford: Routledge. https://www.routledge.com/The-Routledge-Handbook-on-Livelihoods-in-the-Global-South/Nunan-Barnes-Krishnamurthy/p/book/9780367856359.

4

'They Will Be Yearning': Zimbabwean Migration to South Africa and Keeping the Family Connected

Siko Moyo, Sonto Madonsela and Maria C. Marchetti-Mercer

Like most migrants we spoke to for this book, Zimbabweans who have made the choice to move to South Africa as well as their families in Zimbabwe all face the dilemma of balancing losses and gains. One of our participants, Tendai, speaks of both a 'good decision' and a 'bad decision' to express this situation:

> On the other side, you know, it was a good decision to leave because here in Zimbabwe … you can't sustain your family … So it was a good decision so that we can also live, we can also eat … we can also get to wear clothes … But on the other hand, to me it was a bad decision because I grew up without a father, you know. I grew up with my mom … playing both parts … Both roles. To be a dad and be a mom. So, I had to grow up here alone without a father without guidance … so I had to be a man and find myself out. So, for me it was a bad decision because I don't know him … To me it was a bad decision because I never had a father in my life.

As Tendai's regret at not having a father around suggests, it is hard for a child to understand the situation, but a loss of connection is felt equally by the parents. Brief moments of connection, even for adults, are often not enough:

> As much as technology is assisting but then I feel that even the bond between me and my son will [be lost] over time if things remain like this ... The gap will be bigger and bigger over time. So, it's not just ... he doesn't understand the financial side that, okay, my mother is sending finances, my uncle is sending finances, but he is missing that there's a gap that his mother is not there. So, I don't believe finances are everything. Maybe for an adult, for my mother, she can understand that ... we've got food, my daughter is sending food ... But for a person, a little child, they will be wanting that, they will be yearning for their mother's love, to spend time with their mother. It's not enough to just send voice notes and video calls. Yeah, that's what I believe. (Chipo)

Much has been written on the phenomenon of Zimbabwean migration to South Africa, especially as it has played out since the opening of South Africa's borders after 1994 (Crush et al. 2017). In the last decade, South Africa has become the primary destination of choice for people leaving Zimbabwe. Political instability and economic decline in Zimbabwe are driving migration to South Africa at an accelerating rate. An estimated total of between two and three million Zimbabweans may be living in South Africa (Hlatshwayo 2019), but no official figures are available, because data on migration are difficult to collect and interpret.

While the struggling Zimbabwean economy has driven hundreds of thousands of Zimbabweans across the border to seek 'greener pastures' and better economic opportunities, we are also deeply aware that their idealised dreams are often disappointed when they have to face the harsh realities of South African society, including the xenophobia experienced by many migrants in the country (Manik 2007). Most research on

Zimbabwean migration has a socio-economic focus, so that we often fail to comprehend the real stories of Zimbabwean migrants and how, in their quest to save their families from financial hardship, they leave their loved ones behind (Crush et al. 2017). Their attempt to 'rescue' their families by migrating may disrupt the very family system that they seek to protect. That said, it is important to take a family life-course perspective, as migration may have a greater impact at certain stages in the trans-national family life cycle and on certain types of family formations. For example, Wall et al. (2014) note that families with young children and single-parent families are often more negatively affected by the migration of a parent than families with older children, who often benefit from migration opportunities to join their migrant parent.

METHODOLOGICAL REFLECTIONS

The stories of the twenty Zimbabwean participants whom we interviewed differed in their focus, and each one was poignant in its own way. Ten participants who had migrated to South Africa were interviewed in the province of Gauteng; ten were interviewed in Zimbabwe, using a snowball sampling method that made possible matched sampling (see Chapter 2). Some of the participants were adult children who had left behind their parents and their siblings. Some were parents who had left behind their children, as well as their elderly parents. Many of those interviewed in Zimbabwe had seen their children, siblings and parents leave in the hope that they would find better job opportunities and help them survive in the highly precarious socio-economic environment in Zimbabwe.

This chapter was difficult to research, write, and do justice to. The trend of 'circular' migration from Zimbabwe to South Africa, as Jonathan Crush, Abel Chikanda and Godfrey Tawodzera (2015) call it, has deep political and economic roots that are reflected in the daily struggle for belonging, acceptance, employment and legitimation central to the life of many Zimbabwean migrants to South Africa. Nevertheless, despite the centrality of circular migration in the existing literature on Zimbabwean migrants, our findings suggest that, on the part of both migrants and their families left behind, there was acceptance of the move as permanent, albeit punctuated by visits home.

The interviews with Zimbabwean migrants were conducted in South Africa by Siko Moyo, a postgraduate student who hails from Zimbabwe and who left his family behind to come to South Africa to pursue his studies. He began interviewing fellow nationals as part of his own research for his thesis. He regarded his Zimbabwean citizenship as facilitative of the interview process, allowing him to deal with participants with whom he had much in common and to whom he could obtain access fairly easily. Siko is deeply aware of the political situation in Zimbabwe and how many migrants have fled to South Africa to escape political persecution. He was therefore aware that many participants might not be able to divulge certain aspects of why they left Zimbabwe, owing to fear of persecution; this awareness allowed him to create a sensitive atmosphere for his interviews. Siko, like Risuna (who interviewed migrants from Limpopo, see Chapter 3), was self-reflective about detaching himself from his interpretation when analysing his data, suggesting that dual positioning as researcher and migrant created complexity for many of our researchers.

Adopting a snowball sampling method to recruit further participants, Siko also travelled to Zimbabwe to conduct interviews with families left behind. These interviews took place at the height of the Covid-19 pandemic, in December 2020, at a time when visits between families were generally not possible. His ability to travel back 'home' during this time, when most other Zimbabweans were unable to do so, placed him in a particularly privileged position. There were some similarities with and some differences between our findings regarding the use of information communication technologies (ICTs) in the Zimbabwean matched samples and those in the Limpopo families described in the previous chapter. In both places, people struggled with connectivity and the cost of data, but, in general, Zimbabwean families seemed to have a higher level of digital literacy.

The Choice of Stories

We opened this chapter with the words of Tendai and Chipo. For ease of presentation, in this chapter we focus on the stories of these two participants, which are in many ways typical of the experiences of the other people we spoke to. Tendai's story speaks to the experiences of many Zimbabwean children and youths whose parents have moved to South Africa, while Chipo's story speaks to the challenges faced by those parents who had to leave their children behind. Tendai and Chipo are not related or known to each other, but their narratives mirror both these sides of the migratory experience. Tendai was 23 at the time of the interview. His father migrated to South Africa in 2001, so, like many children of migrants, he grew up without a father figure in his life, and with a sense that his family had been 'broken' as a result of his father's migration. Chipo, by contrast, was 40 at the time of the interview. She migrated to South Africa in 2016 in search of employment opportunities and career advancement so that she would be better able to provide for her child, as she was the single parent of a son, aged seven years. She left him in Zimbabwe in the care of her mother.

The stories of our twenty participants varied, but one theme recurred – these migrants left Zimbabwe mainly because their families need support to survive financially, as Tendai's and Chipo's stories make clear. The expression 'greener pastures' was used over and over again, both by those who had migrated and by those left behind. This sense of searching for a utopia, a better future, for a dream that was to come true, was prevalent prior to migration. For many, the harsh reality in South Africa was very different. For them, migration resulted in menial jobs, precarious lifestyles and immense economic pressure, not only to provide for those left behind, but also to survive themselves. Over time, familial relationships were affected, as both Tendai and Chipo told us. Technology plays a crucial role in maintaining regular contact, but this is not always satisfactory. The Covid-19 pandemic worsened the situation for both sides of these migrant families. In most cases, visits had not been possible since the lockdowns began in early 2020, and the economic precarity of many migrants worsened when the pandemic started, increasing the pressures and stresses on family systems.

A BRIEF HISTORY OF ZIMBABWEAN MIGRATION TO SOUTH AFRICA

Migration from what is today Zimbabwe to South Africa has a very long history, even predating the discovery of gold and diamonds in South Africa in the nineteenth century (Wentzel and Tlabela 2006). Indeed, the story of migrant labour in South Africa is intertwined very closely with the histories of neighbouring countries, including Zimbabwe (Van Onselen 2021). More recently, before 1990, most Zimbabweans who migrated to South Africa were white, especially farmers leaving the country after Zimbabwe's independence in the 1980s, or young black male Zimbabweans crossing the border to work illegally on white-owned South African farms or in towns (Crush, Chikanda and Tawodzera 2015). Men were also recruited to work in the South African gold mines. Most of these black migrants came from rural households and worked in South Africa for short periods, returning home once they had accumulated sufficient financial resources; this is known in the literature as a form of circular migration (Potts 2010). During that period, migration was predominantly male-dominated (Crush and Tevera 2010).

In the 1980s, about 200 000 Zimbabweans crossed the border into South Africa annually (Crush and Tevera 2010). According to Marie Wentzel and Kholadi Tlabela (2006), the numbers peaked in the 1990s, following the fall of apartheid, which coincided with a sharp decline in the economy of Zimbabwe. In 2000 alone, approximately 500 000 people crossed the border legally from Zimbabwe into South Africa, while the number of illegal crossings is unknown. By 2008 numbers had more than doubled, to 1.25 million (Crush and Tevera 2010). Recent migration has been characterised by more or less equal numbers of both male and female and young and old, and by people of all education and skills levels.

The rise in inflation, unemployment, poor public service, political oppression and accelerating poverty in Zimbabwe are all push factors that have contributed to the rising emigration. This has led to a significant brain drain of educated and skilled Zimbabweans, who have been pushed out of the country by a deteriorating economy (De Jager and Musuva 2016). As a neighbouring country, South Africa offers Zimbabweans an accessible destination. Brian Latham and Mike Cohen (2011) point out that South Africa is also viewed as economically advanced, compared with other countries in the region. Since the start of the new millennium, many Zimbabweans entering South Africa have claimed that they were merely visiting the country, whereas they were, in fact, joining or visiting parents or other relatives, accessing medical help that was not available at home, buying and selling goods, and making money either to send or to take home (Crush, Chikanda and Tawodzera 2015). Patterns of migration changed between 2005 and 2010: in 2005 Zimbabweans still described going to South Africa as temporary, but after 2005 more than two-thirds of a sample of 493 people indicated that they intended to settle in South Africa permanently (Crush, Chikanda and Tawodzera 2015).

As the economic and political crisis deepened in Zimbabwe, the influx of Zimbabweans into South Africa also increased, making them the largest group of foreign nationals in South Africa. As a result, Zimbabweans have become the victims of resentment, and have been blamed for many of the economic problems in the country, especially the high rate of unemployment (Hungwe 2013). According to Godwin Dube (2017), this resentment is deeply rooted among South Africans, who believe that foreign nationals are taking their jobs and their women, and committing crimes. Zimbaweans are often referred to as '*makwerekwere*', a derogatory term used in South Africa to refer to migrants from other African countries (Hungwe 2013). They have often been the target of xenophobic attacks, particularly in 2008 and 2019.

Many Zimbabwean migrants living in South Africa need to save as much as possible in order to send a meaningful sum of money back home to their families (Mawadza 2008), which places them under great stress. Many live in informal settlements (living in what are known as shacks) and in high-density areas characterised by poor service delivery and a lack of clean water and electricity (Hungwe 2013). Difficult living conditions are worsened by a lack of documentation and the precarious social standing this brings.

ZIMBABWEAN FAMILY RELATIONSHIPS AND ICTs

The impact of migration on individuals and families is complex, as the literature shows, with many challenges and constraints, as well as some opportunities. One important dimension of this complexity requires us to understand the impact of migration on transnational family relationships, in both the destination country and the country of origin, as discussed by authors such as Leon Grinberg and Rebeca Grinberg (1989), Celia J. Falicov (2007) and Maria C. Marchetti-Mercer (2016), who stresses Carlos E. Sluzki's (1979) view of the disruption of social networks as an inescapable consequence of migration. This is the kind of disruption we see in the stories of Tendai and Chipo, who both reported one underlying paradox in the phenomenon of Zimbabwean migration to South Africa: the breakdown of the family system as a consequence of the attempt to rescue this same family. This phenomenon is illustrated throughout our data, so that the stories of the two participants we began with are, in many ways, representative of the other families in the study. Both these stories began as stories of hope for a better future and pride in being able to take care of loved ones. Both are also stories of deep sadness, as the parent–child bond was put under great strain because of separation and distance. It is important to note that the stage in the family life cycle and the age of dependent children at the point when a parent migrates are important considerations when one evaluates the impact of migration. We cannot know the future outcomes of migration for the families in our study. Furthermore, we cannot assume that these family relationships would necessarily have been better if migration had not occurred, given the stressors and strains of life in precarious economic and social contexts.

In what follows, we focus on the experiences shared by participants to better understand their current circumstances.

Tendai's Story

First, let us share the rest of the story of Tendai, whose father left him behind when Tendai was a young boy, and went to look for work in South Africa. This migration has brought opportunities that enabled the family to survive financially and allowed Tendai to pursue university studies. However, it has also brought challenges that have had a negative impact on the father–son relationship, as Tendai's comment, 'to me it was a bad decision because I never had a father in my life', clearly indicates.

Tendai's father migrated to South Africa after finishing college to look for better opportunities. Tendai said: 'So that is when … he left for South Africa and to find better opportunities and to find a job that can sustain the family, the whole family, you know.' As with most migrants in our study of Zimbabwean transnational families, the family approved of the decision to migrate because of the potential advantages it held for the larger family, as is reflected by Tendai's acknowledgement of the decision as 'a good decision', as 'here in Zimbabwe you know you can't sustain your family with what … So it was a good decision so that we can also live, we can also eat, you know, we can also get to wear clothes.' At the same time, Tendai experienced his father's move as having caused serious disruption in the family:

> Like our family … growing up in a family which is not … what can I say? Broken family … we are a broken family … A family should… stay together under one roof. That's a family, you know. [They] should stay under one roof … Share a culture of the family. I don't even know the culture of our family, how we do things … so … That decision affected me because growing up when you don't have a father you face a lot of things. You face bullying, you face … you

> don't know how to be a man, so you just learn how to be a man out here in the streets … Strangers teach you how to be a man but if you are getting it from your father you will know what's right and what's not right, and what's bad. So that was the difficult part for me.

His description of a broken family speaks to the suffering that he experienced because his father was absent during crucial times of his development as a young man. However, he does note the important role that technology played in ameliorating this disruption: 'It's very useful for communication because you'll be communicating always … keep in touch, so yeah, I think social media is very useful right now. If there was no social media, imagine I won't be talking to him. I won't be knowing how he is or is he sick or whatever so but it's useful.' As with many migrant families discussed in this book, WhatsApp, as a free messaging and video-calling application, was commonly the preferred way to communicate because of its ease of use and relatively low cost. However, using WhatsApp requires mobile data or access to Wi-Fi, and the cost of acquiring such data is at times prohibitive. Tendai describes the lengths he goes to in order to get hold of data: '[I have to] hustle […] like I sell alcohol and sometimes I sell other products […] so that I can buy data, I can like buy bundles so that I can keep in touch for communication and research purposes at school. Because we are not given… there's no free data in Zimbabwe – there's no … you know not like other countries or developed countries.'

Tendai argued that communicating through technology also showed care for the other person: 'I can show them that I really care about them so yeah because you're now communicating, you're always in touch. So I don't think it's a barrier to care … if you're communicating it means that person actually cares about you.' The sense of caring was also displayed by Tendai's hiding difficult information from his father so as not to worry him, something that is often seen in migrant families (see, for example, Sampaio 2020): 'During this pandemic you know I faced depression …

And other things … at home so you can't tell a person … you can't express yourself, you know, that you are depressed. That you don't have anything to do, you are not going to school, you're not going to work, you're just sitting idle. So, you can't express your feelings over the phone, so you just hide them and just move on with life.'

The emotional exchange between migrant parents and their children may also be seen as a 'migration paradox', as Deborah Fahy Bryceson (2019, 3052) calls it – migration improves the material condition of children left behind but may often come at the cost of the child's emotional well-being. Studies report an emotional gap between migrant fathers and their children, defined by a sense of dis-comfort, unease, awkwardness in the relationship and a lack of more open communication. These characteristics in essence capture a sense of unfamiliarity that may exist in transnational family relationships (Parreñas 2008), particularly where dependent children are concerned (Wall et al. 2014), which reinforces the importance of the age of children and family life stage in the process.

One way to overcome the distance created in transnational relationships is through visits. Tendai mentioned the importance of visits as a way to reconnect with his father:

> When I visit there … I get to be with him and spend more time with him so it's meaningful to me because we don't see each other more often. So I value that small time … that we have … it's mean-ingful … We try to connect since he is someone … since we have something in common … like we have boxing and I love Orlando Pirates [football club] and he's also a Pirates fan so … and again … I work out, so he works out. So like that's the connection that we have though.

Tangible human connections are made by visiting one's family, rather than just imagining their presence or being in virtual contact via ICTs

(Marchetti-Mercer, Swartz and Baldassar 2021). However, the impact of the Covid-19 pandemic has been severe on families' ability to travel and visit and overcome the sense of distance. It has affected people's ability to attend important family rituals such as funerals, as Tendai described:

> We lost our grandmother right now in May and because of Covid-19 borders were closed and my dad never had an opportunity to come and bury his own mother ... and it was a difficult phase for the whole family and our relationships. Because we had to livestream the whole funeral and it was so painful ... Imagine you ... you have a mother, and your mother is that other side and you can't go and bury her and honour her memory. So, it was very difficult for the whole family. And again you know I miss him a lot and he was supposed to come this year. So he didn't come because of Covid-19.

Nevertheless, what the participants told us about transnational care in times when mobility is constrained, as it was by the Covid-19 pandemic, reveals that even when visits are not possible, family care is not 'put on hold' but continues to be provided across borders through reconfiguration and transformation (Brandhorst, Baldassar and Wilding 2020). But, despite the usefulness of ICTs, Tendai's story constantly revealed the heartfelt pain he experienced from growing up without a father's physical presence.

Chipo's Story

Chipo's story gives the perspective of a parent forced to leave a child behind in order to provide for him. She had to leave her young son in the care of her elderly mother to look for work and further her studies in South Africa. 'I just asked my mother to remain with my son for just a little while, while I'm just trying to settle down.' She constantly agonises over what the impact on her relationship with her son will be in the years to come: 'But for a person, a little child, they will be wanting that, they will be yearning for their mother's love, to spend time with their mother.'

She describes her move as follows: 'It was mostly in search of greener pastures.' Her words reiterate the idealised and aspirational view that many Zimbabwean migrants initially have of South Africa. She also stressed the important role of technology in maintaining relationships with family left behind. WhatsApp was again the preferred means of staying connected with the family:

> We've got a WhatsApp group that we communicate, a family WhatsApp group for myself, my mother and my brother so we constantly keep updated on any family issues. Even in the morning, if it's good morning, if it's Scripture, if it's anything we … that's how we know that we are connected. So every morning we say good morning, how did you sleep? And things like that and then in the afternoon or if there's anything, any issues or if there's … yeah, any issues, that's how we keep connected and communicate.

WhatsApp groups seem to be a way to re-create family interactions in transnational families and facilitate everyday family interactions, albeit at a distance. They have been shown to be highly effective in building and maintaining kinship relationships. Their use indicates what it means to be a family existing in a digital habitat (Lake Yimer 2021). Virtual proximity may be achieved through these groups, which helps to fulfil the desire to remain a connected family despite physical distance. In the face of physical separation and the possibility of virtual connectedness, regular communication plays a role in maintaining family ties and eases the experience of separation (Demirsu 2022).

However, technology is not without its challenges. In many cases, these were associated with cost. Chipo described how she used text messaging and voice recording instead of video calling because of the high cost of data: 'It's mostly texting and voice recordings like let's say for … especially in Zimbabwe where data is a bit expensive. So, video calls they are not … really, we don't use them that much.' Profound asymmetries were noted between the home country and destination country, with communication being cheaper for migrants than for their families, as a study by Mirca Madianou and Daniel Miller (2011) also reported. Different types of ICTs are available primarily to affluent families and people who reside in urban areas (Madianou and Miller 2011). The result is that the migrants' ability to stay connected with left-behind family may be compromised by prohibitive costs and a lack of ICT infrastructure, which reflects inequality in the distribution of ICTs between urban areas (which may be described as more like the Global North) and rural areas (which clearly align with the Global South) (Salma, Kaewwilai and Aziz Ali 2021). It may also be that the high cost of data potentially affects relationship-building, especially in situations where children are not old enough to understand text messages and would benefit from video and voice calling, which offer an important visual presence and an easier way to share emotional connection.

Despite these difficulties, there was a shared sense among participants that ICTs allowed migrants such as Chipo opportunities to continue a relationship of care with their distant family members. Different levels and types of care are exchanged by participants, as Chipo's experience foregrounds. For example, providing for medical and physical health care was very important to her. Chipo found it easier to offer medical care to family members via ICTs, because she was able to seek out medical advice and other forms of practical care in South Africa. It is also more convenient for her to co-ordinate everything, as she does not want to overwork her elderly mother, who is already taking care of her son. This includes arranging for a local pharmacy in South Africa to provide medical advice to her family in Zimbabwe:

> I would say … let's say for example my son … okay, like in the past weeks my son had a bit of a temperature and a runny tummy. So I … with her [Mum] there is like not much that she can do … Well, she can do, but we prefer to do everything from this end. So I had to co-ordinate like the medication. There's a pharmacy that we … we also engage with them here in Cape Town via WhatsApp. I just tell them that my son is not feeling well, these are the symptoms.

And then they call Zimbabwe, my mother, direct to find out what is it that ... what is the problem and things like that for over-the-counter medication then it can be delivered direct to them.

ICTs were also used for providing other practical forms of care such as access to groceries:

Like for groceries there's so many what can I say ... like the Fresh in a Box [groceries sent directly from South Africa] where we buy food from this side or even Mukuru [food vouchers and money]. For Mukuru we even like send ... we just create orders via WhatsApp as well. We create the orders and then you go to Pick n Pay, you pay [from South Africa] and then she's able to collect the money [or goods] from Zimbabwe.[1] So yes, technology has really made life easier for communication and as well as facilitating a lot of things.

Thus the exchange of care in transnational families goes beyond sending financial remittances, as it includes health and practical needs.

What is said and what is not said through virtual communication is a key issue – as an act of care, people may hide information from one another (Sampaio 2020; Baldassar 2007). Chipo describes how once, when her son was ill, her mother did not tell her. Such silence was particularly stressful in retrospect, given the Covid-19 pandemic:

And then I was told that my son had a constant cough and all. And that was before I understood any things about Covid-19 and things like that ... But my mother told me maybe a week later that your son has got this constant cough and ... so I got so upset to say you're only telling me now, my son could be dying and you're only telling me now – why didn't you tell me the first day that he had? But because she knew she sort of like wants to monitor the situation first so that she doesn't cause panic ... But I also do the same, I understand. Instead of me just telling her that oh no I've got this terrible headache, I sort of like just to wait until you know … or find … Not even tell her at all. Unless maybe it's really, really something that is serious maybe I can say, 'Last week you know …'.

Chipo deemed visits very important to close the information gap, which she did not believe can easily bridged by the use of ICTs: 'But for holidays I'd prefer that he comes through, and they also come through and because you might do video calls, you might do voice notes but there's still that gap. You need to see them physically and spend time with them so yeah. So it's both. For ICT it's on a daily basis but for holidays I prefer that they come [in person].' Again, Covid-19 had an impact, not only on the ability to visit, but also on the frequency of communications:

We constantly speak to each other via WhatsApp but then obviously there's … there should be more concern, more care to find out are they okay? Are they … and also educating them on … like what I hear from this side. Because that side they might not have adequate information to say wash your hands, wear [a] mask and things like that. So I would say that definitely communication has increased because of Covid, because of the information that I keep giving to them.

In a time of global distress and uncertainty, it appeared that families needed to stay connected more frequently and more urgently.

Generally, despite the advantages of ICTs and the creative ways in which they have been used, there was a sense of loss in Chipo's relationship with her son: 'And maybe one thing … in as much as technology is assisting … I feel that even the bond between me and my son will [change] over time if things remain like this … The gap will be bigger and bigger over time.' This speaks to the challenges experienced by geographically distant mothers mentioned by Pierrette Hondagneu-Sotelo and Ernestine Avila (1997) and Madianou and Miller (2013).

CONCLUSION

Both stories we have highlighted speak of migrants leaving their loved ones behind in order to rescue the family from financial difficulties. In both cases, their leaving caused an inevitable sense of rupture in the very family they wanted to protect. This implies that, although the children of migrant parents appear to receive better financial support than the children of non-migrant families (Coe 2011), there are also heart-wrenching challenges in dealing with distance, as well as a realistic worry that the separation will damage relationships.

Our findings question the notion that an exchange of care is only possible if people live in the same geographical setting, by showing that family caregiving can be practised by people in different places – something made possible especially because of the role of ICTs. But ICTs cannot solve all the problems of migration. The stories of our participants confirm the significance of the impact of migration on family relationships. They make it clear that ultimately migration involves some form of sacrifice. Chipo's words evoke the pain of this great personal cost: 'I think it's a sacrifice because you get to live without them, and that's something very hard, but I think it's a form of care because you sacrifice a lot. Not being with your family. I've missed out on a lot … I've never played that mother role.' ICTs facilitate care, as we have seen with our Zimbabwean participants, but they cannot eradicate loss. The loss of which Chipo speaks is not just the loss of being able to offer care face to face but also, for her, the loss of a valued role. In order to be a good mother in other respects, she has to face her feeling that 'I've never played that mother role'. It is not possible to know what the future will hold for Chipo and her young son, or for Tendai and his father, and whether regular visits and constant virtual co-presence across distance will enable their relationships to remain connected. What is clear from these stories is how difficult transnational mothering and fathering of young children can be.

NOTE

1   Zimbabweans indicated that payments in US dollars and South African rands are preferred.

REFERENCES

Baldassar, Loretta. 2007. 'Transnational Families and the Provision of Moral and Emotional Support: The Relationship between Truth and Distance'. *Identities* 14, no. 4: 385–409. https://doi.org/10.1080/10702890701578423.

Brandhorst, Rosa, Loretta Baldassar and Raelene Wilding. 2020. 'Introduction to the Special Issue: "Transnational Family Care 'On Hold'? Intergenerational Relationships and Obligations in the Context of Immobility Regimes"'. *Journal of Intergenerational Relationships* 18, no. 3: 261–280. https://doi.org/10.1080/15350770. 2020.1787035.

Bryceson, Deborah Fahy. 2019. 'Transnational Families Negotiating Migration and Care Life Cycles across Nation-State Borders'. *Journal of Ethnic and Migration Studies* 45, no. 16: 3042–3064. https://doi.org/10.1080/1369183X.2018.1547017.

Coe, Cati. 2011. 'What Is Love? The Materiality of Care in Ghanaian Transnational Families'. *International Migration* 49, no. 6: 7–24. https://doi.org/10.1111/ j.1468-2435.2011.00704.x.

Crush, Jonathan, Abel Chikanda and Godfrey Tawodzera. 2015. 'The Third Wave: Mixed Migration from Zimbabwe to South Africa'. *Canadian Journal of African Studies/ Revue canadienne des études africaines* 49, no. 2: 363–382. https://doi.org/10.1080/0 0083968.2015.1057856.

Crush, Jonathan, Godfrey Tawodzera, Abel Chikanda, Sujata Ramachandran and Daniel Tevera. 2017. *South Africa Case Study: The Double Crisis; Mass Migration from Zimbabwe and Xenophobic Violence in South Africa*. Vienna: International Centre for Migration Policy Development; Waterloo, ON: Southern African Migration Programme.

Crush, Jonathan and Daniel Tevera. 2010. 'Exiting Zimbabwe'. In *Zimbabwe's Exodus: Crisis, Migration, Survival* (African Books Collective Series), edited by Jonathan Crush and Daniel Tevera, 1–49. Cape Town: Southern African Migration Project; Ottawa: IRDC.

De Jager, Nicola and Catherine Musuva. 2016. 'The Influx of Zimbabweans into South Africa: A Crisis of Governance That Spills Over'. *Africa Review* 8, no. 1: 15–30. https://doi.org/10.1080/09744053.2015.1089013.

Demirsu, Ipek. 2022. 'Watching Them Grow: Intergenerational Video-Calling among Transnational Families in the Age of Smartphones'. *Global Networks* 22, no. 1 (January): 119–133. https://doi.org/10.1111/glob.12334.

Dube, Godwin. 2017. 'Levels of Othering: The Case of Zimbabwean Migrants in South Africa'. *Nationalism and Ethnic Politics* 23, no. 4: 391–412. https://doi.org/10.1080/1 3537113.2017.1380458.

Falicov, Celia J. 2007. 'Working with Transnational Immigrants: Expanding Meanings of Family, Community, and Culture'. *Family Process* 46, no. 2: 157–171. https://doi. org/10.1111/j.1545-5300.2007.00201.x.

Grinberg, Leon and Rebeca Grinberg. 1989. *Psychoanalytic Perspectives on Migration and Exile*. London: Yale University Press.

Hlatshwayo, Mondli. 2019. 'Precarious Work and Precarious Resistance: A Case Study of Zimbabwean Migrant Women Workers in Johannesburg, South Africa'. *Diaspora Studies* 12, no. 2: 160–178. https://doi.org/10.1080/09739572.2018.1485239.

Hondagneu-Sotelo, Pierrette and Ernestine Avila. 1997. '"I'm Here, but I'm There": The Meanings of Latina Transnational Motherhood'. *Gender and Society* 11, no. 5: 548–571. https://doi.org/10.1177/089124397011005003.

Hungwe, Chipo. 2013. 'Survival Strategies of Zimbabwean Migrants in Johannesburg'. *Journal of Community Positive Practices* 13, no. 3: 52–73.

Lake Yimer, Beneyam. 2021. 'Social Media Usage, Psychosocial Wellbeing and Academic Performance'. *International Quarterly of Community Health Education* (18 July). https://doi.org/10.1177/0272684X211033482.

Latham, Brian and Mike Cohen. 2011. 'South Africa May Deport 1.2 Million Zimbabweans'. *Bloomberg News*. https://www.bloomberg.com/news/articles/2011-01-03/south-africa-says-232-000-zimbabweans-seek-residency-ahead-of-deadline.

Madianou, Mirca and Daniel Miller. 2011. 'Mobile Phone Parenting: Reconfiguring Relationships between Filipina Migrant Mothers and Their Left-Behind Children'. *New Media and Society* 13, no. 3: 457–470. https://doi.org/10.1177/1461444810393903.

Madianou, Mirca and Daniel Miller. 2013. *Migration and New Media: Transnational Families and Polymedia*. London: Routledge.

Manik, Sadhana. 2007. 'To Greener Pastures: Transnational Teacher Migration from South Africa'. *Perspectives in Education* 25, no. 2: 55–65. https://hdl.handle.net/10520/EJC87429.

Marchetti-Mercer, Maria C. 2016. '"If You Uproot a Tree You Leave a Big Hole Behind": Systemic Interconnectedness in Emigration and Family Life'. *Contemporary Family Therapy* 38, no. 3: 339–352. https://doi.org/10.1007/s10591-016-9386-6.

Marchetti-Mercer, Maria C., Leslie Swartz and Loretta Baldassar. 2021. '"Is Granny Going Back into the Computer?" Visits and the Familial Politics of Seeing and Being Seen in South African Transnational Families'. *Journal of Intercultural Studies* 42, no. 4: 423–439. https://doi.org/10.1080/07256868.2021.1939280.

Mawadza, Aquilina. 2008. *The Nexus between Migration and Human Security: Zimbabwean Migrants in South Africa*. Institute for Security Studies Papers no. 162 (May). https://www.files.ethz.ch/isn/98947/PAPER162.pdf.

Parreñas, Rhacel Salazar. 2008. 'Transnational Fathering: Gendered Conflicts, Distant Disciplining and Emotional Gaps'. *Journal of Ethnic and Migration Studies* 34, no. 7: 1057–1072. https://doi.org/10.1080/13691830802230356.

Potts, Deborah Helen. 2010. *Circular Migration in Zimbabwe and Contemporary Sub-Saharan Africa*. Woodbridge, UK: Boydell and Brewer.

Salma, Jordana, Lalita Kaewwilai and Savera Aziz Ali. 2021. 'Migrants' Wellbeing and Use of Information and Communication Technologies'. *International Health Trends and Perspectives* 1, no. 2: 139–160. https://doi.org/10.32920/ihtp.v1i2.1421.

Sampaio, Dora. 2020. 'Caring by Silence: How (Un)documented Brazilian Migrants Enact Silence as a Care Practice for Aging Parents'. *Journal of Intergenerational Relationships* 18, no. 3: 281–300. https://doi.org/10.1080/15350770.2020.1787038.

Sluzki, Carlos E. 1979. 'Migration and Family Conflict'. *Family Process* 18, no. 4: 379–390. https://doi.org/10.1111/j.1545-5300.1979.00379.x.

Van Onselen, Charles. 2021. *The Night Trains: Moving Mozambican Miners to and from the Witwatersrand Mines, 1902–1955*. New York: Oxford University Press. https://academic.oup.com/book/39309.

Wall, Karin, Claudio Bolzman, Loretta Baldassar and Laura Merla. 2014. 'Mapping the New Plurality of Transnational Families'. In *Transnational Families, Migration and the Circulation of Care: Understanding Mobility and Absence in Family Life*, edited by Loretta Baldassar and Laura Merla, 61–77. London: Routledge.

Wentzel, Marie and Kholadi Tlabela. 2006. 'Historical Background to South African Migration'. In *Migration in South and Southern Africa: Dynamics and Determinants*, edited by John Oucho, Pieter Kok, Derik Gelderblom and Johan van Zyl, 71–96. Cape Town: HSRC Press. https://www.hsrcpress.ac.za/books/migration-in-south-and-southern-africa.

'You Do Not Finish All Stories': Malawian Families and the Struggle to Stay Connected

Esther Price and Glory Kabaghe

MALAWIAN MIGRATION TO SOUTH AFRICA

For over a century, people from what was once known as Nyasaland, and then became the independent modern state of Malawi in the early 1960s, have migrated to what is now the Republic of South Africa in search of employment and economic opportunities. Most migrants found work in the mining sector through the Employment Bureau of Africa (TEBA), founded in 1902 (Latsky 2008; TEBA n.d.), whose role was to recruit migrant workers for the South African Chamber of Mines (Chirwa 1997). The programme ended abruptly in the late 1980s when Malawians were accused of bringing HIV and AIDS into South Africa. They were required to test for HIV and AIDS to get a permit to work with TEBA. The Malawian government regarded this as a discriminatory and amoral practice and pulled out of the agreement, resulting in the mass repatriation of Malawian migrant workers recruited under TEBA between 1988 and 1992. The end of this formalised migration resulted in grave adverse effects for former migrant workers, their families and the rural communities that had benefited significantly from remittances (Chirwa 1997).

Migration patterns from Malawi have thus shifted significantly over the last three decades as the needs of the South African job market have evolved. Even without a formalised migration route, the South African informal sector has remained attractive to Malawian migrants, and demand in South Africa for domestic workers and workers in the manufacturing sector has increased. However, Malawian migrants are often forced to take jobs that are considered undesirable by South African workers because of long hours and poor pay. They tend to migrate as individuals with no formalised or social protections, and make the move with very limited resources in the hope of earning a living wage to sustain themselves and their families back home. This leaves Malawian migrants straddling two worlds: they must work, live and survive in one world, but participate economically and emotionally as part of a transnational family in the other.

METHODOLOGICAL REFLECTIONS

As part of this study, we interviewed nine people living in Malawi and seven in South Africa. Esther Price, who had lived in Malawi for some years, did the interviews for the sample in South Africa. She began by inviting a large number of Malawian migrants living in Johannesburg to participate in the research. These prospective participants were approached directly, as well as indirectly, through snowball sampling. In some cases, employers gave their Malawian domestic employees the study details and invited them to contact the researcher directly. In other cases, prospective participants were invited because they were heard speaking Chichewa, Malawi's principal language, while they worked at the Bruma China Mall, which contains many informal Chinese shops, or sold fresh vegetables in informal marketplaces. An interesting pattern emerged: these prospective participants usually made the initial contact using the 'please call me' feature on their mobile phones, but when they were called back, they often asked a myriad of questions about the research, displaying deep suspicion.

Nine non-matched interviews were conducted in Malawi by the second author, Glory Kabaghe. Despite the fact that Glory was living and working in Malawi, she was also confronted with suspicion from prospective participants. One by one, the majority declined the invitation to participate, citing some variation of two main reasons. The first was that participating in the interview would come at a cost for them in the form of lost (hourly) wages, lost time (for example, their lunch break) or lost potential sales at the market during interview time. The second was a sense of mistrust, a concern that the team was directly or indirectly associated with the South African immigration authorities and would report back on individual findings or break confidentiality, especially around 'overstay status'. A variation of this theme was the concern that researchers would report back to employers, and that participants would consequently lose their jobs. Despite repeated assurances of confidentiality and anonymity, it was not possible to persuade many of these potential participants to take part. This reluctance and suspicion were most pronounced in the Malawian sample, although these reactions were also present across other samples, as reported in this book, thus reflecting the experience of precarity among migrants coming into South Africa.

Given these levels of suspicion and the additional challenges of travel restrictions imposed by Covid-19, the aim of achieving a fully matched sample for the Malawian group was abandoned. In the end, however, snowball sampling proved to be effective in recruiting participants because, as one participant reported, 'most people in such situations [having relatives living in South Africa] are usually in the same circles'. This finding suggests that not only migrants but also their families left behind form communities of care based on absence and longing. Scheduling virtual interviews was difficult, especially managing to communicate synchronously online, which highlighted the difference between asynchronous and synchronous virtual communications (asynchronous virtual communications, for example WhatsApp messaging, are much easier, because people can respond in their own time).

THE STORY OF LISA AND PETER

The story of Lisa and Peter, reported from the only matched set of interviews in the Malawian sample, mirrors the stories of many Malawian migrant workers in South Africa and their families, and therefore provides a helpful focus.

Lisa is a married 49-year-old woman. She works in Malawi as a domestic worker. Lisa has one brother, Peter, aged 35, who migrated from Malawi to South Africa in 2013 in search of what several of our interviewees, such as the Zimbabweans discussed in Chapter 4, referred to as 'greener pastures'. There were financial obstacles to the move to South Africa, as Peter did not have the money to pay for a passport or for travel. Lisa and the extended family pooled resources to pay these costs, thus enabling Peter to migrate to South Africa. Lisa has maintained contact with her brother. Initially, she heard from him through the letters he sent. More recently, he has bought a mobile phone, and so they can maintain contact through phone calls, but Lisa points out that they cannot always afford to buy the airtime necessary to communicate by direct calling. Lisa does not have internet services where she lives in Malawi; this makes it impossible for her to benefit from access to cheaper online methods of staying in touch with her brother, and leaves them no option but to use a more expensive airtime connection.

Peter left Malawi in 2013, making the 2 800-kilometre journey to South Africa in the hope of earning enough to care for his parents and older siblings in Malawi. When he arrived, Peter found work as a tailor and was soon able to send regular remittances to Malawi. He has been unable to visit Malawi again, except in 2018, when he went home for his traditional wedding ceremony, an occasion he recalls fondly. His wife accompanied him back to South Africa. Soon after that, Peter and his wife expected a baby. His wife returned to Malawi in 2019 for the birth of their son, with the intention of returning to South Africa once the baby was older. Unfortunately, the Covid-19 pandemic brought significant financial challenges and considerable loss of income. Peter's wife was still 'stuck' in Malawi at the time of the research, and he mentioned with sadness that he and his then 18-month-old son had not seen each other in person yet. Peter was able to call his wife in Malawi more regularly than his other family members, as she had a mobile phone. However, neither had a smartphone, so they had to rely on direct calling, which is costly and often made Peter feel 'left behind'. This story is typical of many we heard.

ON CHOOSING MIGRATION: THE SEARCH FOR 'GREENER PASTURES'

Migrants were asked to reflect on the processes and considerations that led to their decision to leave their country of birth to migrate to South Africa. As in Peter's story, the pressure to escape adverse circumstances in Malawi was the primary motivation, with people hoping to find better conditions in South Africa. This narrative was shared by most migrants and their family members in Malawi, indicating a sense of connectedness and shared decision-making about the need to take action to mitigate hardship in Malawi. Here we see how even those family members who stay behind can be active participants in the migration process, influencing the decision of one or more of their family members to migrate (Haug 2008; De Jong and Gardner 2013), and providing important financial and emotional support to facilitate the move. However, among our participants, the nature of the adverse circumstances faced by these migrants and the families they left behind varied greatly.

When we asked migrants about their recollections of the decision they took to migrate, the most salient theme that emerged across all interviews was the impetus to leave Malawi for economic reasons, to escape poverty and unemployment, and to send remittances home. The theme of creating a better situation ('greener pastures') for their loved ones at home was prominent in the interviews. Joseph explicitly used this phrase: 'Home [Malawi] is the best. In fact, you know, what makes us move like this? ... To fetch for green pastures, you see? Yeah, because, eh ... sometimes you can see you can't pay for condiments very poor … yeah … if you hear something interesting, like "people in South Africa they are working, making money there, helping their family", yeah, so that's why we wandered up to this place.'

While most migrants appeared to be supported by their families in their decision to leave, benefiting from a 'licence to leave' (Baldassar 2001), it is noteworthy that some migrant participants reported shouldering a solitary and sometimes lonely burden and personal decision-making process that saw them migrate to South Africa. Their narratives expressed a sense of duty to save their families from desperate poverty, as Tom's interview illustrates: 'No, it was on me to decide to come … I was just doing this for my own like situation. I had nothing to do at home. I didn't go to school. We were suffering.'

In the recollections of family members who stayed behind in Malawi, the theme of looking for greener pastures was also evident. Mary describes the considerations that led to a decision made collectively as a family, so that her son would be able to migrate to South Africa in the hope of a better life: 'For the boy, who is the third-born, since he finished school, he was not doing anything, he was just drinking alcohol and causing trouble at home … Then from there he asked his older siblings to help him with funds to go to South Africa for greener pastures.'

Most of the family member participants shared stories that indicated family involvement in the decision to migrate. Generally, there was a sense that the move would benefit the family financially as a collective: 'For this decision, we all sat as a family by giving suggestions and we all saw that the situation we were in was hard [financially]. Since her going there would assist us all here' (Brian). Nevertheless, there was sometimes concern about the safety of family members in South Africa: 'But at first we were refusing since she is female, as we heard a lot of [bad] things from people but after our aunt explained well, we thought it wise to let her go' (Brian). Most family member participants spoke of their personal reluctance to visit South Africa because of the 'bad things they see on the news', including crime and xenophobic abuse, which left them worrying about their loved ones.

There were some instances where family members in Malawi mentioned that a migrant made an individual choice to migrate: 'Ah, no, I did not take part in the decision' (Sophie). This corroborates some of the migrant participants' stories of this process. Anne mentioned that her family member made the choice alone, motivated by the desire to join a new partner in South Africa: 'This decision was her own since she told us that she had found a man but who was not from Malawi but South Africa ... hence they settled there. It was marriage that took her there.'

These stories give a sense of the processes and conversations that ultimately led to migration. While most participants migrated primarily for economic purposes, at least one left to escape an abusive relationship or reconnect with family members in South Africa. Economic factors were clearly the most prominent in the decision to migrate, but these were always intertwined with personal concerns and differences between individuals. It is deeply poignant that some women had to move to a country that they and their families regard as dangerous in order to escape danger in their own homes in Malawi.

For some families, shared decision-making contributed to a continuing sense of connectedness, especially among the family members who stayed behind. All families, whether they benefited from shared decision-making or not, experienced challenges in maintaining transnational family life, but those whose decision to migrate was more personal and individual seemed to indicate the greatest rupture in the family status quo.

ADJUSTMENT AND PRECARITY IN MIGRANT WORKERS

Migrant participants found the transition to South Africa extremely challenging. They had to fend for themselves and survive in a foreign country with limited financial resources. Peter, as we have seen, could not even afford a mobile phone during his first year in South Africa. Loveness articulated the common challenge of adjustment: 'It was tough just because it was the first time, you know ... to be in, like, a foreign country. So, for me it was tough. But at least now I'm coping because I've been here for long.'

Concurrent with financial vulnerability were social challenges such as xenophobic hostility from South Africans and precarious living circumstances. This was especially hard during the initial stages of their move to South Africa. Participants reflected on how this hostility left them feeling unwelcome, unsafe and disconnected both from their host communities and from their families back home: 'Xenophobia is a problem ... I get disappointed because, you see, you can walk in like that, you pass by other people, they even call you "Ey, you Nyasa" [Malawi used to be called Nyasaland] ... So they call you in that name instead of calling me my name ... But ... you didn't do anything wrong to them. So, in so doing you feel, ah, it's not good' (Joseph).

This hostility was often experienced in the quest to meet basic needs such as accommodation and shelter, which, as in Peter's case, are considered essential before 'luxuries' such as mobile phones can be purchased. Although information communication technologies (ICTs) can be difficult to access and afford, there is growing awareness that they are actually crucial for connecting with opportunities for employment and shelter in the host country, and just as critical for communicating and interacting with family members back home (see Codagnone and Kluzer 2011). As a result, lack of access to ICTs at the outset can leave newly migrated Malawians feeling extremely disconnected from both the host country and from their kin in their homeland. Sadly, for many, it is only once migrant workers have met their basic needs (shelter and an income) that they can focus on accessing technologies that begin to reconnect them with their homeland kin, as we shall see below.

ICT PREFERENCES AND CONSIDERATIONS

Almost without exception, our migrant participants spoke emphatically about the positive impact of technologies in their lives and those of their families. However, the types and uses of these technologies varied as a function of cost and available resources. Analogue phones and phone booths have largely been phased out in South Africa since personal mobile phones have become the norm. Even though basic mobile phones (other than smartphones) are relatively inexpensive, the costs of data and direct (international) phone calls remain extremely high in South Africa. Participants spoke of the following dilemma: in order to call their families in Malawi more frequently, they need to have access to cheaper methods of calling, such as WhatsApp calls, which use data. However, in order to access these technologies, they need to buy more expensive smartphones and data for themselves and for their families in Malawi. Without smartphones, participants are forced to direct-call their family members at exorbitant cost and with reduced frequency.

This problem was also mentioned by migrants who have managed to obtain smartphones for themselves and their families. When Peter purchased a mobile phone, he also got one for his wife back in Malawi, which made mutual communication easier, but smartphones remain beyond his budget. Other participants also spoke about their dependence on WhatsApp for cheaper and more frequent connections with their loved ones: 'Yeah, because direct call is expensive, yeah, it's R5 [US$0.29] a minute, so that is expensive. You can't chat for 30 minutes, ah, you have to spend more money, but if I have got R10 [US$0.58], 200 megabytes, ah you can't finish it for an hour [on WhatsApp]. Something like that' (George).

Overall, ICTs seem to afford families an opportunity to satisfy the human need for connection by means of various forms of trans-national caregiving, as discussed below. Paradoxically, though, the challenges of affordability seem to take some of the human aspect out of the experience of connectedness. As soon as one such moment of connection has ended, the quest for resources begins again in the hope of meeting family members' expectation of another call – it remains a never-ending struggle for the emotional survival of the transnational family.

TRANSNATIONAL CARE FUNCTIONS IN MALAWIAN MIGRANT FAMILIES

Several themes emerged in the interviews about transnational care.

ICT-Mediated Financial Care through Remittances

A core theme that emerged relating to the use of ICTs was the provision of financial support, most notably through remittances. It has been reported that migrants with low skills and poor earnings tend to send more remittances back to Malawi than their highly skilled counterparts, who earn more (Niboye 2018). This finding has largely been attributed to the fact that the migration of low-earning, less skilled migrants is often seen as being only for the short term or as temporary, and also to the fact that they are often forced to leave close family behind owing to the financial constraints associated with moving with the entire family (Chirwa 1997).

All the migrant participants in this sample spoke about using their phones to send remittances to Malawi via SMS or WhatsApp. Newer banks such as Mukuru Bank have found ways of using ICTs to offer inter-country money transfers at a fraction of the cost associated with more traditional services such as MoneyGram. There are multiple services for money transfers in the South African market, focused largely on other African countries, and this is a key feature of sub-Saharan African economies (Kitimbo 2021). Mukuru Bank's financial services platform leads the way in Africa when it comes to money transfers through the provision of affordable and reliable financial services to emerging consumers across Africa, in Europe and in China at a subsidised cost. By contrast, MoneyGram is the second-largest money transfer company in the world, offering money transfer services, bill payments, and a range of corporate products and services. One can send money with MoneyGram online, in-app, or via an agent, and pay by cash, wire transfer, debit card or credit card. However, MoneyGram is expensive to use, especially for people who earn money through small businesses and casual labour, as most migrants from Malawi to South Africa do. ICTs have thus made it possible for migrant workers to send money instantly and affordably without additional costs such as transport or lost wages when they take time off work to send remittances. Financial care can, therefore, be given more instantly now, with the widespread availability of ICTs.

From Remittances to Virtual Co-presence: Avenues of Emotional and Moral Support

Emotional support and moral support have been identified as critical components of transnational caregiving. They are widely considered to be the main ways in which strong bonds are created and maintained in transnational families (Baldassar et al. 2016). For example, Joseph spoke about the need to remain present in the lives of his family:

> Yeah, we have to chat. I have to hear the problems there about my children. I have to hear the life of my children at school, yeah I have to do like this each and every week. Yeah, so we are doing this in order the parents must remember that we sometimes, in the years to come, we will be back home. Because if you are in a foreign country you are not calling your parents; you are not communicating with them; they think that you are here for ever and ever. You are here for good. But, you have to, to contact them ... yeah.

These words express the need to provide emotional and moral support to his children to compensate for his physical absence, while simultaneously expressing his own need for care from and for his parents. His emotional care needs are implicit in his need to be held in mind and remembered, demonstrating the bidirectionality of this type of care. The language in his narrative speaks of a heavy burden of obligation and demand as he 'has to' make those connections. ICTs have made the fulfilment of those demands more immediate, but have put extra pressure and a burden on migrants who, before ICTs, would have phoned home and sent letters only occasionally. In the excerpt above, Joseph uses the phrase 'have to' five times – this reads like a litany of obligation (to care for others) as well as need (for care of self).

Support from loved ones back home is also an important theme. As we pointed out earlier, Lisa and other family members had to assist her brother in his move to South Africa. For all migrant participants with children, their parents, family-in-law or siblings in Malawi have at some point taken care of children who have had to stay behind. George reflected on the role his parents play in caring for him by raising and providing for his two children to supplement the remittances he sends: 'I have got two children, but the one who is taking care of these children is my father and my mother. Because I already told them that my situation is not fine … I am not working better, so … my father is providing school fees for my children, their food. Except clothing … clothing I am doing myself but the school fees and other things is my father doing it.' The adverbial clause 'because I already told them that my situation is not fine' may speak to a kind of resignation to living in constrained circumstances, and the shame of having to admit to this. Clearly, the circulation of transnational caregiving is important, with ICTs supporting this interaction (Baldassar and Merla 2014).

Barriers to Transnational Caregiving

Participants reflected on some of the challenges they experience in trying to connect with their family. For migrant participants, survival needs remain paramount. For most, phone calls and connection with family can only occur after rent, food, bills and remittances have been taken care of. Peter longs to connect more frequently with his parents, as well as with his wife and son, but he cannot, owing to finances. Even when he does, direct calling only affords him short calls with little opportunity to share his own experiences and receive support: basic needs must be prioritised over connection. Peter's story highlights how the most vulnerable migrant workers are often left feeling further disconnected from loved ones, as they are forced to rely on expensive direct calling as their only means of communication. This often reduces the migrant family member to the one whose main role in the family is to provide financial support.

For migrant participants with smartphones for themselves and for their family in Malawi, access to technologies such as WhatsApp has widened the portal of connectedness, creating more opportunities to establish virtual co-presence and connection. Joseph said:

> Most of the time I have to use the phones. Especially the WhatsApp, it's fine because ... WhatsApp costs cheap [*laughs*] I have to call my family in Malawi; sometimes we chat for even an hour, even 30 minutes, even more than that ... calling the parents, the family members in Malawi, there is no challenges or difficulties. Everything is fine, as long as you have data. It's fine because it doesn't matter if you are not working better [earning more], at least you have to find R10 [about US$0.58] for that [*laughs*] just for a WhatsApp call.

For some participants, such as Peter, using data calling technologies is not possible because they do not have a smartphone. For others, the barrier is lower literacy levels, which cut people off from these technologies, leaving them feeling more disconnected from family members.

The relationship between connectedness with homeland kin and access to ICTs is movingly demonstrated in the following extract from the story of Tom, a migrant worker who has had no access to a mobile phone ever since his was stolen two years ago: 'So far, I don't have any access. As long as I go and maybe if I borrow a phone from someone then I use it. But so far, I don't have any access to the phone ... so I am all alone here. I don't talk much to them.' Tom's sense of feeling alone and disconnected from his family is palpable, and he has only an unreliable and limited portal of connection on the rare occasion when he is able to borrow a mobile phone to call home.

Joseph, another migrant participant, reflected on life in South Africa before ICTs became widespread and how he felt disconnected from his family. He stressed the critical role of ICTs in creating a shared presence and, ultimately, opportunities for ambient co-presence (Madianou 2016) with his family members in Malawi:

> Yeah, in the past. Um … in, in 2001, when I write my wife a letter, it can take three months … for you to receive that letter. Maybe to respond or to respond you. Three months, you see … It was very hard, then little by little, um, things are changing. We had phones, those big ones, yeah. So was calling, communicating with my wife. This time … every day you can talk to your family and each and every child you can chat with her because of WhatsApp.

This highlights the importance of access to smartphone technologies in order to afford transnational families the opportunity to move from shared presence to 'ambient co-presence' and an increased awareness of the everyday activities of distant kin (Madianou 2016). Ambient co-presence refers to a sense of 'always on' co-presence across distance, which is afforded by simply owning or having easy access to ICTs, and is described by Mirca Madianou (2016, 183) as a peripheral but intense awareness of distant others, which is made possible by today's ubiquitous media environments. This feeling of ambient co-presence is created by the constant contact between migrant and family and the capacity to connect with each other at any time, leading to a sense that family members are constantly there for you, despite the distance.

However, attaining a sense of ambient co-presence is often constrained by challenges in achieving internet and data access. Like the migrant participants, family members who stayed behind reported that they often have to forgo opportunities to connect if competing basic needs in the household exceed the available resources – then airtime and data become unaffordable luxuries: 'Hmm, most times finding money is a problem and hence when we find money we prefer to buy food than to actually buy data' (Catherine). This sentiment was shared by Elsie: 'You find that you want to give a very important message and you also have a problem to buy a bundle of 1 000 kwacha [about US$0.97]), but that 1 000 kwacha, you can still buy something needed for the house so you just go and buy what is needed in the house, the bundle is not really relevant. I can buy it some other time when I get money or someone will maybe share me to buy the bundle later.' Marta expressed her sense that there are not enough opportunities for connection from Malawi: 'The difficult thing is that we only talk to each other than face to face. We of course do video calls and chat but you know we cannot chat until we finish all stories than face to face discussions, hence you find that you have run out of airtime and you do not finish all stories.'

Another challenge was poor network connectivity in Malawi, which often has an impact on the capacity to make video calls or send voice notes: 'For example, when you are texting, there is no problem, but when you want to make a video call, or sometimes when you want to send documents, they get there late, and even voice notes fail to download due to poor network, yeah' (Elsie). This observation was also supported by Anne, who said: 'Yes, most times we have problems with network, like I use Airtel and network is always a problem. And secondly, the charges here in Malawi on phone they charge a lot, and also bundles finish so fast, even a one-month bundle does not take you through that long but a few days. But for her to call us, it is easier because we can talk for so long and they do not charge her as much there.'

Anne's words reveal the underlying belief that her loved one in South Africa is better able to call the family in Malawi because of cheaper calling costs. However, the stories of migrant participants in South Africa tell a different story. This illustrates a disconnect in the narratives pertaining to the economic struggles of migrant workers, who are often under tremendous pressure to provide financially and may perhaps withhold information to protect family at home from worry, as has also been described by Loretta Baldassar (2007b).

I Dream of Home: ICTs as a Proxy for Visits

Participants spoke about missing home and feeling somewhat 'left behind' as they miss out on important occasions, events and milestones. These may all be categorised as forms of personal, hands-on and practical care and support that require physical co-presence and that are best exchanged through visits (Baldassar et al. 2016; Finch 1989). These types of transnational care, requiring visits, remain unattainable for most Malawian migrants.

Peter spoke about feeling left behind because he has missed out on his young son's entire life. He has visited Malawi only once since his migration in 2013: 'Last I went was 2018. It was October, ja, 2018. Even [now] I haven't seen my baby yet. Because my wife was here with me all this time. She went back in 2019. She went back to have the baby but she's not yet back because of Covid-19 and the finances as well.' Peter's words reveal his longing to be physically present with his wife and baby, but these personal and practical care needs cannot be met, not even through the mediating portal afforded by ICTs.

None of our seven migrant participants in South Africa had visited Malawi in a long time, owing to the distance and to costs, which were exacerbated by the Covid-19 pandemic, involving the cost of polymerase chain reaction (PCR) tests to be allowed to travel. For many, visiting Malawi undermines their goal of saving money for their ultimate return home. Some mentioned that travelling home by road, a journey of about 2 800 to 3 300 kilometres, depending on where in Malawi 'home' is, takes up to three days each way because of severe backlogs and delays at the borders – they have to cross at least three borders, whether they go via Zimbabwe and Mozambique, or via Zimbabwe and Zambia. In addition, there are financial costs associated with lost wages, bus tickets, and money to sustain families and meet their expectations upon arrival. There are expectations about them being financially resourced when they return home from working in 'eGoli' (the City of Gold), as Johannesburg is often called. Loveness's experience is typical: 'That's a long time. I didn't go for five years. So I very much miss them. But you know, to go home is expensive so when you go there you need more money. Like you can't go and to spend there so I just decided not to go, maybe I can just go once and for all.' In the absence of visits, ICTs remain critical, as Peter remarked: 'I cannot go home … Yeah, and I just say that it's not about the internet, access to technology or what what, no. It's about me and how much I got. I earn little money and that is all I have. Without the phone, then there is nothing.'

Imagined Co-presence as Care in Transnational Families with Ubiquitous Media

Malawian migrants and their family members seemed to hold each other in mind, to think of each other constantly. Migrant participants spoke about being preoccupied with ensuring that their loved ones were doing well, suggesting a strong duty of care: '… always keeping in touch, to be connected to my family in Malawi. I have to communicate with them, my parents in Malawi. Each and every weekend I have to take time to chat with them there in Malawi. They have to tell me about their problems there, about my children. I have to send something small to help my children in Malawi. Yeah. Always I am keeping in touch. I know everything about my family in Malawi' (George).

Concurrent with the need to make sure that homeland kin were well, there was a deep sense of not wanting to burden family at home with the migrants' struggles in South Africa. Once again, this supports Baldassar's (2007a) research, which concluded that family members on both sides choose what to share during virtual co-presence opportunities, in ways that may unintentionally create a disconnect. Interestingly, when migrants choose not to disclose the difficulties they face, family members back home may sense this and often watch the news or learn about some adverse occurrences in South Africa, especially through news media, causing them great concern and worry, especially when their migrant family members do not communicate or share these occurrences: 'They, they are always saying, "Come back home" … If they can hear people are fighting, they calling me same time. Because the TVs are everywhere.

Even the rural areas you see in the house there is a solar panel, then ... there is TVs, they can see the DStv there. They can see what is happening. So ... they always hear, wish for you to come back home' (Joseph).

REFLECTIONS

Overall, Malawian migrants in this sample expressed a strong sense of a duty of care toward their family members back home. While navigating the complicated socio-political landscape in South Africa, they work hard to secure enough funds to support themselves *and* their families back home. In addition, they feel pressure to save money for their eventual return to Malawi. Invariably, migrants and stay-home family members spoke about the importance of ICTs in connecting with their families. Those who were able to phone more frequently reported a greater sense of connection with their family, including feeling a sense of ambient co-presence. However, as Lisa's and Peter's stories show, maintaining this connection is often fraught with challenges. The biggest barrier to transnational caregiving through ICTs is cost. Smartphones emerged as an absolute necessity for such communication, but they remained a luxury, limited to those who have the necessary financial resources. Despite the initial cost, smartphones permit cheaper calls than the roughly R7 per minute for regular calls (at the time of the research), and cheaper calls allow for longer and more frequent virtual and even ambient co-presence opportunities. ICT connections are an important portal through which transnational caregiving processes are exchanged. Sadly, Malawian migrants are usually unable to access this resource during the most challenging times of their migration experience, namely, upon arrival and during periods of financial precarity, leaving them at risk of disconnection and despair.

As with meeting physical needs, transnational caregiving appears to be stratified by the availability of monetary resources. At the most basic level, there are remittances, which allow financial care to be shared. This appears to the most basic form of transnational care, one that remains fundamentally non-negotiable. Research suggests that caregiving between migrants and non-migrants is bidirectional (Carling 2008; Wilding 2006), but in this sample financial care appears to be mostly unidirectional, from the migrants to the family at home. When the basic needs to share financial care have been met, migrants and their families can then allow for other needs to be met, such as emotional and moral support, and information-sharing about milestones and developments (admittedly, financial support can also be considered a form of emotional care). However, in instances where migrants experience financial precarity or have no access to the internet, as with Lisa and Peter, they are forced to use expensive direct calls to call home to hear from their family. Their own needs for emotional and moral support remain unacknowledged and largely unmet. During times of financial precarity, care becomes limited and unidirectional. ICT-mediated connections using WhatsApp have emerged as the most important route to migrant well-being, as they allow them and their families in Malawi to feel better connected and integrated.

REFERENCES

Baldassar, Loretta. 2001. *Visits Home: Migration Experiences between Italy and Australia*. Melbourne: Melbourne University Press.

Baldassar, Loretta. 2007a. 'Transnational Families and Aged Care: The Mobility of Care and the Migrancy of Ageing'. *Journal of Ethnic and Migration Studies* 33, no. 2: 275–297. https://doi.org/10.1080/13691830601154252.

Baldassar, Loretta. 2007b. 'Transnational Families and the Provision of Moral and Emotional Support: The Relationship between Truth and Distance'. *Identities* 14, no. 4: 385–409. https://doi.org/10.1080/10702890701578423.

Baldassar, Loretta and Laura Merla. 2014. *Transnational Families, Migration and the Circulation of Care: Understanding Mobility and Absence in Family Life*. New York: Routledge.

Baldassar, Loretta, Mihaela Nedelcu, Laura Merla and Raelene Wilding. 2016. 'ICT-Based Co-presence in Transnational Families and Communities: Challenging the Premise of Face-to-Face Proximity in Sustaining Relationships'. *Global Networks* 16, no. 2 (Special Issue): 133–144. https://doi.org/10.1111/glob.12108.

Carling, Jørgen. 2008. 'The Human Dynamics of Migrant Transnationalism'. *Ethnic and Racial Studies* 31, no. 8: 1452–1477. https://doi.org/10.1080/01419870701719097.

Chirwa, Wiseman Chijere. 1997. '"No TEBA: Forget TEBA": The Plight of Malawian Ex-migrant Workers to South Africa, 1988–1994'. *International Migration Review* 31, no. 3: 628–654. https://doi.org/10.1177/019791839703100305.

Codagnone, Cristiano and Stefano Kluzer. 2011. *ICT for the Social and Economic Integration of Migrants into Europe*. JRC Scientific and Technical Reports. Seville: European Commission Joint Research Centre Institute for Prospective Technological Studies.

De Jong, Gordon F. and Robert W. Gardner, eds. 2013. *Migration Decision Making: Multidisciplinary Approaches to Microlevel Studies in Developed and Developing Countries*. Amsterdam: Elsevier.

Finch, Janet. 1989. *Family Obligations and Social Change*. Cambridge: Polity Press.

Haug, Sonja. 2008. 'Migration Networks and Migration Decision-Making'. *Journal of Ethnic and Migration Studies* 34, no. 4: 585–605. https://doi.org/10.1080/13691830801961605.

Kitimbo, Adrian. 2021. 'Mobile Money and Financial Inclusion of Migrants in Sub-Saharan Africa'. In *Research Handbook on International Migration and Digital Technology*, edited by Marie MacAuliffe, 251–266. Elgar Online. https://doi.org/10.4337/9781839100611.00029.

Latsky, Henriette. 2008. 'A Taste of the Employment Bureau of Africa (TEBA): Mining the Past'. *ESARBICA Journal: Journal of the Eastern and Southern Africa Regional Branch of the International Council on Archives* 27: 128–146. https://doi.org/10.4314/esarjo.v27i1.31024.

Madianou, Mirca. 2016. 'Ambient Co-presence: Transnational Family Practices in Polymedia Environments'. *Global Networks* 16, no. 2: 183–201. https://doi.org/10.1111/glob.12105.

Niboye, Elliott P. 2018. 'International Labour Out-Migration in Mzimba District, Malawi: Why Persistent?' *International Journal of Research in Geography* 4, no. 2: 9–21. https://doi.org/10.20431/2454-8685.0402002.

TEBA. N.d. 'The TEBA Story'. http://www.teba.co.za/about_main.html.

Wilding, Raelene. 2006. '"Virtual" Intimacies? Families Communicating across Transnational Contexts'. *Global Networks* 6, no. 2: 125–142. https://doi.org/10.1111/j.1471-0374.2006.00137.x.

6

(Dis)connections: The Paradox of Intergenerational WhatsApp Communication in Transnational Kenyan Families

Ajwang' Warria

TRANSNATIONAL MOVEMENT AND COMMUNICATION

The Kenyan diaspora is extensive, but most Kenyans who have left the country maintain a strong connection with their Kenyan identity, family and home country (Opiyo et al. 2016; Stuhlhofer 2022). The literature indicates that transnational family obligations, emotional ties and synchronous (real-time) communication are facilitated by free or affordable technology through internet and social media, which provide 'a sense of mattering and belonging' (Plaza and Plaza 2019, 3) and connection. This chapter investigates how WhatsApp has become a virtual transnational bridge that links Kenyans in South Africa and Kenya and provides them with intergenerational connections. It highlights the problem that these intergenerational connections are not always smooth, and may require (re)construction over time and additional supportive technologies. These dynamics in intergenerational family relationships can be usefully understood in relation to the insights gained into generational connectivity spanning distance, as discussed in the literature and in this chapter.

Migration often has beneficial outcomes, but it has also been recognised as having a negative impact on families when geographical distance challenges the emotional connections between family members, reconfiguring families and relationships of care in the context of migration, especially in the past, when communication was difficult (Akanle, Fayehun and Oyelakin 2020; Baldassar 2017). Today, technology plays a crucial role in supporting intergenerational (and international) connectivity (Reis, Mercer and Boger 2021). Of the technologies available, WhatsApp is the preferred mode of communication among Kenyan families and friends or loved ones, enabling them to create and nurture multi- and bidirectional care and support links. Indeed, according to a recent study of Kenyans in Austria by Eunice Wangui Stuhlhofer (2022), family chats can be a lifeline when they enable connection and solace; however, for some people or at certain times, the constant and synchronous thread of communication can become overwhelming, cause anxiety and contribute to distress and social overload (Baldassar et al. 2016). Healthier family communication and high engagement in approaches to coping contribute to improved psychological well-being when individuals are faced with challenges (Geçer and Yıldırım 2023).

The term 'transnational families' in this chapter is used loosely to refer to family members separated from each other and from the physical practices of maintaining family life. Despite their geographical separation, members of many transnational families maintain a feeling or sense of collective welfare and participate in ways of being with the purpose of strengthening ties, and sustaining unity and familyhood across and from a distance (Barglowski 2021; Bell and Biyand Erdal 2015; Bryceson 2019; Kędra 2021a). As in the study by Olayinka Akanle, Olufunke A. Fayehun and Gbenga S. Oyelakin (2020), when I use the term 'left behind', I do not use the term to express negativity or disadvantage, but to refer to migrants' family members who remain in their countries of origin.

KENYANS AND THEIR HISTORY OF MIGRATION

According to George Odipo, Charles Owuor Olungah and Dalmas Ochieng Omia (2015), 'Kenyans have a long history of international, cross border, intra-regional labour migration' (43). The *World Migration Report*, published in 2022, indicated that Kenya's population in 2020 stood at 73.77 million, with 0.50 million Kenyans living abroad (McAuliffe and Triandafyllidou 2022). A recent report by Julia Faria (2021) gives the slightly higher figure of more than 535 000 Kenyans living abroad. The United States is one of Kenyans' preferred destinations (Faria 2021), as is the United Kingdom (McAuliffe and Triandafyllidou 2022). Peter Owiti Opiyo et al. (2016) reported that in 2016 there were fewer than 20 000 Kenyans in South Africa, and even fewer in the five South East Asian countries under the accreditation of the Kenya Mission in Bangkok. However, as with other migration patterns, it is difficult to obtain accurate estimates of numbers of Kenyan migrants (Mwaniki and Dulo 2008; Odipo, Olungah and Omia 2015).

The migration of Kenyans dates back to when the various ethnic groups (categorised as Bantus, Nilotes and Cushites) resettled in their present-day communities (Mwakikagile 2014). This was followed in the twentieth and twenty-first centuries by migration from rural to urban areas in Kenya – a process of urbanisation often linked to colonisation, development and poverty. The British colonial government exerted political control over the region and over the social interactions of its inhabitants. Since Kenya gained independence in the early 1960s, the government has done little to encourage Kenyans to look for opportunities abroad, but has rather encouraged the return of those who had left, especially for further studies (Ghai 2005). Over time, however, many Kenyans who went abroad decided to stay there, because of the harsh political and economic realities in Kenya (Grimm 2019). In addition, Kenyan families that could afford to do so began sending some family members abroad as an investment and as part of a form of family-based economic insurance (Egwurube 2020). Although the intersections between social class and communication orientation are not the focus of this chapter, it is important to note that a family's social class can shape the experiences of individual migrants (Barglowski 2021) and their family functioning, and contribute to immigrant optimism (Barglowski 2019) and migrant capital (Erel and Ryan 2018).

According to John Oucho, Linda A. Oucho and Vollan Ochieng (2014), internal migration continues to reflect regional inequalities that still operate in the country, as Kenyans move out of poor, underdeveloped and remote rural home areas to urban destinations with more favourable economic opportunities. In this chapter, however, I focus on migration to South Africa from Kenya.

Care is both a resource and a relational practice that unfolds across spaces, places and generations. Communication activities and practices are part of daily routines in families – regardless of setting. The term 'digital kinning', coined by Loretta Baldassar and Raelene Wilding (2020), refers to the importance of care and caring relationships maintained over geographical distance through information communication technologies (ICTs) (Bryceson 2019). Both internal and external migration for most Kenyan migrants and their families left behind are driven by several factors, including labour opportunities, high unemployment rates, political instability and ethnic violence, climate change and individual aspirations. With regard to international migration, the choice of the destination country is influenced by factors such as historical and personal links, ease of acculturation and cultural affinity, perceived affluence and geographical proximity. Whatever the reason for migrating, staying in regular communication is, for many Kenyans, part of cultural expectations, a survival strategy, something that provides a sense of belonging and status, and a means to maintain psychosocial and emotional well-being. In this way, family pressure, family bonds, life cycle, economic capital and the use of current digital technology (Bryceson 2019) can be seen to influence migration intentions globally.

METHODOLOGICAL REFLECTIONS

Like that of many Kenyans at home and abroad, my own personal history embraces movement and migration. My parents and older siblings lived in Tanzania in the 1970s before relocating to Kenya. Furthermore, at the time of writing this chapter, I occupied two spaces in time: retrospectively, I am an individual who was left behind when my siblings left Kenya to take up opportunities overseas; and as a Kenyan migrant with a young family in South Africa at the time of writing this chapter, I retain transnational ties in Kenya. My research interest lies in exploring familyhood in migration and cross-border situations. Hence, my shifting positionality may be reflected in some of the discussions. It is possible that similarities between my own circumstances and those of my participants prompted my curiosity (and that of my participants) and a desire to learn more about my own experiences of migration. Although my participants did not know me personally, and despite my status as a researcher and interviewer, in some instances I was treated as a proxy relative because of my status as a co-member of Kenyan culture. This is an experience that has also been reported by other researchers (for example, by Baldassar 2007). For face-to-face interviews I was invited into the homes of some research participants, I asked questions (and they asked questions), we shared a meal and I was treated as part of the family. This speaks to the cohesion felt by migrants in the destination country in which cultural and national identity transcends all other identity roles.

Convenience, purposive and snowball sampling were used to recruit the fifteen participants. The data sources include interviews with ten Kenyans who had left Kenya for South Africa, and five unmatched families that were left behind in Kenya. The interviews in South Africa were a mixture of face-to-face and online interviews using Zoom and WhatsApp. My colleague Josephine Arasa, from the Psychology Department in the School of Humanities and Social Sciences at the United States International University – Africa (Nairobi), collected the data in Kenya, while I collected data in South Africa. In Kenya, Josephine interviewed four participants in person and one online. Josephine recalls that it was difficult to recruit participants because of a persistent fear that she was 'spying', acting *mala fide*, in order to gather information for the authorities. As with the experiences of the Malawian participants described in Chapter 5, the anxiety of many of these potential participants was rooted in their relatives' status as illegal immigrants in South Africa. Despite the challenges, these interviews added to the depth of the data that we had collected from Kenyan migrants themselves by describing the lived experience of those left behind, while also confirming many of our initial findings about patterns of care among Kenyan migrants. For example, families left behind confirmed that their relatives had migrated for educational or professional reasons, and that those left behind were not financially dependent on the migrants – in fact, in many instances, the migrants were financially dependent on their relatives in Kenya. Our findings subverted much of the supposed common knowledge about migrants and their families, and also provided some unexpected and important empirical evidence that confirms the heterogeneity of migration experiences among African populations.

The fact that interviews were possible through WhatsApp and Zoom implied access to these technologies and digital literacy among all those who were part of the sample. The Kenyans we interviewed in South Africa had mostly migrated for educational or professional reasons, and their migration was not forced by the political situation, as was that of most of the Democratic Republic of Congo sample (see Chapter 7), or by extreme poverty, contrary to some of our other samples. They were also generally better educated than most of the members of our other samples. All the Kenyans interviewed in South Africa had a postsecondary qualification – mostly a Master's degree or a doctoral qualification. All these participants were Kenyan citizens with South African permanent residency. This immigration status means that they have South African identity documents and can legally work in South Africa. All had financial security, as was evident from their jobs in well-paying professions, the affluent neighbourhoods or suburbs where they lived, and the cars that they drove. They could be described as belonging to middle-class families and they often visited their families in Kenya once or more frequently a year. Most of the participants interviewed in South Africa and all the participants interviewed in Kenya had children. The children of the South African participants were enrolled in private schools and some had dual citizenship (South African and Kenyan).

FINDINGS ON CONNECTION

The various themes that emerged from the interviews are discussed below.

Embedded Benefits of Intergenerational Connectivity

Maintaining ties for Kenyans transnationally means many things, more than just remitting cash, sending gifts to their families or connecting telephonically or through social media. These individual and collective connections are about identity, status, belonging and maintaining positions in the community, as well as being influential (Kioko 2010).

Intergenerational connectivity has been researched from various perspectives, including a focus on the functionality of the technology and its sociological effects (Reis, Mercer and Boger 2021), its role during Covid-19 (Popyk and Pustułka 2021) and one of its potentially darker sides, silencing (Sampaio 2020). It is important to recognise that digital connectivity can reduce the sense of separation and loss that is often associated with migration (Plaza and Plaza 2019). It allows for an exchange of caregiving between the sending and receiving areas, and this may involve satisfying the need for emotional support (Kędra 2021a; Merry et al. 2019). For example, family members send each other videos, audio messages and pictures of family members, practices that contribute to the maintenance of bonds and relationships (Baldassar and Merla 2014; Kędra 2021b). Video calls enable grandparents to see how their children and grandchildren are faring, without being in the same physical space. Moreover, grandparents can enquire about issues that concern them, and their children can also request advice on parenting. Absko, a parent based in Kenya with an adult migrant child in South Africa, mentioned that 'the beauty of it is you might not physically be with your child for guidance and counselling but are able to counsel them and just give them direction'. This speaks to the culturally constructed notion that parenting responsibilities extend beyond geographical proximity and do not stop simply because offspring are physically absent.

Similarly, there is care that extends from those who have left to those who have remained behind. This bidirectional caregiving provides an avenue for sourcing advice: distant family members still occupy an important space and are the preferred fundamental social network for support. Thus, as Deborah Fahy Bryceson says, the 'transnational family constitutes a multi-dimensional spatial and temporal support environment for migrants' (2019, 3043). This is aided by the notion of co-presence – being there without necessarily being physically present – mediated and enabled by technological advances (Baldassar 2008; Kędra 2021b); in other words, a mediated absent-present (Twigt 2019).

Migration is a process. Digital connections supplement reunions and visits, facilitating the emotional work associated with the continuum of the migration experience. (Again, the fact that the Kenyan sample was better resourced is reflected in the option of visits, which was not available for many interviewees in the samples from other African countries.) Text messages are synchronous, intimate and casual – and may therefore hold more appeal than emails. Visual components in WhatsApp offer ways to express intimacy and give a sense of prox-imity, as family members are able to see each other and converse in real time (Fernandez-Ardevol and Rosales 2017; Hillyer 2021). Our participants tended to choose WhatsApp for transnational family care because it allows for the exchange of video and audio recordings, photos and text, and because of the ease of such exchanges. The visual content shared in communication is important as a way of ensuring intimacy and a sense of gathering the truth through visual evidence. Furthermore, these technologically mediated connections also assist in regularising contact, building relationships and preparing for actual physical meetings. One participant indicated that it reduces the distance when people meet: 'It facilitates constant contact … through the technology, you build a momentum for the physical visit … it's like a preamble to the physical visit' (Absko).

The connectivity also acts as a means of enabling the transmission of culture, feeling like 'a part of this bigger family and teaching young children that it's very important to have close family ties' (Absko). This point was also made by two Kenyan participants in South Africa. Family members seemed invested and hopeful in the experience of co-presence as influenced and kept alive by possibilities of future visits and reunions (Baldassar 2023).

The significance of 'seeing' through WhatsApp video calls can also be better understood if one considers age and intergenerational relations. Mary, who has an adult daughter in South Africa, appreciated that they could see each other and that she could rely on her own judgement to ascertain the well-being of her daughter. She said: 'We are able to see her … like the other day I was talking to her and I realised that she has lost weight. So, I am able to see her, and I am able to see her gestures … I learn a lot and I get a lot of information.' Mary is able to continue to be a parent and a provider of care transnationally (Barglowski 2021), a role that is experienced and performed through the WhatsApp communication framework. Mary's comments also show the complexities of visual communication, expressions of daily stresses and the burden of coping with what one sees on these video calls. They illuminate, too, a powerful psychosocial content of connected care; her words illustrate both joy and a tinge of sadness, hope, anxiety and worry. WhatsApp video calls enhance narratives of care, including gendered narratives of practices of care, but they can also perpetuate family fragility, care drain and connection strain.

Digital Connectivity and Engagement: Care and Obligation

The sense of family support that is received provides a sense of connectedness and fosters a close connection with the home country. It allows the bridging of distances and engagement with family. There are also mutual activities to keep each other involved and updates on life happenings, for example, by sending pictures. However, in all these activities, some are left out and disconnected. This creates a troubled feeling linked to disengagement, a sense of uneasiness, pain, unfulfilled responsibility and a helpless feeling of not knowing how to engage further. Monica, now in South Africa, has two young children, both born in Kenya. In line with the ethnic norms that require her to establish bonds with family and her ancestors, she said that with WhatsApp communication the family is 'able to see us and see their grandchildren'. The communication element of seeing each other is important in the interactions, as it facilitates connections 'even if it's just on the phone'. Shiku, also in South Africa, communicates with her mother in Kenya often, especially since her father died. She says that 'on a video call, you see the excitement. Sometimes she phones me like every evening.' Monica further indicated that with her family-in-law it has just not been possible to see each other on a video call, despite all the effort they have put in. With a sad trailing voice, she said, ending with a sigh: 'It's just voices ... so they're missing out, we have tried. Quite a loss to not know.' The family-in-law are left out of regular connection, particularly because they do not have access to video calls. Voice is important in communication, but having both audio and visual elements in communication seems to enhance the relationship and interaction.

As we have seen from the work of Maria M. Kioko (2010) on the Kenyan diaspora, individual and collective connections are about identity, status, belonging and maintaining positions in the family and in the community, and being influential. These social relations are also extended to fellow migrants, in demonstrating a sense of cultural obligation and solidarity and, ultimately, belonging. From my observation, Kenyans from different ethnic groups are able to relate better to each other when they are outside the country and away from the everyday reminders of ethnic differences in their home country. Several of the Kenyans interviewed in South Africa participate in fundraising initiatives to support the sending areas; these enable them to create co-presence with people left behind, establish room for engagement, and allow them to practise patriotism. Communication and connections can also occur in times of distress; these offer an opportunity to express other forms of trans-national care. Such forms of care have often been learned from the older generations (kinship care), and are expressed as monetary or other contributions that can assist the family in distress. Shiku, who is married to a Zimbabwean and who now lives in South Africa, has experienced this generosity from kinship networks in the past. She said: 'It's just being there.' This implies being available, accessible and present to offer comfort when the family is not close by.

In the context of Kenya's history of corruption and in the spirit of transparency, informal welfare monetary contributions on WhatsApp are often accompanied by an announcement of the amount that each person contributes. This information is shared with others, 'sharing who is con-tributing what' (Nuro) – making care visible. Sharing this information can indicate to what extent the monetary target has been met, but it may also create a sense of digital competition and surveillance. This could potentially be an exclusionary activity for Kenyans in South Africa who cannot contribute financially or who are only able to give a little or in non-monetary terms.

WhatsApp connections between family members (Kędra 2021b), linking groups of migrants with groups of people who remain in Kenya, not only reinforce connection, but also underscore implicit rules of connection – such as those governing who should be helping whom finan-cially, and to what degree. As Sarah Vuningoma, Maria Rosa Lorini and Wallace Chigona (2021) found, the use of mobile phones in migrant com-munities in South Africa enhances social connectedness – with family and friends in the country of origin and with fellow migrants in the country of resettlement – as well as with people in the destination country, to forge bonds with the destination community. In addition, cyber communities provide different categories of migrants with a digital lifeline (Alencar, Kondova and Ribbens 2019) – avenues to seek socialisation and a sense of continued belonging, especially when they feel marginalised in local host communities, as Rumika Suzuki Hillyer (2021) found in a study on Japanese migration. Crucially, though, these communities provide ways in which relationships may be policed. For example, a study of the Trinidadian diaspora by Dwaine Plaza and Lauren Plaza advances the debate on transnational care by arguing that the 'moral obligation dimension is crucial to understanding the caring about and caring for kin relationships' (2019, 2). The notion of kinship morality is a set of moral discourses that informs people's behaviours towards their families, whether they are close together or far apart. Therefore, people tend to negotiate relationships within these (un)scripted moral and ethnic guidelines. These caring, social, norm-influenced commitments transcend boundaries of blood, marriage, residence, culture and country, and are expressed in many ways and through different tangible and intangible activities and actions.

Tensions and Complexities in Intergenerational Care Connections

Much emotion is expressed about transnational connections, notably the reciprocity of caring. For example, elderly parents who are in need of care also contribute to care and connections mediated by WhatsApp.

Shiku recalls how excited her parents and everyone were about getting a WhatsApp-enabled phone – little did they know that this would turn Shiku's mother into what she calls 'a super connector'. The large increase in contact and the intensity mediated by video calling influenced not only the care given but also the care received, as shaped by the intergenerational communication. The connections are tiring for Shiku, but she does not want to hurt her mother's feelings or show disrespect or a lack of regard by letting her know that her contacts are too frequent and 'too much', as this would be seen as a cultural intergenerational (family) silencing. The complexity of (dis)connection arises in this case from the fact that Shiku's mother is allowed to be the central caregiver in the home setting owing to her respected and acknowledged bio-cultural status as a parent. Shiku has struggled to cope with the care connection demands that her mother places on her and Shiku's husband when her mother contacts them every day. This increased frequency resulted in a large increase in the number and intensity of contacts, leading to disconnection rather than connection. At the same time, Shiku is also able to appreciate the value of communication through WhatsApp and how it has helped with the loss and grief of her father's death. This finding supports the notion of psychological well-being and coping in situations where there is a high level of communication and engagement (Geçer and Yıldırım 2023) and familyhood across distance (Kędra 2021b).

A WhatsApp group can also be a site of conflict between members of the group, as well as a source of internal conflict, especially when one knows that there is not much influence one can exert from a distance. This may be a form of silencing brought about by distance and mediated by blood relations. Like some participants in a study by Dora Sampaio (2020), Shiku concealed her emotions by not expressing them to her mother (or her sister), as a way to protect family exchanges and communication while enacting care.

Connecting on a family WhatsApp group, whether by choice or by circumstance, pushed the study participants to reflect on who they are, their relationships and how others understand them. Features of identity are contributors to communication, as they can act as social markers. Wamalwa, who only has male siblings, spoke about the conflicts that arise on the family groups and through the recognition of the family connection: 'Because we were brought up in the same home and were linked with each other closely, we know why they initiate that.' Intergenerational interdependencies and the interrelations between masculinity and care (dis)connections are also evident in the powerful gendered resolution of the tension, as Wamalwa adds that 'there are certain members in the family who calm each other down based on the fact that probably they were born, let's say, close to each other and they probably lived with each other. We try and help each other as much as possible.' Even when men show care or connect with each other, there is a resistance to intimate nurturing. Then connection takes place in ways that are historically connected to masculinity and notions of care (Ellemers 2018). These may include what Bing Sun, Hongying Mao and Chengshun Yin (2020) refer to as 'distracting strategies'. These strategies are evident in the way Wamalwa feels the need to qualify his response about the connection among his brothers.

According to A. Bheemeshwar Reddy and Madhura Swaminathan (2014), age and intergenerational relations have an impact on care and connectivity. In particular, there are challenges to connecting that are not dissimilar to those faced by rural South African families (see Chapter 3). Having access to a technological device does not automatically mean that one knows how to use it, and this applies especially to older family members. Muli and Neki, who are both fathers of two young children and both live in South Africa, noted that the type of technology their parents are currently exposed to was absent when they were growing up, but they had to get them WhatsApp-enabled phones in order to connect. Muli pointed out that his parents were not tech-savvy and that 'it wasn't just a lesson but lessons upon lessons on how to use WhatsApp ... luckily my brother was able to help them more'. Neki also connected the challenges experienced to his parents' age by saying that 'they find it difficult accessing the WhatsApp and it's been hard because every time I try to call on WhatsApp, they don't know how to answer so it's been very tricky for them'. Thus, the elements of intergenerational digital literacy and facilitation are crucial in understanding technology-mediated communication (Baldassar et al. 2022).

These challenges also speak to the cost of care and the kind of resourcing – both tangible and intangible – needed to ensure that communication happens. The study participants provided assistance in purchasing the smartphone device and teaching family how to use the device and WhatsApp – indicating that the performance of care and support work is not limited to physical at-home situations for transnational families, but may involve more than just one family member. Generally, it was felt that the benefits outweigh the costs.

Intergenerational communication can be constrained by the dilemma of a double burden: the desire to communicate, on the one hand, and the cost of communication, on the other. Transnational parenting, even on WhatsApp, can be expensive. Zippy, who has an adult child in South Africa, said: 'Actually in a sense, knowing I have no other avenue of parenting and guiding my children, this has become my basic requirement – I have actually factored having Wi-Fi and having data as priority budget items in my monthly expenditure budget.' Care and connection matter, and the financial independence to communicate can facilitate one's agency and help one perform parenthood.

Although group chats are ideal for quick updates, WhatsApp may not be good enough as a medium for sharing important aspects of people's lives, providing emotional support, and sharing deep intimate emotions. Under any circumstances, receiving bad or traumatic news or resolving conflict and tensions can be emotionally draining and can induce feelings of powerlessness and emotional distress. This can be made worse in the digital world where traditional boundaries are being reshaped.

Communication is not only about pleasant issues, and the communication of bad news through the use of technology was highlighted by study participants. Shiku, who has lived in South Africa for more than ten years, recalled the time when her father was ill and had been taken to hospital. The next day she received a 'text in my sister's [WhatsApp] group saying Dad had just died ... I mean that is technology. It is not the best [*anxious laughter*] ... but if I guess, my smaller sister was also dealing with her own. I wouldn't blame her – how she passed the communication.' The efficiency of the technology in allowing for instant communication was undercut in this case by the lack of rules on how to use the technology in a humane way. As Shiku says, with resignation, 'that is technology' – technology can leave psychosocial and emotional needs unfulfilled. This may become especially difficult when transnational family members are experiencing major life events. The issue here is not the device itself, but how it is used and how to promote empathetic communication and mitigate further psychosocial distress (Baldassar et al. 2016; Choe et al. 2019). It is not impossible for emotional wounds, dilemmas and conflicts to be addressed via a WhatsApp message or group. Simon, who is in Kenya but has relatives in South Africa, said: 'When a matter requires more expounding, when a matter requires more encouragement, more comfort, then the telephone becomes more important'. The use of a phone call was also strongly supported by Shiku, who noted: 'There is always a process of how to communicate … You don't just put it on a WhatsApp group, you know. There has to be proper channels or an elder takes the phone, calls and communicates with you.'

CONCLUSION

This chapter set out to explore transnational intergenerational care, support and well-being, and confirmed that WhatsApp is a central mode of addressing those needs for this Kenyan sample, which was better resourced than many other samples in this book. It was not possible to conclude that transnational intergenerational connectivity coheres in only one way. The findings from this chapter suggest that, firstly, WhatsApp as a mode of communication can indeed help nurture connections across borders and distance, and thus serve as a transnational care link connecting intergenerational family members. Secondly, WhatsApp is used to solidify connections of cultural obligation and provide support. Thus, performing familyhood transnationally through WhatsApp allows for elements of digital physical co-presence. Thirdly, communication through WhatsApp poses some challenges in terms of what and how things are communicated, and how frequently. Finally, WhatsApp can be a lifeline and a rare connection with the country and people left behind and in the country of resettlement, as well as between migrants in the diaspora or settlement areas.

Conversational strategies and communication voids may sometimes hinder caring if there is silence or a form of silencing, but sometimes silence can also contribute to sustaining well-being in contexts where families are separated by distance. Further studies should explore family networks and strategies that assist and protect transnational families in their silencing practices, but still contribute to their well-being.

REFERENCES

Akanle, Olayinka, Olufunke A. Fayehun and Gbenga S. Oyelakin. 2020. 'The Information Communication Technology, Social Media, Intergenerational Migration and Migrants' Relations with Kin in Nigeria'. *Journal of Asian and African Studies* 56, no. 6: 1212–1225. https://doi.org/10.1177/0021909620960148.

Alencar, Amanda, Katerina Kondova and Wannes Ribbens. 2019. 'The Smartphone as a Lifeline: An Exploration of Refugees' Use of Mobile Communication Technologies during Their Flight'. *Media, Culture and Society* 41, no. 6: 828–844. https://doi.org/10.1177/0163443718813486.

Baldassar, Loretta. 2007. 'Transnational Families and the Provision of Moral and Emotional Support: The Relationship between Truth and Distance'. *Identities* 14, no. 4: 385–409. https://doi.org/10.1080/10702890701578423.

Baldassar, Loretta. 2008. 'Missing Kin and Longing to Be Together: Emotions and the Construction of Co-presence in Transnational Relationships'. *Journal of Intercultural Studies* 29, no. 3 (Special Issue: Transnational Families – Emotions and Belonging): 247–266. https://doi.org/10.1080/07256860802169196.

Baldassar, Loretta. 2017. 'Transformations in Transnational Ageing: A Century of Caring among Italians in Australia'. In *Transnational Aging and Kin-Work*, edited by Parin Dossa and Cati Coe, 120–138. Series on Global Perspectives on Aging. New Brunswick, NJ: Rutgers University Press.

Baldassar, Loretta. 2023. 'Migrant Visits over Time: Ethnographic Returning and the Technological Turn'. *Global Networks* 23, no. 1: 160–173. https://doi.org/10.1111/glob.12393.

Baldassar, Loretta and Laura Merla. 2014. 'Locating Transnational Care Circulation in Migration and Family Studies'. In *Transnational Families, Migration and the Circulation of Care: Understanding Mobility and Absence in Family Life*, edited by Loretta Baldassar and Laura Merla, 25–58. New York: Routledge.

Baldassar, Loretta, Mihaela Nedelcu, Laura Merla and Raelene Wilding. 2016. 'ICT-Based Co-presence in Transnational Families and Communities: Challenging the Premise of Face-to-Face Proximity in Sustaining Relationships'. *Global Networks* 16, no. 2: 133–144. https://doi.org/10.1111/glob.12108.

Baldassar, Loretta and Raelene Wilding. 2020. 'Migration, Aging, and Digital Kinning: The Role of Distant Care Support Networks in Experiences of Aging Well'. *The Gerontologist* 60, no. 2: 313–321. https://doi.org/10.1093/geront/gnz156.

Baldassar, Loretta, Raelene Wilding, Lukasz Krzyzowski and Joanne Mihelcic. 2022. 'Digital Citizenship for Older Migrants in Australia: The Need for a Comprehensive Policy Framework'. In *Vulnerable People and Digital Inclusion: Theoretical and Applied Perspectives*, edited by Panayiota Tsatsou, 139–160. Cham: Springer International.

Barglowski, Karolina. 2019. *Cultures of Transnationality in European Migration: Subjectivity, Family and Inequality*. Oxford: Routledge.

Barglowski, Karolina. 2021. 'Transnational Parenting in Settled Families: Social Class, Migration Experiences and Child Rearing among Polish Migrants in Germany'. *Journal of Family Studies* 29, no. 2: 893–910. https://doi.org/10.1080/13229400.20 21.2007786.

Bell, Justyna and Marta Bivand Erdal. 2015. 'Limited but Enduring Transnational Ties? Transnational Family Life among Polish Migrants in Norway'. *Studia Migracyjne – Przeglad Polonijny* 3, no. 157: 77–98.

Bryceson, Deborah Fahy. 2019. 'Transnational Families Negotiating Migration and Care Life Cycles across Nation-State Borders'. *Journal of Ethnic and Migration Studies* 45, no. 16: 3042–3064. https://doi.org/10.1080/1369183X.2018.1547017.

Choe, Eun Kyoung, Marisa E. Duarte, Hyewon Suh, Wanda Pratt and Julie A. Kientz. 2019. 'Communicating Bad News: Insights for the Design of Consumer Health Technologies'. *Journal of Medical Internet Research Human Factors* 6, no. 2: e8885. https://doi.org/10.2196/humanfactors.8885.

Egwurube, Joseph. 2020. 'Acculturation, Adjustment and Syncretism: The Social and Cultural Identity Mix of Black African Immigrants in Selected American Cities'. In *Changing Societies: Cultures in Movement in Coastal Cities*, edited by Vincent Mariet, Muthia Chandra, Letyzia Taufani, Martine Raibaud, David Waterman and Micéala Symington, 11–33. Newcastle upon Tyne: Cambridge Scholars.

Ellemers, Naomi. 2018. 'Gender Stereotypes'. *Annual Review of Psychology* 69: 275–298. https://doi.org/10.1146/annurev-psych-122216-011719.

Erel, Umut and Louise Ryan. 2018. 'Migrant Capitals: Proposing a Multi-level Spatio-temporal Analytical Framework'. *Sociology* 53, no. 2: 246–263. https://doi.org/10.11 77/0038038518785298.

Faria, Julia. 2021. 'Main Destinations for Kenyan Emigrants 2020'. Statista. https://www.statista.com/statistics/1231434/number-of-kenyan-emigrants-by-country-of-destination/.

Fernandez-Ardevol, Mireia and Andrea Rosales. 2017. 'Older People, Smartphones and WhatsApp'. In *Smartphone Cultures*, edited by Jane Vincent and Leslie Haddison, 55–68. London: Routledge.

Geçer, Ekmel and Murat Yıldırım. 2023. 'Family Communication and Psychological Distress in the Era of Covid-19 Pandemic: Mediating Role of Coping'. *Journal of Family Issues* 44, no. 1: 203–219. https://doi.org/10.1177/0192513X211044489.

Ghai, Dharam. 2005. 'How Can Kenyans Abroad Contribute to National Development?' *Development in Practice* 15, no. 5: 668–676.

Grimm, Adam. 2019. 'Studying to Stay: Understanding Graduate Visa Policy Content and Context in the United States and Australia'. *International Migration* 57, no. 5: 235–251. https://doi.org/10.1111/imig.12561.

Hillyer, Rumika Suzuki. 2021. 'Staying Connected: Effects of Online Platforms on Transnational Family Relations and Social Capital'. *Contemporary Japan* 33, no. 1: 3–23. https://doi.org/10.1080/18692729.2020.1847389.

Kędra, Joanna. 2021a. 'Performing Transnational Family with the Affordances of Mobile Apps: A Case Study of Polish Mothers Living in Finland'. *Journal of Ethnic and Migration Studies* 47, no. 13: 2877–2896. https://doi.org/10.1080/1369183X. 2020.1788383.

Kędra, Joanna. 2021b. 'Virtual Proximity and Transnational Familyhood: A Case Study of the Digital Communication Practices of Poles Living in Finland'. *Journal of*

Multilingual and Multicultural Development 42, no. 5: 462–474. https://doi.org/ 10.1080/01434632.2020.1839084.

Kioko, Maria M. 2010. 'Diaspora in Global Development: First Generation Immigrants from Kenya, Transnational Ties, and Emerging Alternatives'. *Journal of Global Initiatives: Policy, Pedagogy, Perspective* 2, no. 2: 151–168. https://digitalcommons. kennesaw.edu/jgi/vol2/iss2/4.

McAuliffe, Marie and Anna Triandafyllidou, eds. 2022. *World Migration Report 2022.* Geneva: International Organization for Migration.

Merry, Lisa, Dominic Mogere, Dan Odindo and Nancy Edwards. 2019. 'Transnational Family Support and Perspectives from Family Members Back Home: A Pilot Study in Kisumu, Kenya'. *Journal of Global Health Reports* 3: e2019025. https://doi. org/10.29392/joghr.3.e2019025.

Mwakikagile, Godfrey. 2014. *The People of Kenya and Uganda.* Dar es Salaam: New Africa Press.

Mwaniki, David L. and Charles O. Dulo. 2008. *Managing the Migration of Human Resources for Health in Kenya: The Impact on Health Service Delivery.* EQUINET Discussion Paper Series 55. Harare: EQUINET.

Odipo, George, Charles Owuor Olungah and Dalmas Ochieng Omia. 2015. 'Emigration Mobility Trends and Patterns in Kenya: A Shift from South–North to South–South Migration'. *International Journal of Development and Economic Sustainability* 3, no. 4: 29–48. https://profiles.uonbi.ac.ke/ochiengomia/files/emigration-mobility-trends-and-patterns-in-kenya_publication.pdf.

Opiyo, Peter Owiti, Darmp Sukontasap, Jiraroj Mamadkul and Raymond Udoffe Brown. 2016. 'Strategies to Increase the Number of Kenyan Diaspora in Southeast Asian Countries under the Accreditation of Kenya Mission in Bangkok'. *Open Journal of Political Science* 6, no. 2: 123–133. https://doi.org/10.4236/ojps.2016.62012.

Oucho, John, Linda A. Oucho and Vollan Ochieng. 2014. *Is Migration the Solution to Poverty Alleviation in Kenya? Rural–Urban Migration Experiences of Migrants from Western Kenya to Kisumu and Nairobi.* Migrating out of Poverty, Working Paper 21. University of Sussex.

Plaza, Dwaine and Lauren Plaza. 2019. 'Facebook and WhatsApp as Elements in Transnational Care Chains for the Trinidadian Diaspora'. *Genealogy* 3, no. 2: 1–22. https://doi.org/10.3390/genealogy3020015.

Popyk, Anzhela and Paula Pustułka. 2021. 'Transnational Communication between Children and Grandparents during the Covid-19 Lockdown: The Case of Migrant Children in Poland'. *Journal of Family Communication* 21, no. 3: 223–237. https:// doi.org/10.1080/15267431.2021.1929994.

Reddy, A. Bheemeshwar and Madhura Swaminathan. 2014. 'Intergenerational Occupational Mobility in Rural India: Evidence from Ten Villages'. *Review of Agrarian Studies* 4, no. 1 (July): 95–134. https://doi.org/10.22004/ag.econ.308509.

Reis, Logan, Kathryn Mercer and Jennifer Boger. 2021. 'Technologies for Fostering Intergenerational Connectivity and Relationships: Scoping Review and Emergent Concepts'. *Technology in Society* 64 (February): 101494. https://doi.org/10.1016/j. techsoc.2020.101494.

Sampaio, Dora. 2020. 'Caring by Silence: How (Un)documented Brazilian Migrants Enact Silence as a Care Practice for Aging Parents'. *Journal of Intergenerational Relationships* 18, no. 3: 281–300. https://doi.org/10.1080/15350770.2020.1787038.

Stuhlhofer, Eunice Wangui. 2022. 'In Pursuit of Development: Post-migration Stressors among Kenyan Female Migrants in Austria'. *Social Sciences* 11, no. 1 (December): 1–18. https://doi.org/10.3390/socsci11010001.

Sun, Bing, Hongying Mao and Chengshun Yin. 2020. 'Male and Female Users' Differences in Online Technology Community Based on Text Mining'. *Frontiers in Psychology* 11 (26 May). https://doi.org/10.3389/fpsyg.2020.00806.

Twigt, Mirjam A. 2019. 'Mediated Absent Presence in Forced Displacement'. *Popular Communication* 17, no. 2: 171–184. https://doi.org/10.1080/15405702.2018.1540784.

Vuningoma, Sarah, Maria Rosa Lorini and Wallace Chigona. 2021. 'How Refugees in South Africa Use Mobile Phones for Social Connectedness'. In *C&T '21: Proceedings of the 10th International Conference on Communities and Technologies; Wicked Problems in the Age of Tech, June 20–25, 2021, Seattle, WA*. https://doi.org/10.11.45/3461564.3461569.

7

Making a World of Care: DRC Refugees' Barber Shop Stories

Thembelihle Coka and Maria C. Marchetti-Mercer

SETTING THE SCENE

In the heart of what was once the central business district of Johannesburg, you are overwhelmed by the daily commotion of traffic, taxis, car guards, pedestrians and noise (Winkler 2013). You hear a range of shouted conversations in many African languages, in voices raised to be heard over the cacophony. This part of South Africa is a place of refuge for many from other parts of the continent. It is also a dangerous and uncertain place, where crime and illegal activities are commonplace, and where, in order to get about, you have to make your way past sex workers, informal pavement traders and many others trying to get by, as they do in other cities of the world (Oliveira 2011). It is also a place where there has been, and may well again be, a pattern of xenophobic attacks by South Africans on foreign nationals (Mogoboya and Montle 2020).

In this world, which is simultaneously one of refuge, hope, possibility, fear and despair, you will find a barber shop. The shop is owned by Charles, a refugee from the Democratic Republic of Congo (DRC). As you step through the doors of the shop, you hear African music and the voices of people waiting to have their hair done. The shop is small, but it is carefully organised, especially compared with the chaotic world outside. On one side of the room are male barbers attending to the hair of male clients, and across the central table, on the other side, female hairdressers work on braiding the hair of their female clients, attending to their eyebrows, or performing other rituals of beautification. The very existence of this haven of peace and order in the prevailing context of threat and despair – a place where, for all the clients, looking good and having dignity matter – tells a story of resilience. And the place is not just about the customers' hair or their eyebrows, the cuts or the weaves. As one client put it in his own language, commenting on his new hairstyle, 'Nobody does it like home here [in South Africa]'. The shop is a place to pause on a challenging journey which has been long and is still not over. Thembelihle (Lihle for short), the first author of this chapter, had many conversations in this place, a barber shop owned by a DRC refugee, learning more about these people's lives. Lihle had to negotiate the difficulties of being both a researcher who wanted detailed information and an empathetic listener who was deeply affected by the moving stories that the barber shop owner and his customers shared. As in other chapters, pseudonyms are used – in this case, these are even more essential than elsewhere in this book, because people from the DRC are at risk in South Africa as foreigners, and are especially set apart by the fact that French is their language of general communication,[1] and they have more limited English at their command than most Malawian and Zimbabwean migrants, for whom English is a second language.

The DRC is a member of the Southern African Development Community (SADC), whose website states: 'Conflicts in southern Africa and neighbouring regions over the years have resulted in the movement of millions of refugees seeking asylum in neighbouring countries. SADC as a region has recognised the need to balance the potential security risks associated with hosting refugees against the benefit of regional integration that encourages the movement of people for economic development' (SADC 2012). As is well known, the DRC has a long and ongoing history of conflict (Ayres 2012; Kennes and Larmer 2016; Laudati 2013; Venugopalan 2016; Williams 2013). Almost four million people have died, including the late President Laurent-Désiré Kabila, who was assassinated in 2001; around 3.4 million people have been displaced (Mahlangu 2016). The dire political situation in the DRC and concurrent violence form the backdrop to our participants' reasons for fleeing their country of origin for South Africa. Although it is possible for DRC citizens to be accepted into South Africa as asylum seekers or refugees, that does not guarantee a warm welcome from local communities.

METHODOLOGICAL REFLECTIONS

Lihle initially intended to interview refugees at a non-governmental organisation that accommodates refugee populations and assists them in dealing with their traumatic experiences. However, she was not granted permission by the organisation to conduct interviews on the premises, because the refugees are deemed a vulnerable population that require immediate counselling, as many have not yet dealt completely with their traumatic experiences. She then acquired access to a barber shop in Johannesburg owned by a refugee from the DRC. During her interview with the owner, she realised that all the other workers (and customers) were DRC refugees as well. She therefore undertook eight interviews with willing participants (five male and three female) in this setting, which serves as a safe space, thus providing us with a unique glimpse into the formation of a makeshift and newly emerging community of migrants, far away from home. Her participants had all been living in South Africa for between six and twenty-one years.

Most individuals who migrate from the DRC are fleeing the threat of death, forced conscription or worse. They often realise that they are leaving their families behind in a very precarious situation. They have no idea whether and when they might visit home again, if ever, and often do not know what has become of those they left behind. Technology is extremely basic in the communities back home, where people lack devices, connectivity, data, money and digital literacy. The community that has formed here is composed of individuals who have experienced deep trauma. Many experience survivors' guilt, which was shared by members of this group, but may be incomprehensible to outsiders. For these reasons, there was no way to conduct interviews with family members back in the DRC.

MEETING SOME OF OUR PARTICIPANTS

One of the people with whom conversations were held in the barber shop was Chris. He was born and raised in the DRC. He fled in 2001 owing to unbearable conditions and a lack of employment. He had to use several buses, travelling through Zambia and Zimbabwe, to reach South Africa. He is married to the young woman he has loved since their childhood, and she followed him to South Africa in 2004. They have one child together. His mother tongue is French, but he tries to speak English, although he sometimes finds it difficult. He had been in South Africa for 19 years when he was interviewed.

He works in the hair salon as a barber, and he has been working there since he came to South Africa. His parents died when he was very young, and he grew up with siblings and other family members. It took him a while to become integrated in South Africa, but he finds South Africa safer and less violent than the DRC, even though he has been a victim of crime in his adopted country. Working at the barber shop enables him to provide for his family, but since he does not earn much, he finds it hard to send money to his family back home in the DRC. He therefore prioritises the needs of his immediate family in South Africa.

To communicate with his family in the DRC, he uses his wife's mobile phone and sometimes a colleague's mobile phone, as he considers his colleagues his new family. It was observed during the interviews that when the mobile phone belonging to one of Chris's colleagues rang, Chris took the phone and went outside. The owner of the phone was not concerned and did not even ask where Chris was taking the phone.

He clearly trusted Chris, so sharing a mobile phone did not seem to be a big deal. Two of the other barbers were often seen sharing lunch, using their hands. The shared phone and shared food seemed part of the same strategy of survival together, and part of the creation of a new kind of family and kinship far away from home.

Ray is a regular client at the salon. Like Chris, he is also from the DRC. He fled the DRC in 1999 at the age of 19, while he was doing his first year at medical school at the University of Lubumbashi. He feared for his country, which, as he saw it, was in the hands of former rebels. He left his mother, biological brother, cousins and nephews in the DRC. His father died when Chris was seven years old, and his mother died in 2016. Ray had a friend in Lusaka, Zambia, who visited the DRC often, and together they travelled to South Africa, hoping for a better future. However, when Ray and his friend arrived in South Africa, it was difficult for them to get access to bursaries, as they were not South African. A Catholic priest offered some financial support, but it was not enough. Ray tried for a time to work and study but was unable to maintain this, so he dropped out of university. He began working full-time as a security guard, earning a very small salary. He registered for some university modules through correspondence courses. He is now an entrepreneur, has a fleet of cars, which he rents to Uber drivers, and is working with a Congolese friend. He owns a number of properties in South Africa, and, together with another friend, who is a quantity surveyor, he owns a construction company. Ray has a South African wife and is currently applying for citizenship. He has four children, two girls and two boys, all born in South Africa. He has a good relationship with his parents-in-law, and describes as his extended family those gathered around him in the barber shop, which he uses, as he puts it, 'to hotspot', since he always has a lot of data on his mobile phone. He uses WhatsApp to communicate with his family back in the DRC, and his access to data is important in all his family connections.

Ray's story of success contrasts with the story of many others we heard. Many of these are stories of lives that have remained precarious, of the ongoing struggle to survive, and of trying to keep in touch with family back in the DRC. One of the most devastating effects of the refugees' flight from their homeland is the dispersal of the original family unit. While the stories of how people fled differ – whether they fled as an individual or together with members of the family unit – the impact on the family system has always been far-reaching. Becoming a refugee is different from other forms of migration: in most instances, refugees are unable to return to their families and friends back home, because it would put their lives at risk or because of limited finances (Nkomo 2019). Consequently, one of the major challenges facing people displaced by conflict is how to reconnect with those family members and loved ones left behind.

Refugees entering the country are issued with documentation by the South African government that is supposed to allow them to work in the country and to access some resources (Kalitanyi and Visser 2010). However, these documents are commonly ignored by potential employers, especially when it comes to formal, well-paid jobs; hence, the refugee populations from African countries often seek employment in the informal sector (Johnston and Bacishoga 2013) and in the lower economic sector (Smit and Rugunanan 2014). Consequently, they may struggle to afford data or internet access, especially if they need to conserve all available financial resources to prioritise survival (World Bank 2011). There may be immense pressure on them to provide for their immediate families in South Africa. Nevertheless, buying data or having access to the internet is the only way for them to remain in contact with their families in their country of origin, as they are unable to undertake visits back home, given the ongoing political violence and costs.

BARBER SHOP STORIES: THE STRUGGLE FOR CONNECTION

It was obvious from all our participants' stories that significant push factors led them to flee from their country of origin. Their flight was linked for most participants to a lack of security and persisting violence: 'The time I left home, there were so many things that took place there, so I could not tolerate the violence there' (Nelson). Generally, the political situation in the DRC remains unstable and they felt they had no choice but to leave: 'It was not by choice nor a good reason … actually, I flee from it because of insecurity reasons that was happening there' (Boris). Participants also experienced severe financial hardship. For example, Chris mentioned that 'as a man you have to fight, for looking for a job, I was sitting not doing anything … and I was not involved'.

The specific vulnerability of young boys and men was highlighted by Luce: 'My brothers left home to look for jobs and running away from the rebels, from becoming soldiers … they were collecting young guys and … Once they come here, young boys like our age, they take you by force.' While young boys were the main target, in some cases the entire family was a target of extreme violence. For example, Samuel notes: 'My other family was butchered and killed because the military wanted me to become a younger soldier.'

Most of the participants departed from the DRC as individuals, leaving their families behind, as it would have been difficult to undertake the journey with their families: 'You never know what is going to happen on your way, that time it was like everybody has to fly on their own' (Boris). Elderly parents were not able to join the participants because of difficulties inherent in the journey, as no transportation was available, or because of deteriorating health: 'Mother is the one that was alive, but she was old and not healthy' (Luce). The journey from the DRC was fraught with danger, difficulty and complications, and there was often no time to plan the trip – not even to gather enough resources to sustain them on the way, as Luce described: 'I grabbed my daughter with nothing. I left her clothes and just took a little bit of food.' Several participants experienced traumatic experiences en route to South Africa. Boris recalled: 'You are running. You see a body of [a] person lying down. You see a person running, you get shot down and you continue running.'

South Africa was not necessarily the planned destination when they fled from the DRC. Ray explained: 'The time when I left, I passed by Uganda, then I went to Tanzania and then those countries alone that I found myself in South Africa.'

Participants experienced different levels of negative emotions when they were separated from their families. For example, Boris mentions that 'when you're leaving your family you don't know when you will ever see them again'. Participants reported that after arriving in South Africa, they experienced complete isolation from their family members: 'It was difficult for me to communicate with the family, no number, no contact to find someone' (Boris). Luce specifically mentioned missing the communal aspects of sharing a meal with the family: 'I cannot remember when last did I speak to the whole family, neither share dinner with them and it's been 19 years now'. Participants also described missing and longing for their home: 'Home sweet home, but it's not easy for them to come here to meet with my family [from] back home' (Nelson). There was also a sense of worry, thinking that their families did not know what had happened to them: 'Because my family that was left, they couldn't reach me … they thought that I died along the way' (Samuel).

All the participants mentioned facing several challenges when they arrived in South Africa, lacking any support systems. For example, Nelson said: 'I felt lost. I was in a new country. I didn't know anyone.' Often it was years before they could get in touch with families. A particular challenge experienced by some was the loss of their documents along the way. When they got to South Africa, they found difficulty in securing new documents: 'You don't have the green ID, then even the poor of the poorest jobs like security, you are not going to get a job in security. It is very difficult for the newcomers' (Ray).

Having academic qualifications from their home country did not necessarily help them. Luce commented: 'Unfortunately here I was nothing. I had to start from the bottom.' Arriving in South Africa seemed to offer only limited employment opportunities. This often led to their taking up informal work, such as becoming street vendors or working in a barber shop. Luce remembered: 'I walked into every salon in CBD asking for any kind of jobs but with no luck … It was hard to survive because I could not get a job to support my daughter.'

The challenges they encountered in obtaining work often resulted in financial problems. This was made worse because they faced pressure to provide for their families back home, if they retained any contact at all. Boris lamented: 'I may not lie, due to the income that I have, it's difficult for me to provide, since I also don't have enough on my side and can't provide for them that side.'

Participants reflected on challenges such as having no sense of belonging when arriving in South Africa, and the lack of emotional and social support from South African nationals: 'Once you arrive, you do not have a family. You start over, a new life again' (Chris). Then, Chris found the barber shop owner, Charles, who assisted the newcomers by creating jobs for them, helping them to achieve a sense of belonging. Boris said: 'I found some people who could speak the same language with me, that I associated myself with them. Like brothers, like a friend, like a family.' Boris's comment raises the issue of language as a barrier – the participants were all French speakers and experienced language difficulties when they arrived, which added to their sense of alienation – not being able to speak any local language made it extremely difficult: 'I did not know how to communicate with anyone and they did not understand my language' (Boris).

THE MOBILE PHONE SOLUTION

All our participants found having mobile phones or access to such phones very helpful. They reported using mobile phones in two ways; first, to assist them in integrating into the new society and, second, to get in touch and stay in touch with their families back home. As regards the integrative aspect, Chris explained: 'When I integrate to the country, a phone, start looking for other friends to add some number of members, the brothers.' As regards staying in touch, Ray happily commented: 'If we have an urgent message now you just dial someone and then the message goes across. It is no more the time when you have to send letters through the post office and wait for weeks and months for you to get the feedback.'

An interesting phenomenon in this sample was mobile phone-sharing as a practice both among the participants and among their families back home. For example, Chris shared 'with [his] wife all the time'.

They also support each other by sharing their mobile phones with fellow refugees in their presence: 'I share my cell [mobile] phone with anyone next to me at work and someone who is closer to me' (Chris).

Participants reported using a number of mobile phone services such as normal voice calls, mobile internet voice calls and video calls. Most of the participants liked WhatsApp in particular because it offers features such as video calling, audio recording, voice calls, sending and receiving of images and data, as well as immediacy and an affordable rate: 'WhatsApp came. It was a much better way because it is much cheaper. You can call them using voice calls for such a long time … We always communicate via WhatsApp or by a normal call' (Ray). These useful features allowed some of the participants and their families to keep in contact: 'We always communicate via WhatsApp … we always use a voice recorder, and [with] their WhatsApp calls, the family will send videos to see what is going on that side' (Nelson). Another important feature is the video call feature, which allows visual communication: 'You can video-call and look at the person. You see the smile on the person' (Boris).

Social media were highlighted as an important tool for communication, especially Facebook, which was experienced as an effective way of staying in touch with families back home. For example, having lost contact with his family, Jaiden took a chance in the hope of re-establishing contact: 'I did register with my real name in Facebook because I was hoping that someone will recognise me and show my family' (Jaiden). Similarly, Luce used Facebook to look for her brother, who left the DRC when he was young: 'I searched for him and found him on Facebook. I had so much joy when we finally met. I now stay with him.'

As with other samples (see Chapters 3, 4 and 5), and as also reported by Loretta Baldassar (2007), participants tended to hide unpleasant information from family members back home. Mado admitted: 'When you're physically present when a person you get to engage in more meaningful conversation … a phone can be very deceiving.'

As regards their families back home, participants mentioned that they had a number of issues that made communication challenging – for example, poverty and lack of access to resources, both financially and because of rural conditions: 'The people that I am reaching are still poor and some don't have the smartphone' (Boris). The families back home also have problems with electricity, making it difficult to charge phones and get internet connection, according to Nelson: 'Sometimes there is even a problem for electricity, maybe the phone is off.'

In terms of their own challenges, participants reported financial problems linked to the use of information communication technologies (ICTs), notably costs related to data. They need money to get data and they do not make enough at the salon, for example, to sustain all their needs: 'I buy data, depending on how much I make on that day in the salon' (Boris). When they do not have enough data, this makes communication with family difficult. Participants did, however, point out that buying data is cheaper than buying airtime. Ray explained: 'In Congo DRC the telecommunication is very expensive for the country, calling Congo for one minute it'll cost you about R15 [US$0.82]. You have a minute.' Often participants have to prioritise their immediate families' expenses before thinking of buying data or providing for their families back home: 'Before I even buy data, I have to know that I pay rent for my kids ... So, I cannot be providing for someone who is far. Before, I provide for the one who is near to me' (Nelson).

Because of financial limitations, as well as security issues in some cases, visits are almost impossible, making their dependence on technology even heavier: 'Although we would think of going to visit her or her come this side, we cannot because we can't afford the journey' (Luce).

DISCUSSION

It is clear that technology plays an important role in the lives of the participants. Firstly, in this sample, all had access to mobile phones, either their own or borrowed from others, and they indicated that these were valuable, given the physical and geographical separation from their families. This echoes other international research such as that of Mary Chamberlain and Selma Leydesdorff (2004), highlighting the use of mobile phones and ICTs in offering continuous interaction between families separated by geographical space.

Secondly, mobile phones allowed participants to be updated about events in their home country, giving them a chance to be in contact. Prior to the advent of mobile communication, they would have had to use handwritten letters, sent through the post office, and it took a long time for these letters to be delivered (if they were delivered at all) and for them to be answered, but now mobile phones offer instant communication (Harney 2013).

Participants also found mobile phones useful to connect with their families and avoid feeling alienated in South Africa, since most of them did not know anyone when they arrived. Frequent interaction with their families back home may therefore provide a sense of care and security among this refugee population, but, as Safa'a AbuJarour and Hanna Krasnova (2019, 1792) warn, reliance on family communication may also limit their chances of integration outside their group.

Connecting with fellow refugees, especially Congolese who speak the same language, was important, and again mobile phones assisted in this regard. Participants used mobile phones to create informal networks, to share general information and create relationships with fellow Congolese refugees. These findings concur with those of Sarah Vuningoma, Maria Rosa Lorini and Wallace Chigona (2020) and Kevin Allan Johnston and Kasky Bisimwa Bacishoga (2013), who argue that the use of mobile phones promotes integration among refugees, contributes to reducing alienation, and promotes connectedness within refugee communities. This helped participants with community-building. Frequent interaction with fellow refugees also helped establish trust, as Raelene Wilding also reported (2009).

One key to maintaining shared social worlds for our participants and for those left behind in the DRC was sharing mobile phones. The example we described early in this chapter is not unusual – food is shared, phones are shared. It was phone-sharing that struck us most in our data, even though social media were also definitely used, as has been shown in other refugee communities (Xu and Maitland 2016). Our finding about phone-sharing raises interesting questions regarding how to think about ICTs in the context of migration in Africa. For our participants, phones are shared in a relatively secure physical space – the barber shop. This shop, which caters largely to migrants and refugees, seems to be crucial for creating a world in which, even in a situation of deprivation, sharing is supported in a fairly safe space and is life-affirming. The barber shop itself creates a constructed, family-like atmosphere and new kinship-like ties, but phone-sharing adds another layer of connected identity. The shared phones bring refugees together in a care network. Sharing also plays a very public role in showing the new 'kin' the reality and importance of prior but distant ties. As one shop patron hands over his or her phone to another, or to an employee, what is being performed is not just an act of kindness. It is also an enacted recognition of the importance of origin and a life story for people who are in other ways rootless, whose individual family stories and histories of migration are of little interest in the hurly-burly and precarity of life in contemporary Johannesburg. The phones themselves allow for disembodied contact with those still in the DRC, as well as a recognition of the embodied reality of the importance of connection to the past, even for people who left the DRC decades ago.

It is possible to interpret this finding in the light of research on the refugee experience in general. We know, for example, that separation from one's family can have negative psychological consequences (see, for example, Mazzetti 2008). Corresponding research exploring the importance of social support in the lives of refugees highlights the role that other refugees in similar positions can play in alleviating those difficulties (Liamputtong and Kurban 2018). This supports the work of Ignacio Correa-Velez, Sandra M. Gifford and Adrian G. Barnett (2010) and

Norah E. Mulvaney-Day, Margarita Alegria and William Sribney (2007), who have all foregrounded the positive influence that close relationships can play in the mental and physical health of refugees. Celia J. Falicov (2007) has highlighted the importance of ethnic community networks in helping migrants deal with the challenges associated with migration. These re-creations of social networks correlate strongly with health, mental health, and stable identities (Vega et al. 1991).

But there may be something more at stake here. Something is happening through the use of ICTs, and especially their communal and very public use in the barber shop. This not only creates an alternative, Johannesburg-based family or kinship network, but also potentially links those left behind to one another through the common contact by way of the barber shop. We realised in hindsight that a question we should have asked our participants was what they told those back home about the barber shop in Johannesburg, and whether any families in the DRC came into contact with each other through the fact that they have relatives in Johannesburg. There is a rich literature on the creation of new migrant communities, but much less has been written on the issue of how those left behind may, together and across traditional family and kinship lines, create their own new networks. We do not yet fully understand the role of mobile phones and phone-sharing in the creation of new networks, both virtual and in person, and we need to know more about this. Especially since Covid-19, more and more lives are lived at least partially online. These stories from the barber shop in Johannesburg point us to the importance of studying the interfaces and interpenetrations between local and virtual worlds and networks.

NOTE

1   Their language situation is complex. For general communication between people from various regions in the DRC and outside it, French is the lingua franca. While one of the DRC's over 200 languages may be their mother tongue, they tend to use French, which was very deeply ingrained in the colonial era as the official language of the country, and which has remained the official language even after independence in 1960, even though there are four national languages: Kituba (Kikongo), Lingala, Swahili, or Tshiluba (Translators Without Borders 2023).

REFERENCES

AbuJarour, Safa'a and Hanna Krasnova. 2019. 'Understanding the Role of ICTs in Promoting Social Inclusion: The Case of Syrian Refugees in Germany'. In *Proceedings of the 25th European Conference on Information Systems (ECIS), Guimarães, Portugal, June 5–10, 2017*, 1792–1806. https://aisel.aisnet.org/ecis2017_rp/115.

Ayres, Christopher J. 2012. 'The International Trade in Conflict Minerals: Coltan'. *Critical Perspectives on International Business* 8, no. 2: 178–193. https://doi.org/10.1108/17422041211230730.

Baldassar, Loretta. 2007. 'Transnational Families and the Provision of Moral and Emotional Support: The Relationship between Truth and Distance'. *Identities* 14, no. 4: 385–409. https://doi.org/10.1080/10702890701578423.

Chamberlain, Mary and Selma Leydesdorff. 2004. 'Transnational Families: Memories and Narratives'. *Global Networks* 4, no. 3: 227–241. https://doi.org/10.1111/j.1471-0374.2004.00090.x.

Correa-Velez, Ignacio, Sandra M. Gifford and Adrian G. Barnett. 2010. 'Longing to Belong: Social Inclusion and Wellbeing among Youth with Refugee Backgrounds in the First Three Years in Melbourne, Australia'. *Social Science and Medicine* 71, no. 8: 1399–1408. https://doi.org/10.1016/j.socscimed.2010.07.018.

Falicov, Celia J. 2007. 'Working with Transnational Immigrants: Expanding Meanings of Family, Community, and Culture'. *Family Process* 46, no. 2: 157–171. https://doi.org/10.1111/j.1545-5300.2007.00201.x.

Harney, Nicholas. 2013. 'Precarity, Affect and Problem Solving with Mobile Phones by Asylum Seekers, Refugees and Migrants in Naples, Italy'. *Journal of Refugee Studies* 26, no. 4: 541–557. https://doi.org/10.1093/jrs/fet017.

Johnston, Kevin Allan and Kasky Bisimwa Bacishoga. 2013. 'Impact of Mobile Phones on Integration: The Case of Refugees in South Africa'. *Journal of Community Informatics* 9, no. 4: 1–20. https://doi.org/10.15353/joci.v9i4.3142.

Kalitanyi, Vivence and Kobus Visser. 2010. 'African Immigrants in South Africa: Job Takers or Job Creators?' *South African Journal of Economic and Management Sciences* 13, no. 4: 376–390. https://doi.org/10.4102/sajems.v13i4.91.

Kennes, Erik and Miles Larmer. 2016. *The Katangese Gendarmes and War in Central Africa: Fighting Their Way Home*. Bloomington, IN: Indiana University Press.

Laudati, Ann. 2013. 'Beyond Minerals: Broadening "Economies of Violence" in Eastern Democratic Republic of Congo'. *Review of African Political Economy* 40, no. 135: 32–50. https://doi.org/10.1080/03056244.2012.760446.

Liamputtong, Pranee and Hala Kurban. 2018. 'Health, Social Integration and Social Support: The Lived Experiences of Young Middle-Eastern Refugees Living in Melbourne, Australia'. *Children and Youth Services Review* 85: 99–106. https://doi.org/10.1016/j.childyouth.2017.12.020.

Mahlangu, Winnie. 2016. 'Challenges Faced by Congolese Refugees after Arriving in South Africa'. Honours report, University of the Witwatersrand. https://hdl.handle.net/10539/25538.

Mazzetti, Marco. 2008. 'Trauma and Migration: A Transactional Analytic Approach toward Refugees and Torture Victims'. *Transactional Analysis Journal* 38, no. 4: 285–302. https://doi.org/10.1177/036215370803800404.

Mogoboya, Mphoto J. and M. Edward Montle. 2020. '(Re)examining the Need for Ubuntu as an Antidote to Xenophobia in South Africa through a Glimpse into Mpe's *Welcome to Our Hillbrow*'. *Ubuntu: Journal of Conflict and Social Transformation* 9, no. 1: 71–86. https://hdl.handle.net/10520/EJC-1d58a4994a.

Mulvaney-Day, Norah E., Margarita Alegria and William Sribney. 2007. 'Social Cohesion, Social Support, and Health among Latinos in the United States'. *Social Science and Medicine* 64, no. 2 (January): 477–495. https://doi.org/10.1016/j.socscimed.2006.08.030.

Nkomo, Thobeka S. 2019. 'Exploring Congolese Refugees and Asylum Seekers' Survival Strategies in South Africa: Implication for Social Work Practice'. *Journal of Human Behavior in the Social Environment* 29, no. 4: 499–518. https://doi.org/10.1080/10911359.2018.1556142.

Oliveira, Elsa Alexandra. 2011. 'Migrant Women in Sex Work: Does Urban Space Impact Self-(re)presentation in Hillbrow, Johannesburg?' MA dissertation, University of the Witwatersrand. http://hdl.handle.net/10539/10267.

SADC (Southern African Development Community). 2012. 'Refugee'. https://www.sadc.int/themes/politics-defence-security/public-securit/refugees/.

Smit, Ria and Pragna Rugunanan. 2014. 'From Precarious Lives to Precarious Work: The Dilemma Facing Refugees in Gauteng, South Africa'. *South African Review of Sociology* 45, no. 2: 4–26. https://doi.org/10.1080/21528586.2014.917876.

Translators Without Borders. 2023. 'The Four National Languages of the DRC'. https://translatorswithoutborders.org/four-national-languages-drc.

Vega, William, Bohdan Kolody, Ramon Valle and Judy Weir. 1991. 'Social Networks, Social Support, and Their Relationship to Depression among Immigrant Mexican Women'. *Human Organization* 50, no. 2: 154–162. https://doi.org/10.17730/humo.50.2.p340266397214724.

Venugopalan, Harish. 2016. 'Understanding the Conflict in Congo'. *ORF Issue Brief*, 139 (May): 1–12. New Delhi: ORF.

Vuningoma, Sarah, Maria Rosa Lorini and Wallace Chigona. 2020. 'The Use of Mobile Phones by Refugees to Create Social Connectedness: A Literature Review'. *International Journal of Information and Communication Engineering* 14, no. 8: 586–590. https://publications.waset.org/10011361/the-use-of-mobile-phones-by-refugees-to-create-social-connectedness-a-literature-review.

Wilding, Raelene. 2009. 'Refugee Youth, Social Inclusion, and ICTs: Can Good Intentions Go Bad?' *Journal of Information, Communication and Ethics in Society* 7, nos 2–3: 159–174. https://doi.org/10.1108/14779960910955873.

Williams, Christopher. 2013. 'Explaining the Great War in Africa: How Conflict in the Congo Became a Continental Crisis'. *Fletcher Forum of World Affairs* 37, no. 2 (Summer): 81–100. https://www.jstor.org/stable/45289589.

Winkler, Tanja. 2013. 'Why Won't Downtown Johannesburg "Regenerate"? Reassessing Hillbrow as a Case Example'. *Urban Forum* 24, no. 3: 309–324. https://link.springer.com/article/10.1007/s12132-012-9178-5.

World Bank. 2011. 'The Impacts of Refugees on Neighboring Countries: A Development Challenge'. Washington, DC: World Bank. https://openknowledge.worldbank.org/handle/10986/9221.

Xu, Ying and Carleen Maitland. 2016. 'Communication Behaviors When Displaced: A Case Study of Za'atari Syrian Refugee Camp'. In *Proceedings of the Eighth International Conference on Information and Communication Technologies and Development ICTD 2016*, 1–4. https://doi.org/10.1145/2909609.2909642.

8

The Luxury of Longing: Experiences of ICTs by South African Emigrants to Non-African Countries and Their Families

Maria C. Marchetti-Mercer and Leslie Swartz

Tsitsi Dangarembga's wrenching novel of life in contemporary Zimbabwe, *This Mournable Body* (2018), paints a vivid picture of lives curtailed by limited choices and restricted opportunities. The occupational scientist Gail Whiteford (2000) uses the term 'occupational deprivation' to refer to the kind of state in which many of the characters in Dangarembga's book, including the main character, may be said to live. Her description is useful: 'Occupational deprivation is, in essence, a state in which a person or group of people are unable to do what is necessary and meaningful in their lives due to external restrictions. It is a state in which the opportunity to perform those occupations that have social, cultural and personal relevance is rendered difficult if not impossible. It is a reality for numerous people living around the globe today' (Whiteford 2000, 200). Many of the stories we have told thus far in this book are stories of occupational deprivation – we have worked with people who, indeed, have had minimal opportunity to do things that they would like to do (the notion of performing 'occupations' would be the occupational science term, which does not, however, refer only to work-related activities). We have spoken with people who are essentially on the wrong side not only of digital inequity and injustice, but also of what occupational scientists term 'occupational injustice' (Durocher, Gibson and Rappolt 2014; Peters and Galvaan 2021).

METHODOLOGICAL REFLECTIONS

In this chapter we describe the experiences of a very different cohort of participants from the ones discussed earlier. These are mostly middle-class South African families of various races, in which at least one member has emigrated from South Africa. They were the focus of the first research project mentioned in Chapter 1, managed by Maria C. Marchetti-Mercer and Leslie Swartz, which explored South African transnational families and how they negotiate the burden of care of elderly parents. A total of 23 families participated in this study. We interviewed 24 elderly parents whose adult children had migrated from South Africa. We also spoke to 7 siblings of migrant children still living in South Africa who were involved in the care of their parents, as well as 17 adult children who had migrated abroad from South Africa. All these interviews took place before the Covid-19 pandemic, some face to face and others online. These were matched samples.

When it came to interviewing these participants, we were faced with mirrors of our own personal stories. We both moved from our countries of origin to South Africa at a young age and left behind our roots as well as many significant familial relationships. Many of the stories that participants shared with us thus resonated with our own migration experiences. In recent years, both of us have had family members, colleagues and friends leave the country, so the experiences of loss shared by participants were very familiar. As authors we acknowledge that our own fresh experiences of seeing friends and colleagues leave South Africa may have affected our perceptions of the data and interviews. The stories told by participants often resonated with our own interactions with and loss of people we know.

REASONS FOR MIGRATION

The majority of our migrant participants made the choice to migrate freely, to improve their employment, educational and living opportunities. Unlike many of the African migrants discussed in the preceding chapters, these families had ready access to information communication technologies (ICTs) to maintain contact and the possibility of reciprocal visits was also more likely for this sample.

In line with general trends of South African international migration highlighted in Chapter 1 (see Crush 2000; Höppli 2014; Marchetti-Mercer 2016), these participants had chosen Canada, New Zealand, Australia, the United States, the United Kingdom and the United Arab Emirates (UAE) as their destinations. Those who migrated were mostly highly skilled, reflecting the phenomenon of what has been dubbed the 'brain drain' (see, for example, Marchetti-Mercer, Swartz and Baldassar 2021). Some wanted to pursue further educational opportunities. They mostly tended to migrate with their nuclear families, but there were cases where adult children migrated alone, leaving parents and siblings behind.

Their motivations for migration were unlike those discussed in the book thus far. They made a choice to migrate, and financial remittances played little part in their relationships with the family members they left behind. Indeed, several of the older people interviewed were proud of the fact that they did not receive financial assistance from their children. The only evidence of financial support sometimes took the form of assistance for visits to the countries to which their children had migrated (Marchetti-Mercer et al. 2020). Of interest was the finding that among the white and Indian participants left behind, there was a sense that the migration was permanent, while in black families there was a strong expectation and hope that eventually adult children would return (Marchetti-Mercer et al. 2020).

Like other migrants, this group of participants relied heavily on ICTs to stay in touch with their loved ones. Unlike other samples, however, they had good access to ICTs and could afford them relatively easily.

EXPERIENCES OF MIGRATION AND MAINTAINING CONNECTION

The findings are divided into positive experiences and negative experiences of ICTs by those who left and those who stayed behind. Visits are briefly discussed as a supplementary form of communication available to most of this sample.

The Strengths of ICTs as a Mode of Communication

This sample generally expressed positive experiences with regard to the use of ICTs. Kim was a typical example: 'I don't feel that far away from them and because I can talk to them and see their faces, I don't feel … alienated' (Marchetti-Mercer and Swartz 2020, 1867). Some commented on the fact that technological advances have resulted in less expensive ways of communicating. Those who had experienced more traditional ways of communicating, such as letter writing and phone calls, appreciated this shift – letters were a slow form of staying in touch, and international phone calls were expensive. Pulane reminisced: 'You don't know an air[mail] letter? You see it's a reflection of the changing times. Air letters were the main form of communication we had' (Marchetti-Mercer et al. 2020, 1745). The participants in our sample relied strongly on smartphones and applications often linked to these, such as WhatsApp and FaceTime. Many also used Skype, which was a popular choice to stay connected. For example, Gill said that she uses Skype because it is much cheaper than phone calls: 'Ever since then, I would try to call back home once a week to my parents. The kids is a bit more intermittent but … we try to keep in touch via Skype' (Marchetti-Mercer and Swartz 2020, 1868). Pearl commented: 'We Skype and then fortunately there is WhatsApp now because we had to use a landline, which was expensive, so now we Skype or we use WhatsApp, we talk almost twice to three times a day' (2020, 1868).

Social media were mentioned as asynchronous ways of staying connected. In the words of Gerry: 'And you have photos there and everybody can see, so you don't see each other, but you feel like you know them. You feel like you know them because you see them all the time, how they change, you just don't see them in real life, that's all' (Marchetti-Mercer and Swartz 2020, 1870). Peter also reflected on how the advent of Facebook had brought about a change in family interactions: 'I think probably in 2008, no 2007, we had Facebook ... [it] became a little easier to post photographs of the kids and I think my mom and, um, family, they got a bit closer to us and the children with posting video clips of rugby and gymnastics and what not, you know, so because [unclear] became more useful in [that] they are capturing the moments and posting them instantly' (2020, 1870).

The use of Skype is striking, because it was not mentioned by the participants in the African samples interviewed. Skype usually requires a computer or laptop on both sides of the communication. Its use therefore indicates the more advanced technological resources available to these participants. At the time, some mentioned WhatsApp (relatively new on the South African scene when we collected these data), which implied smartphone use in a period when smartphones were less readily available than they are now. This resource, which was mentioned frequently by our African participants in Chapters 3 to 7, has become much more widely used since we collected the data on this middle-class group. Skype provided an opportunity for visual contact, as George explained: 'The eye contact in Skype to me removes most of my problems ... with the technology' (Marchetti-Mercer and Swartz 2020, 1869). Gill described her mother's excitement at being able to see her: 'I just remember my mother was so excited when she could see me, and talk to me' (2020, 1869).

In contrast to the experience of many of the African participants, especially those discussed in Chapters 3 to 6, grandchildren did not stay behind with their grandparents when adult children emigrated to other countries in search of employment. The creative use of technology by grandparents left behind was also highlighted in our findings (Marchetti-Mercer and Swartz 2020). For example, Susan, a grandparent in South

Africa, described a way used to connect people in different continents to participate in a family christening:

> And my one little grandchild here had a ... my mother did a blessing for her, instead of a christening and Lily in Australia is the god-mother. So we put her on the Skype on the cellphone on the chair and the chair was empty but it had a cellphone on it with Skype on it and Lily attended the whole lesson and she made comments and was part of it, and she read a speech that she had written, well, a speech, something for her little goddaughter on the Skype. (Marchetti-Mercer and Swartz 2020, 1869)

ICTs also made it possible for three sisters and their mother to share an important family moment while waiting for the result of one sister's pregnancy test, as Susan recalled: 'I thought, isn't that incredible, there are my three daughters sharing one of the most important moments even though they are so far apart' (Marchetti-Mercer and Swartz 2020, 1869).

When Technology Does Not Provide All the Answers

Older people tended to struggle with unfamiliar technology, much like older people from the samples discussed in the earlier chapters. One striking difference was that in most instances the emigrants had the financial means to buy their parents the relevant equipment in order to communicate with them, as Jai proudly said: 'And the one from Australia he is the one who sent me the iPad. He said that this is what will keep you occupied. Slowly I learned how to use it'. Mama Maria added, 'This is the phone that Annie sent me from America. So I can WhatsApp, save pictures of [my grandchildren?] Danny and Simon' (Marchetti-Mercer and Swartz 2020, 1870). The technological challenges experienced by older people were highlighted by Mary: 'So what we did is we brought my parents as well as his parents each an iPad, so to make it easier to be able to Skype, and my parents have really gotten into the whole technology and getting in touch and stuff' (2020, 1871).

These struggles with technology sometimes led children to become frustrated with their parents when technology made it more difficult for older people to communicate with them, as Lindiwe acknoweledged: 'Oh, but my dad is terrible with technology so with him it's SMSs [texting] or I have to call him' (Marchetti-Mercer and Swartz 2020, 1871). Mary, who enthused about her own parents' embrace of technology, expressed annoyance with her mother-in-law: 'His mom not so much … Ja she's not good at it … it doesn't seem like she's prepared to learn either. So it's been really hard' (2020, 1871). However, in all instances, technology was readily available and there were no instances of participants not being able to communicate because they could not afford the appropriate device or access to the internet and mobile data.

There were some complaints about the quality of internet in South Africa as compared with that in the First World countries to which participants had emigrated. Gill remarked: 'It has a lot to do with the connectivity. The, the bandwidth … the bandwidth is not good enough to carry the … image well. But we always try to … to have a little bit of image and then a little bit of conversation' (Marchetti-Mercer and Swartz 2020, 1871). Priscilla, a parent in South Africa, said: 'Well, my biggest problem with Skype normally is the fact that it's … our technology is not good enough, so I battle' (2020, 1871).

Unlike those migrants for whom technology remains mostly a luxury, these participants took access to ICTs for granted, and instead mentioned the potentially traumatic aspects linked to the use of technology, as was highlighted by Carla (a sister in South Africa): 'And as I say, it's, you say goodbye more often' (Marchetti-Mercer and Swartz 2020, 1871). Matilda and John indicated that for two years they had preferred not to use Skype to communicate with their brother and sister: 'It's almost more upsetting … I find Skype being traumatic. Absolutely traumatic' (2020, 1871).

In this context where ICT access is almost taken for granted, what resurfaced most strongly was the wish for physical co-presence, in line with similar findings reported by Maria C. Marchetti-Mercer, Leslie Swartz and Loretta Baldassar (2021). The lack of physical contact experienced in relationships mediated by technology often created feelings of distress among participants. For example, Lesley lamented: 'It's not the same as to have someone holding you and hello Mum, I'm here for a cup of coffee' (Marchetti-Mercer and Swartz 2020, 1872). This was also emphasised by Ruth: 'It's not the same as talking to the person … you always feel you want to be with her … Love together' (2020, 1872). Similarly, Kim spoke of the inability to carry out ordinary, everyday social interactions: 'I do miss the fact that you know, we can't just go to a movie together or have dinner together or something' (2020, 1872).

Carla commented specifically on the inability to have physical contact with her sister living abroad: 'And I am not very good at talking over a telephone especially with a delay. But you still can't touch them, so there is that touch, that direct contact that you miss' (Marchetti-Mercer and Swartz 2020, 1872). This absence of physical contact was also hard for Mitchell, even with Skype: 'It actually sometimes can be even worse because you can see the person right in front of you but you … you can't hug them and you can't hold them and it just makes them feel even worse than if they were just talking over the phone' (2020, 1873).

Elderly participants in particular foregrounded the lack of physical closeness they experienced and a sense of nostalgia for more traditional ways of communication. Gogo preferred the old ways of communicating: 'We talk on the "YapYap".[1] It's bad you know, I don't like communicating that way. And I love letters and writing' (Marchetti-Mercer and Swartz 2020, 1872). There was a strong sense of loss experienced by grandparents regarding their lack of involvement in their grandchildren's lives. Susan spoke sadly of this loss: 'Because I have a lot of communication, but I think the actual physical separation, not being able to go to children's birthday parties' (2020, 1874).

Some grandparents missed especially physical proximity to young grandchildren. Lauren remarked: 'You know that longing just to put your arms around them and hug them.' Cornelia commented: 'Ja, not really knowing, seeing the grandchildren on Skype is much different than handling a baby in your arms' (Marchetti-Mercer and Swartz 2020, 1874). Despite the visual element, many felt that even Skype left much to be desired when communicating with small children. Gill explained:

> Because of Skype, so she was a tiny little baby when I could see her on Skype, which is great, but then as she developed, um I realized that it is not always easy for the child of three, four years old to communicate via Skype, they, for them, the physical, the three-dimensionality and the physical of being hugged cannot be replaced, so sometimes I was quite distressed about what, how the kid interacted with me, but I also reflected and realized that for her I am just a two- ... two-dimensional image. (Marchetti-Mercer and Swartz 2020, 1874)

In times of crisis when people usually need family support, the distance was felt even more poignantly, as Peter commented: 'After [the] death of [my] grandparent ... I felt so far removed from being able to comfort them and to share with them [the] grief ... and I think what I found was at times when I needed support and involvement from friends and others, ah, that's when you miss the contact' (Marchetti-Mercer and Swartz 2020, 1873).

The flip side of the availability of ICTs was a sense, especially among those abroad, that at times technology could be intrusive, infringing upon participants' sense of privacy. Kim recalled her interactions with her mother: 'She used to get very emotional when I would tell her you call me too much and she didn't want to hear but I needed to tell her so she got it.' Similarly, Warwick described his mother's attempts to constantly phone him: 'Yeah, but it's happened where she has tried to call me as I have been driving and it's like you know, you put, reject the call and she is like, she is not having any of that and she keeps calling back and you are eventually, like listen I am driving … [*laughing*] … What are you up to? … You can run but you can't hide' (Marchetti-Mercer and Swartz 2020, 1873).

In many instances technology was experienced as stressful when participants wanted to hide difficulties and problems, as described by Cornelia: 'If you talk to Mother on the phone, she will always tell you it's going fine, and then when we start Skyping then I see, okay, she doesn't stand up to come to the computer anymore, she just sits, then I know it's not going well' (Marchetti-Mercer and Swartz 2020, 1873). Colleen also commented on the fact that families sometimes tend to hide things from each other: 'What tends to happen is your family, they don't tell you everything that's happening to them, because they have a fear of worrying you, being so far away … So Skype will never change that, it's a human thing. So, say, for instance, one of my parents got sick, they won't tell me until it's really needed to tell me' (2020, 1873–1874).

Visits to Overcome Separation

Some participants in this sample could afford to travel from the destination country to South Africa, but more frequently the direction was from South Africa to the emigrants' new home. Having real-time interaction with grandchildren through visits may have helped overcome some of the difficulties of physical separation that were not resolved by online communication. Gill is a case in point:

> I do think that … if you have not seen them at all in physical and only communicate with them through Skype that would be more of a challenge, because I do have at least once a year some interaction with them … whether we holiday together every two years, we all holiday together, my family. Um, that, it does make a difference, so they do have a memory of me in physical. So the Skype then is an add-on. If they did not have that physical memory,

it might have been more challenging. (Marchetti-Mercer and Swartz 2020, 1875)

The importance of visits to mediate this relationship was also highlighted by Colleen:

For instance, we went to visit South Africa, my mom and dad aren't strangers to them, they're part of their lives ... So if it wasn't for things like that, it would be far harder, just to do the phone call and keep that relationship between especially the grandchildren with their grandparents. If you have that connection, you could use phone calls, but if you've never met a person, to form a bond, it's far easier to do it that way. (Marchetti-Mercer and Swartz 2020, 1875)

However, visits were also not without challenges, despite the more considerable financial means of this sample. Given the fact that these participants emigrated to countries geographically very far away, such as Canada, New Zealand, Australia, the United States, the United Kingdom and UAE, the costs associated with these trips were considerable (even though most of our participants came from middle-class backgrounds). According to Susan, 'Quite a few people that I know of cannot afford to go and visit their children and their children cannot afford to visit them ... my heart goes out to them' (Marchetti-Mercer, Swartz and Baldassar 2021, 432). In some instances, age and health issues also affected people's ability to travel. Others felt uncomfortable with having to stay as a guest in someone else's house, especially when they had to go for longer to offset the cost of travelling so far. As Jai said: 'That's too long, to be in the same environment with the same people; I'm very set in my ways. I'm in my comfort zone and I do my thing when I want it' (2021, 432).

Significantly, all the participants in this sample saw visits as a form of 'emotional refuelling', as it touched on the emotional dimensions linked to family life (Marchetti-Mercer, Swartz and Baldassar 2021).

DISCUSSION

The sample discussed in this chapter differs from those explored in Chapters 3 to 7, in that these migrants from South Africa and their families who stayed behind are middle-class or affluent people – people of means with full access to the benefits they can derive from using ICTs. This access is a key difference, which highlights a number of vital issues.

For these international migrants and their families, using ICTs whenever they wanted meant instant, easy communication. Whereas data bundles are more expensive in South Africa, and not as readily available, in the better-resourced destination countries chosen by these emigrants they are cheap, with faster speeds, and easily accessible. Older participants especially, like those in a study by Valerie Francisco (2015), appreciated this benefit of ICTs – they could still recall writing letters, how difficult it sometimes was to write them, and the long wait for a reply, even though some, like Gogo, were nostalgic about letter writing. Our findings regarding these South African emigrants and their families are in line with those exploring the concept of the transnational, interconnected family described by other authors working in countries outside Africa (see Bacigalupe and Cámara 2012; Baldassar 2007a, 2007b, 2008, 2016; Madianou and Miller 2013a, 2013b).

Unlike participants in our other samples, generally these participants took ICTs for granted – all of them could afford smartphones and other technology. However, what is interesting is that this well-off group, a group able to take the availability of ICTs for granted, found these media problematic in some ways (Marchetti-Mercer and Swartz 2020). They mentioned problems they experienced in using ICTs extensively. Rather than challenges in accessing ICTs, they faced challenges with issues that emerged during frequent use of these media. They were immensely grateful for ICTs, but they could not see them as a 'cure' for distance (Marchetti-Mercer and Swartz 2020) – they could begin to articulate the problems associated with using them. They mentioned three main problem areas. The first of these is users' level of familiarity with ICTs. The second is the 'disembodied' nature of the communication. The third relates to the ways in which ICT use can be experienced as traumatising. We discuss each of these concerns briefly below.

Familiarity with ICTs

Several of the participants from other samples (see Chapters 3 to 7) mentioned the struggles of some of their older family members to use the technology, which excluded them from frequent use of the functionalities of WhatsApp and other ICT options. This theme also came up even in the present sample, who have much greater access to the technology. Both older people and much younger people may struggle with the ICTs, as prior studies also show (Baldassar et al. 2016). Marchetti-Mercer and Swartz (2020, 1871) note that older people in particular may be intimidated by the technology and find it difficult to adapt to it (for example, Lindiwe mentioned her father's unease with technology, and Mary said her mother-in-law was not 'prepared' to learn). When adult children emigrate, ICTs seem to offer an easy way to keep in contact, but parents' and grandparents' inability or unwillingness to use ICTs may frustrate attempts to use this way to stay in touch, a situation epitomised by the comment of a family member about the use of this 'apparently simple tool' (2020, 1876). In addition, the ability to use ICTs is also affected by ageing bodies, when hearing, eyesight and mobility decline. When the available ICTs cannot be used effectively, this may exacerbate a sense of loss in both the migrants and those left behind, sometimes causing conflict.

Not Being There 'in Body'

For both the old and the young, physical absence may be something they cannot overcome, and ICTs cannot make up for that loss. At one end of the spectrum, young children may not understand how computer-mediated communication works, and may be unable to grasp the concept of online co-presence. Marchetti-Mercer and Swartz cite a young participant in their study who asked, when a visiting grandparent was about to board her plane back to South Africa: 'Is Ouma [Granny] going back into the computer now?' (2020, 1874). An older child who can initiate a WhatsApp or Skype call would understand how these ICTs are used, but for a young child this may indeed be confusing. At the other end of the spectrum, grandparents speak about the lack of a meaningful relationship with children and grandchildren when they cannot hug them in person (Marchetti-Mercer 2017). An online conversation cannot replace in-person contact, but adults, specifically some grandparents, are able to adopt creative ways, such as puppet shows for the grandchildren over Skype (Marchetti-Mercer and Swartz 2020), to overcome distance. In a better-resourced sample, such as the one discussed in this chapter, mutual visits are also an option to achieve the kind of physical, in-person contact that participants in all our samples speak of with longing, irrespective of ICT use (Baldassar 2023).

We have noted the longing for quotidian interactions that offer comfort and intimacy in our prior studies, such as Lesley's poignant comment about the simple pleasure of a hug and sharing a cup of coffee (Marchetti-Mercer and Swartz 2020, 1872). In this respect, our present findings also confirm our previous finding that issues of distance are less important for bodies considered 'normal', but the distance is a real and practical issue for those living in bodies that need more direct physical care and assistance (Swartz and Marchetti-Mercer 2019). Baldassar (2007a, 2023) presents a similar argument, concluding that visits to maintain mutual relationships of care are vital. Our awareness of these issues intensified in a world where the Covid-19 pandemic and travelling restrictions added to the issues of cost, distance and (in the case of participants in our other samples) real physical risk and political instability (Brandhorst, Baldassar and Wilding 2020; Merla, Kilkey and Baldassar 2020).

ICTs and Trauma

Pauline Boss (2016) has noted that ambiguous loss is an integral aspect of the migratory experience. We also found this to be a source of sadness and sense of ambivalence among the transnational families in our sample. It seems that ICTs may in fact be a hindrance more than a help in some ways, because if ICTs make continual contact possible, families do not get a chance (or may not try) to come to grips with the very losses inherent in migration and to mourn them – as Cornelia pointed out, 'You say goodbye more often' (Marchetti-Mercer and Swartz 2020, 1871). ICTs can also deepen the sense of the impossibility of physical touch (a point linked to the theme discussed above), when 'you can see the person right in front of you but you ... you can't hug them and you can't hold them', as Mitchell expressed it (2020, 1873). Grandparents who stayed behind often commented sadly that seeing their grandchildren online, especially new babies and young grandchildren, was a bitter-sweet experience for them, because it was not the same as holding the child in person (2020, 1874). In times of crisis, the distance was felt even more intensely.

Constant contact through ICTs may interfere with the process of developing new and more satisfying local, embodied relationships and networks. As a result, those who emigrate may struggle to indi-viduate from their family in the home country, especially if they have difficulty achieving control, autonomy and privacy, and setting bound-aries (Bacigalupe and Cámara 2012). When such issues arise, ICTs can be used to exclude the voices of those who are absent, whether it is the voices of family in the home country or of adult children abroad. Our findings in this group confirmed a point made in other samples: ICTs make it easier to remain silent about bad news, difficulties and challenges, so as not to worry those who cannot be there physically to share in the problem – 'It appears easier to hide difficult news from each other when only interacting in a virtual world' (Marchetti-Mercer and Swartz 2020, 1877).

Elsewhere, Swartz (2015) has suggested that the idea of 'trauma', as codified in the *Diagnostic and Statistical Manual of Mental Disorders*, may depend implicitly on assumptions about an orderly and predictable world. The world of the participants in the sample discussed in this chapter is very different from that inhabited by most of the research participants whose stories we shared in several of the preceding chapters. Although large-scale surveys show that rates of mental disorder are strongly associated with social and economic inequality and with poverty (Lund et al. 2010; Ngui et al. 2010), the naming of distress and its codification into what is viewed as a problem or a disorder in a particular healing system may depend on whether people feel there is anything to be gained by this codification and naming (Swartz 2015). In short, it may not help to describe something as a problem if one does not have the resources to do anything about it.

Given these considerations, it is useful in the context of this book to compare the experiences of our participants, as described in Chapters 3 to 7, with those of emigrants and their families who live much less socio-economically and politically constrained lives.

REFLECTIONS ON OUR FINDINGS

It is particularly meaningful to reflect on our more affluent participants' experiences, which were collected in a pre-Covid-19 period when conducting Skype interviews seemed to be groundbreaking and the use of technology in maintaining family relationships seemed to be strictly the domain of middle-class migrant families. In the last two years, however, we have witnessed a surge in the use of technology in maintaining family relationships and other social ties as lockdowns and travel restrictions have created distance, even in families living in the same geographical space. Now, Skype and similar platforms do not seem like novelties, as millions of grandparents across the world have spent months separated from their families and have been unable to see and touch their grandchildren in person. The central role that technology can play to ameliorate distance in families has taken centre stage in a world where Covid-19 has determined who may see whom and how, both in person and online (Brandhorst, Baldassar and Wilding 2020; Merla, Kilkey and Baldassar 2020).

Overall, these migrants from South Africa, as well as their families still in South Africa, expressed far more reservations and concerns about how ICTs are used than did most participants in our study (many of the other samples were more concerned about having access to ICTs). It would be useful to consider the issues raised by these better-resourced migrants and those they left behind in further studies, given that, despite complaints, both sides continue to use ICTs. One issue we did not consider in sufficient detail in our earlier publications was the impact of what Mirca Madianou and Daniel Miller (2013a, 2013b) term 'polymedia'; this has important implications for considering the different positionings of our more wealthy participants compared with the majority of participants mentioned in this book. Madianou and Miller argue:

> Once users have obtained either a computer or a smartphone, and once the hardware and connection costs are met, then the cost of each individual act of communication itself becomes largely inconsequential. So today a typical urban young adult of a lower- to middle-class income in many parts of the world can choose between calling though a landline, mobile phone or Voice Over Internet Protocol (VOIP) through applications such as Skype, with or without webcam; alternatively she or he can send a text or an email, use Instant Messaging (IM) or a variety of social networking applications. (2013b, 170)

Through their fieldwork with Filipino and Caribbean families, these authors show that once the thresholds mentioned above are met, media users can begin to exercise more choice over what kinds of media they prefer to use. We would argue, along with these authors, that this aspect of choice may also be the choice not to use certain platforms or to express reservations about them (see also Baldassar et al. 2016). As Madianou and Miller further note, however, there are three central preconditions for this exercise of choice, and these are access, affordability and literacy. They also comment that polymedia 'remains an aspiration and not the current state for much of the world' (2013b, 175). For most of the people we interviewed for this book, some or all of the preconditions of access, affordability and literacy were not met, and it is indeed true that for them polymedia in the sense discussed by Madianou and Miller could be described as an 'aspiration'. We may take this even further – for something to be an aspiration one has to have a sense of possibility of things being different, and we are not convinced that for many of our participants, especially those 'left behind' in conditions of poverty, there was this sense. Aspiration itself may be something of a luxury then – a luxury experienced by the wealthier people we discuss in this chapter. Emerging research on the role of ICTs in supporting the 'agentive futures' of older migrants thus provides an interesting and relevant case (Baldassar, Stevens and Wilding 2022; Ho et al. 2022; Nguyen, Baldassar and Wilding 2022).

Is what we are seeing in this chapter simply an example of the possibility that people with more privilege may have higher expectations of a world that they have greater ease in navigating? This may be part of the picture, but it may also be that if and when a greater degree of digital justice is achieved, those who currently have poor access may begin to be more concerned about what the limits of ICT contact may be, and about issues of choice within a polymedia landscape. At present, the struggle just to *have* this contact predominates in much of what people have said to us. Paradoxically, a situation in which there is more caution about ICTs and their benefits may be a sign of better socio-economic circumstances in people's lives. However, if people are given the option to have virtual co-presence or none at all, or access only by letters and phone calls, presumably most would prefer virtual co-presence, despite the challenges that may come with different forms of ICT use.

NOTE

1 The term 'Yap Yap' was used by the participant – we assume that it refers to WhatsApp, presumably using Whatsapp Call rather than video calling, and similar modes of communicating.

REFERENCES

Bacigalupe, Gonzalo and Maria Cámara. 2012. 'Transnational Families and Social Technologies: Reassessing Immigration Psychology'. *Journal of Ethnic and Migration Studies* 38, no. 9: 1425–1438. https://doi.org/10.1080/1369183X.2012.698211.

Baldassar, Loretta. 2007a. 'Transnational Families and Aged Care: The Mobility of Care and the Migrancy of Ageing'. *Journal of Ethnic and Migration Studies* 33, no. 2: 275–297. https://doi.org/10.1080/13691830601154252.

Baldassar, Loretta. 2007b. 'Transnational Families and the Provision of Moral and Emotional Support: The Relationship between Truth and Distance'. *Identities* 14, no. 4: 385–409. https://doi.org/10.1080/10702890701578423.

Baldassar, Loretta. 2008. 'Missing Kin and Longing to Be Together: Emotions and the Construction of Co-presence in Transnational Relationships'. *Journal of Intercultural Studies* 29, no. 3 (Special Issue: Transnational Families – Emotions and Belonging): 247–266. https://doi.org/10.1080/07256860802169196.

Baldassar, Loretta. 2016. 'De-demonizing Distance in Mobile Family Lives: Co-presence, Care Circulation and Polymedia as Vibrant Matter'. *Global Networks* 16, no. 2: 145–163. https://doi.org/10.1111/glob.12109.

Baldassar, Loretta. 2023. 'Migrant Visits over Time: Ethnographic Returning and the Technological Turn'. *Global Networks* 23, no. 1: 160–173. https://doi.org/10.1111/glob.12393.

Baldassar, Loretta, Mihaela Nedelcu, Laura Merla and Raelene Wilding. 2016. 'ICT-Based Co-presence in Transnational Families and Communities: Challenging the Premise of Face-to-Face Proximity in Sustaining Relationships'. *Global Networks* 16, no. 2: 133–144. https://doi.org/10.1111/glob.12108.

Baldassar, Loretta, Catriona Stevens and Raelene Wilding. 2022. 'Digital Anticipation: Facilitating the Pre-emptive Futures of Chinese Grandparent Migrants in Australia'. *American Behavioral Scientist* 66, no. 14: 1863–1879. https://doi.org/10.1177/00027642221075261.

Boss, Pauline. 2016. 'The Context and Process of Theory Development: The Story of Ambiguous Loss'. *Journal of Family Theory and Review* 8, no. 3: 269–286. https://doi.org/10.1111/jftr.12152.

Brandhorst, Rosa, Loretta Baldassar and Raelene Wilding. 2020. 'Introduction to the Special Issue: "Transnational Family Care 'On Hold'? Intergenerational Relationships and Obligations in the Context of Immobility Regimes"'. *Journal of Intergenerational Relationships* 18, no. 3: 261–280. https://doi.org/10.1080/15350770.2020.1787035.

Crush, J. 2000. *Losing Our Minds: Skills Migration and the South African Brain Drain.* Migration Policy Series no. 18. Southern African Migration Project. Cape Town: IDASA. http://samponline.org/wp-content/uploads/2016/10/Acrobat18.pdf.

Dangarembga, Tsitsi. 2018. *This Mournable Body.* London: Faber and Faber.

Durocher, Evelyne, Barbara E. Gibson and Susan Rappolt. 2014. 'Occupational Justice: A Conceptual Review'. *Journal of Occupational Science* 21, no. 4: 418–430. https://doi.org/10.1080/14427591.2013.775692.

Francisco, Valerie. 2015. '"The Internet Is Magic"': Technology, Intimacy and Transnational Families'. *Critical Sociology* 41, no. 1: 173–190. https://doi.org/10.1177/0896920513484602.

Ho, Elaine Lynn-Ee, Leng Leng Thang, Shirlena Huang and Brenda S.A. Yeoh. 2022. '(Re)constructing Ageing Futures: Insights from Migration in Asia and Beyond'. *American Behavioral Scientist* 66, no. 14: 1819–1827. https://doi.org/10.1177/00027642221075265.

Höppli, Thomas. 2014. *Is the Brain Drain Really Reversing? New Evidence*. Policy Research on International Services and Manufacturing Working Paper 1. Cape Town: PRISM, University of Cape Town.

Lund, Crick, Alison Breen, Alan J. Flisher, Ritsuko Kakuma, Joanne Corrigall, John A. Joska, Leslie Swartz and Vikram Patel. 2010. 'Poverty and Common Mental Disorders in Low and Middle Income Countries: A Systematic Review'. *Social Science and Medicine* 71, no. 3: 517–528. https://doi.org/10.1016/j.socscimed.2010.04.027.

Madianou, Mirca and Daniel Miller. 2013a. *Migration and New Media: Transnational Families and Polymedia*. London: Routledge.

Madianou, Mirca and Daniel Miller. 2013b. 'Polymedia: Towards a New Theory of Digital Media in Interpersonal Communication'. *International Journal of Cultural Studies* 16, no. 2: 169–187. https://doi.org/10.1177/1367877912452486.

Marchetti-Mercer, Maria C. 2016. '"If You Uproot a Tree You Leave a Big Hole Behind": Systemic Interconnectedness in Emigration and Family Life'. *Contemporary Family Therapy* 38 (September): 339–352. https://doi.org/10.1007/s10591-016-9386-6.

Marchetti-Mercer, Maria C. 2017. '"The Screen Has Such Sharp Edges to Hug": The Relational Consequences of Emigration in Transnational South African Emigrant Families'. *Transnational Social Work* 7, no. 1: 73–89. https://doi.org/10.1080/21931674.2016.1277650.

Marchetti-Mercer, Maria C. and Leslie Swartz. 2020. 'Familiarity and Separation in the Use of Communication Technologies in South African Migrant Families'. *Journal of Family Issues* 41, no. 10: 1859–1884. https://doi.org/10.1177/0192513X19894367.

Marchetti-Mercer, Maria C., Leslie Swartz and Loretta Baldassar. 2021. '"Is Granny Going Back into the Computer?" Visits and the Familial Politics of Seeing and Being Seen in South African Transnational Families'. *Journal of Intercultural Studies* 42, no. 4: 423–439. https://doi.org/10.1080/07256868.2021.1939280.

Marchetti-Mercer, Maria C., Leslie Swartz, Vinitha Jithoo, Nthopele Mabandla, Alessandra Briguglio and Maxine Wolfe. 2020. 'South African International Migration and Its Impact on Older Family Members'. *Family Process* 59, no. 4: 1737–1754. https://doi.org/10.1111/famp.12493.

Merla, Laura, Majella Kilkey and Loretta Baldassar. 2020. 'Introduction to the Special Issue "Transnational Care: Families Confronting Borders"'. *Journal of Family Research* 32, no. 3: 393–414. https://doi.org/10.20377/jfr-420.

Ngui, Emmanuel M., Lincoln Khasakhala, David Ndetei and Laura Weiss Roberts. 2010. 'Mental Disorders, Health Inequalities and Ethics: A Global Perspective'. *International Review of Psychiatry* 22, no. 3: 235–244. https://doi.org/10.3109/09540261.2010.485273.

Nguyen, Hien Thi, Loretta Baldassar and Raelene Wilding. 2022. 'Lifecourse Transitions: How ICTs Support Older Migrants' Adaptation to Transnational Lives'. *Social Inclusion* 10, no. 4 (Life Course Justice and Learning): 181–193. https://doi. org/10.17645/si.v10i4.5735.

Peters, Liesl and Roshan Galvaan. 2021. 'A Scoping Review Exploring "Opportunity" in Occupational Science: Possibilities for Conceptual Development'. *Journal of Occupational Science* 28, no. 2: 249–267. https://doi.org/10.1080/14427591.2020.1 832906.

Swartz, Leslie. 2015. 'Care and the Luxury of Trauma: A South African Story'. *Palliative and Supportive Care* 13, no. 2: 399–404. https://doi.org/10.1017/S147895151400042X.

Swartz, Leslie and Maria C. Marchetti-Mercer. 2019. 'Migration, Technology and Care: What Happens to the Body?' *Disability and Society* 34, no. 3: 407–420. https://doi. org/10.1080/09687599.2018.1519409.

Whiteford, Gail. 2000. 'Occupational Deprivation: Global Challenge in the New Millennium'. *British Journal of Occupational Therapy* 63, no. 5: 200–204. https://doi. org/10.1177/030802260006300503.

PART 3

FINAL CONSIDERATIONS

9

Analysis of Important Data Emerging from the Study

**Maria C. Marchetti-Mercer, Leslie Swartz
and Loretta Baldassar**

The preceding chapters have presented specific examples of migration: internal migration in South Africa, immigration from sub-Saharan Africa to South Africa, and emigration from South Africa to non-African destinations. The purpose of this chapter is to explore the differences among these specific groups of migrants and their families, as well as the commonalities. Such comparisons may in themselves be contested, because the participants come from vastly different cultural, ethnic and socio-economic backgrounds, with much diversity within groups. There are also differences in their motivations for migrating, their migration pathways and their access to technology (the main focus of our research). At first glance, the six samples – the rural–urban migrants and their families; the Zimbabwean, Malawian and Kenyan (im)migrants and their families; the refugees from the Democratic Republic of Congo (DRC); and middle-class (e)migrants to non-African destinations and the family members who stayed behind – seem completely distinct, with no obvious similarities, except that at some stage some left their places of origin, while others stayed behind. The lived realities of our participants did indeed differ immensely, with some focusing more on their gains and others more on their losses. What they all shared was a desire to maintain familial relationships across geographical distance and over time, and their use of information communication technologies (ICTs) to do so, to push their experience further towards a sense of gain.

We begin by recapping the prominent themes in each sample, focusing on the unique experiences of each group. We then turn to the overarching themes that speak to the universality of migration patterns and the roles played by technology in transnational families.

RURAL–URBAN MIGRATION IN SOUTH AFRICA

The movement from rural to urban areas by many black South Africans is not a new phenomenon, as discussed in Chapters 1 and 3. Despite the democratic dispensation in place since 1994, even after the demise of apartheid, conditions in South Africa's rural areas remain extremely difficult. Consequently, migration from rural to urban areas continues, especially among younger people, to escape a cycle of poverty and to seek economic and educational advancement: 'There is no work here apart from when a person leaves and goes to Gauteng. If you choose to reside here in our village, you will be jobless … All my children who left, left for work reasons' (Peter). Families tend to approve of the decision to migrate because of the potential economic benefits the move holds for the larger family system: 'We saw that [migration] as the potential remedy for the hunger we were suffering' (Lebo).

Inevitably, the move has a significant impact on family dynamics. On the one hand, there is a possibility (but no guarantee) of gain for the individual who migrates, and of remittances for those who stay behind. On the other hand, interpersonal and social changes are experienced by the migrants and those who stay behind: 'It was painful when they left; it is unbearable. What is hard for me is the fact that I am left alone' (Mmabatho). This sample confirmed the value of mobile phones to maintain relationships at a distance. Participants expressed an overall sense that technology was very helpful, offering the possibility of immediate communication, as well as new ways of 'do[ing] family relationships'. Nsovo said: 'ICTs have changed the way we do relationships but has really helped with keeping in touch with our loved ones who are far and wouldn't have been able to if there weren't these platforms.' There was a concern that, because face-to-face connection was not possible without video calls (or internet options such as Skype, which are not commonly available to this sample), there was a likelihood that family members could hide important information from each other so as not to cause unnecessary concern: 'Yes, you can lie … I can say I am fine even though I feel like … he can see this person is not well' (Florence). Because of this drawback, WhatsApp video calls were valued above phone calls, SMSs (texting) or WhatsApp messaging for their ability to provide more information – people could 'see' each other, making it harder to hide things like ill-health. One constraint is the cost of smartphones to run such applications. Moreover, the use of technology was hindered by impediments associated with ageing: 'We have poor vision and also we struggle with regard to how to dial the numbers' (Mmabatho). Limited digital infrastructure and network problems also contributed to difficulties in communicating across distance: 'While you are still talking on important issues … sometimes the network plays havoc on the communication' (Star). There were also broader issues with regard to digital literacy, particularly for older participants. Merriam asked: 'Ah, do I know what data is, my child?' Sibongile lamented: 'My granny can't use social media, so if I want to talk to her about something, I have to call and talk … to her.' Overall, economic limitations placed real constraints on people's digital access: 'When we have money, we use it for other things because they are the priorities' (Peter).

Those who migrated experienced a number of challenges such as language difficulties in the new urban environment, often similar to those mentioned by migrants moving to a different country: 'There's a difference because around here they don't speak my language and I don't know their language. I don't even like going out because of that' (Mbali). Urban migrants depended on technology not only to stay in touch with their families, but also to navigate their new environment and gain access to educational or employment opportunities. Economic constraints remained a challenge in respect of access to smartphone technology and data. For some, ICTs are not enough to bridge the gap in a culture where family connection is particularly highly valued. These individuals saw visits as opportunities to overcome interpersonal distance, allowing family members to see each other and often to solve problems: 'Through visits we can resolve problems amongst us through word of mouth and also physically through the exchange of handshakes where necessary' (Peter). However, visits were not always possible because of the expense and the physical challenges faced by older participants who could not travel long distances.

In one sense, geographical distance is socially constructed. By this we mean that distance is experienced differently, depending on socio-economic status (as the sample of out-migrants to non-African destinations, discussed in Chapter 8 and below, also suggests). Even though these participants moved only from rural to urban areas within the same country, migrating across relatively short distances compared with others described in this book, this migration required enormous social and psychological adaptation and also a process of 'technological migration' for both those who migrated and those who stayed behind. This sample underlined the economic disparities and concomitant digital divide that people in and from rural South Africa must grapple with. They experience technology as mostly useful to maintain relationships with family members in other places, but the cost of data and smartphones, as well as poor and unreliable network infrastructure, makes ICT use highly challenging. Much has been written about inequality in South Africa, but the immense (often unseen) digital divide between better-resourced segments of the population and disadvantaged communities with limited resources is no less important than other forms of inequality.

AFRICAN MIGRATION TO SOUTH AFRICA

Migration from Zimbabwe

Zimbabwean participants conveyed a sense of inevitability about migration to South Africa, given the dire political and economic situation in their country. Bonga explained: 'Like everybody this side of the country, or like everybody in this country, they had to take the trip to South Africa to look for opportunities.' Generally, families supported the move, as they believed it would hold benefits for the whole family: 'I know it was a good decision to leave because here in Zimbabwe you know you can't sustain your family' (Tinashe). Participants' comments indicated a widespread shared expectation that South Africa would provide 'greener pastures' and more economic opportunities, a hope that was realised for some. However, Zimbabwean migrants often experience economic and social hardships in South Africa, making the pressures and challenges to provide for their families back home immense: 'I'll also say there is a huge financial support that's coming' (Mgcini). These pressures have been worsened by the Covid-19 pandemic.

ICTs, especially in the form of WhatsApp technology, are experienced as useful, but their use is limited by financial constraints on both sides: 'It is not everyone who can afford those data bundles … it's not everyone who can afford those smartphones … So it becomes a challenge for some' (Mthembeni). In some instances, participants made direct calls in emergencies, despite the prohibitive cost: 'But then when it's urgent like something needs to be done, maybe them sending money, that's when then I call' (Mthandazo). Lack of technological skills and digital literacy posed a challenge to many older family members back home, and this was sometimes compounded by the physical disabilities associated with ageing: 'Or sometimes I do speak to my grandmother, so I understand the troubles she would go through with reading' (Kwando). Lack of access to data and the internet was also mentioned. One gain was various examples of relationships of care using ICTs mentioned by this sample, including, but not limited to, financial remittances, such as sending medication or food vouchers, or co-ordinating care for the elderly.

WhatsApp family groups were common and were seen as an attempt to re-create some 'normal' family interaction: 'It's just become an important way of staying in touch and updating your family not only [on] day-to-day moves, but your minute-to-minute moves as well; you can actually tell ... talk to a family member about what you are doing, every step of the way' (Tendai). Virtual forms of communication had their limits, however, and again there were examples of family members who hid potentially difficult information from one another. Tinashe admitted: 'During this pandemic ... I faced depression ... You can't tell a person ... you can't express yourself ... that you are depressed. That you don't have anything to do, you are not going to school, you're not going to work, you're just sitting idle ... so you just hide [these things] and just move on with life.' As with the rural migrants in South Africa, there was evidence that some of the limitations of online or virtual forms of co-presence could be addressed through (occasional) visits and, failing that, video calls, which permitted family members to 'see' each other:

> It allows us to see, what we are saying is actually a reflection of what is happening on the ground like in terms of each individual's well-being. You get to see and confirm if that is what is on the ground ... the fact that I am able to talk to you, really, actually helps us to know that someone is okay ... following those lives and just checking on each other, or sometimes just showing each other what you are doing, what you have done. (Mgcini)

Prior to Covid-19, for those who could afford them, visits took place regularly in both directions, but these were curtailed by the pandemic: 'I used to go there but now because of Covid, I haven't been there in a year. The whole year, I haven't been there. So we have been really affected, especially not seeing my son for a year' (Innocentia). The inability to visit further increased the importance of and reliance on ICTs to support family connection across distance.

Malawian Migration

Historically, many Malawians have left their country to seek employment in South Africa. The trend continues because of the difficult socio-economic conditions prevalent in Malawi. Like the Zimbabweans who migrate, some held an idealised perception of the 'greener pastures' they would find in South Africa: 'Then from there he asked his older siblings to help him with funds to go to South Africa for greener pastures' (Mary). However, adjustment to South Africa generally proved to be very difficult: 'Ah no. I don't feel I'm belonging … It doesn't matter where I'm living here now, now I am approaching two years now. It's two years but I'm not feeling like I am belonging' (Victor). Malawian migrants reported often experiencing xenophobia, making their situation in South Africa precarious.

In general, there was support from their families for the decision to migrate: 'For this decision, we all sat as a family by giving suggestions and we all saw that the situation we were in was hard [financially]. Since her going there would assist us all here' (Brian). However, there was also a sense of concern regarding family members' safety in South Africa.

The stories of migrants also seemed to reflect their hope that migration was not permanent and their goal was ultimately to return to Malawi: 'Yes, we want to live in Malawi. Even myself I like to live in my country' (Victor). There was a strong sense of financial obligation towards those left behind, which was not always easy to meet, given the precarious situation of migrants in South Africa, and again it was clear that this precarity was deepened by the Covid-19 pandemic.

The Malawian sample saw mobile phones as useful tools to communicate with their families: 'A lot! Yes, a lot! It … it is easy, I don't feel alone. Because I am able to … if I … when I have money, I can make a phone call and I can hear my sister's voice' (Abby). WhatsApp was the preferred application because it is free, although one needs data to use it. The opportunity to 'see' loved ones was experienced as an advantage, especially through WhatsApp video calls: 'We also do video calls … to check up on each other and see how we are all doing' (Marta). However, video-call technology requires smartphones, which less-resourced migrants cannot always afford. Even when these phones are available, people need money to buy data, which was challenging given other financial needs: 'Hmm, most times finding money is a problem and hence when we find money we prefer to buy food than to actually buy internet data' (Catherine). The cost of personal visits and smartphones led some of this sample to rely on direct phone calls, which are more expensive but accommodate older family members who are not technologically literate: 'My father, I use direct calls … He doesn't use WhatsApp, and can't write, so it's hard for me to call him … maybe in three months or what. I'm not calling him like often but … not like every day. Just because to call him straight it's very expensive' (Beatrice). For financial reasons, visits tended to take the form of migrants travelling back home, but they cost money and time, and were severely curtailed by the Covid-19 pandemic.

Kenyan Migration

This sample differed from the previous two African samples in the sense that most Kenyan migrants who came to South Africa and whom we interviewed had a higher level of education than others discussed so far, and they migrated to pursue educational or further professional opportunities. The expectation of financial remittances for family members left behind was absent or not as strong as in the other African samples. In many instances, money was actually sent from home to these migrants in South Africa (especially in the case of students) and, when money was sent back home, it was for special occasions such as weddings or funerals. There was a strong shared sense that technology allowed families to maintain family life with members across distance. Again, WhatsApp family groups were prevalent: 'Most of the communication is through WhatsApp. We have formed family groups, so we keep each other abreast with whatever is happening in our lives ... It helped build bonds' (David). The greater access to smartphone technology and the ability to afford data ensured that this sample experienced ICTs as a useful way to re-create continued living family interactions: 'Internet usage has enabled families to draw closer and even teach the young children, you know, the younger ones coming up that, you know, it's very important to have close family ties, and with technology now, there is no excuse' (Absko). Video calls were regarded as a useful way to 'see' and check in on each other's well-being so as not to 'hide' important information: 'And then we are able to see one another, we are able to "face-to-face". We are able to face-talk' (Mary).

There was some evidence of technology being used specifically to parent children in another country, by way of offering psychological and moral support: 'The beauty of it is you might not physically be with your child for guidance and counselling, and counsel them, you know, just to give them direction. But the beauty of it, they are available 24 hours' (Nuru). This was also reinforced by Absko: 'I have no other avenue of parenting and guiding my children.'

Financial provision had to be made to ensure access to the internet to facilitate communication. Network problems in Kenya were mentioned as sometimes being an obstacle to communication: 'Sometimes you get that there's no internet and probably there's something that you really need to get or something that ... maybe there's some information you want to pass over to her urgently. Then when you get home probably the lights are not there, so there's no internet so that makes it quite difficult for us to communicate' (Mary). Direct phone calls were also sometimes used, especially in emergencies, but were deemed expensive: 'I think that's why I got my parents a smartphone to see if I can use data to make calls instead of you know being billed at the end of the month on normal calls. Because calling ... making normal calls in Kenya, international calls is quite expensive' (Henry). Visits, even prior to the Covid-19 pandemic, were potentially expensive and logistically complicated, as they involved obtaining visas, which was a complicated process, but technology has helped overcome this constraint: 'Since I'm not able to visit, the communication … I'm able … because I'm able to communicate it makes the visiting an option since I can still not be physically together but still, I think the use of smart technology has made it what … has made it convenient and better so we are able to … despite not being able to visit each other we are still able to communicate or keep in touch' (Aaron).

DRC Refugees

This sample is strikingly different from the others, as this group of participants did not have a choice about leaving their country of origin. Most of them were forced to flee because of the violence and political instability in the DRC: 'It was not by choice nor a good reason … actually, I flee from it because of certain reasons and insecurity that was happening there, that place' (Boris). Young boys, especially, were afraid of being recruited as child soldiers. Most participants migrated as individuals, leaving their families behind. They underwent a dangerous and often traumatic journey to South Africa, which was not necessarily their chosen destination, but this is where their journey ended.

Arriving in South Africa, they faced many challenges, particularly if they had lost their documents along the way. Most experienced extreme isolation, as they lacked support systems: 'I felt lost, I was in a new country. I didn't know anyone' (Nelson). They also faced maltreatment from xenophobic South African nationals or became victims of crime. Luce recalled: 'He hit me, and my daughter started crying, thanks to the man, he stopped, but he took all the little that we had.' They also struggled to find employment even if, in some instances, they had good academic qualifications: 'Unfortunately here I was nothing. I had to start from the bottom' (Luce). They expressed a strong longing for their families back home as well as concern over their well-being; sometimes they expressed guilt at having left their family behind: 'When you're leaving your family, you don't know when you will ever see them again' (Boris).

The DRC refugees in our sample indicated that, for them, mobile phones are useful tools, not only to connect with their families back home but also to integrate into South African society: 'Communication is the most important thing in life, if you cannot find someone, or see someone at least, if you can talk to the person and [when he or she] hears your voice the person can be happy' (Boris). WhatsApp was the preferred application, as it offers immediate communication and also allows video calls, which enable people to 'see' family back home: 'You can video-call and look at the person. You see the smile on the person' (Boris). There were also examples of using social media such as Facebook as an effective way of locating and then staying in touch with families back home: 'I did register with my real name in Facebook because I was hoping that someone will recognise me and show my family' (Jaiden). Nevertheless, the theme of hiding difficult information from distant family members surfaced again: 'When you're not physically present ... you [do not] know exactly how they feel because a phone can be very deceiving' (Samuel).

The significant financial limitations these DRC refugees experienced had an impact on their ability to access data and stay connected: 'Before I even buy data, I have to know that I pay rent, for my kids' (Nelson). Participants also mentioned that their families back home experienced problems related to costs, networks and infrastructure. To overcome this difficulty, there were examples of phone-sharing on both sides of the migratory spectrum: 'I share my cell [mobile] phone with anyone next to me at work and someone who is closer to me' (Boris). These refugees actively sought out other refugees as a means of providing and receiving support in the context of a society where they often feel very alienated and of a situation where there is almost no possibility of returning back home to visit: 'I found some people who could speak the same language with me, that I associated myself with them. Like brothers, like a friend, like a family' (Boris). This was very evident in the experiences in the barber shop discussed in Chapter 7. As with other groups, there was a mixture of gains and losses – precarious financial and personal security, although the poverty and insecurity were possibly not as extreme as that experienced in the DRC, as well as a loss of culture and family, even when the participants in this sample found a new 'family' of people in South Africa to communicate and share with.

OUT-MIGRATION TO NON-AFRICAN COUNTRIES

This sample of migrants comprised middle-class migrant families across all racial groups, mostly educated and in professional positions, reflecting the phenomenon of the brain drain, which has been prevalent in South Africa since the early 1990s. These migrants chose countries such as Canada, Australia, New Zealand, the United Kingdom, the United States and the United Arab Emirates (UAE) as their destinations. Most (e)migrated with their nuclear families, leaving behind elderly parents. Those who stayed behind were ambivalent about their children's migration. On the one hand, they could understand the potential benefits for their children and grandchildren in terms of professional opportunities or quality of life: 'I knew his decision was for the best, you know, as hard as it is for us, it was for the best' (Lauren). On the other hand, they described the heartache and anguish of their children's and especially grandchildren's migration: 'I was torn apart by the time it got to her departure' (Dudu).

The majority of these better-resourced participants had no problem in accessing the technology required to maintain relationships with family members. They used a variety of platforms, including WhatsApp, FaceTime and Skype. They welcomed the accessibility of these ICT platforms: 'I don't feel that far away from them, and because I can talk to them and see their faces, I don't feel … alienated … you can actually just check in with them you know, if you need to ask them a question' (Kim). Older people did struggle with technology at times and had to be aided by younger family members, which sometimes caused frustration: 'Oh, but my dad is terrible with technology so with him it's SMSs or I have to call him'

(Lindiwe). There remained a sense that people wanted to 'see' each other, and that technology, even Skype, lacked the intimacy of physical contact and interaction: 'It actually sometimes can be even worse because you can see the person right in front of you but you … you can't hug them and you can't hold them and it just makes them feel even worse than if they were just talking over the phone' (Mitchell).

Participants also used WhatsApp groups: 'Then we also have a family WhatsApp group as well. So, if anyone needs to say something to all of us at once, it will be on that WhatsApp group' (Lindiwe). Facebook was also seen as a useful platform: 'And you have photos there and every-body can see, so you don't see each other, but you feel like you know them. You feel like you know them because you see them all the time, how they change, you just don't see them in real life, that's all' (Gerry). Participants tried to find creative ways to use technology to relate to their young grandchildren; one grandmother, for instance, used hand puppets.

Despite these very positive reports on extensive ICT use, there were some reservations. As with other samples, families also tended to hide dif-ficult information from each other so as not to create unnecessary con-cern: 'What tends to happen is your family, they don't tell you everything that's happening to them, because they have a fear of worrying you, being so far away … So, say for instance one of my parents got sick, they won't tell me until it's really needed to tell me' (Colleen). Grandparents in par-ticular felt the loss of not being able to be part of their grandchildren's lives: 'Ja, not really knowing, seeing the grandchildren on Skype is much different than handling a baby in your arms' (Cornelia). These limitations of ICT-based communication are offset, however, by instances where migrants experienced their parents' communication as too frequent or too intrusive: 'She has tried to call me as I have been driving and it's like you know, you put, reject the call and she is like, she is not having any of that and she keeps calling back and you are eventually, like listen I am driving … [*laughing*] … What are you up to? … You can run but you can't hide' (Warwick).

Visits were experienced as a way of emotionally refuelling relationships: 'It's almost like you have a fuel tank that is refilled' (Annie). There were many examples of grandparents visiting their migrant children and grandchildren to provide practical support: 'I don't go as a tourist to Sydney; I go as a mother and granny ... and I make cakes and I kill myself working' (Susan). However, even this group mentioned cost as a factor, as well as difficulties associated with travelling very long distances, especially for older people.

MOBILITY AND TECHNOLOGY ACCESS AND RIGHTS: CENTRAL, OVERARCHING CONCERNS

Since the advent of the internet in the 1990s, there has been increasing enthusiasm about the possibility that technology might bring about the so-called death of distance (Baldassar 2007b; Cairncross 2002).

As discussed in Chapter 1, the crucial role of ICTs in connecting and maintaining migrant (transnational) families has been shown in much of the literature (Baldassar 2007a, 2007b, 2008, 2016; Horst 2006; Madianou 2016; Marchetti-Mercer 2012a, 2012b, 2016, 2017; Wilding 2006). Some authors have also explored the possibility of new kinds of relationships and ways of being together across distance, through the creation of 'virtual families' (Falicov 2005) and 'virtual intimacies' (Wilding 2006). There is no doubt that ICTs have revolutionised the capacity of families to stay together across distance. We agree with Gonzalo Bacigalupe and Maria Cámara, who argue that exploring the role of ICTs in keeping families connected holds enormous 'potential for transforming the psychology of immigration' (2012, 1435). All our participants reported some measure of support and reassurance through their ability to connect with family using ICTs, and truly appreciated how much harder it would be to maintain family and support networks, and understood how much more diminished their networks would be, without ICTs.

Despite our findings regarding the gains enjoyed from ICT use, in foregrounding the important role of ICTs in the lives of transnational migrants we cannot assume that they all share the same technological tools or the same level of access to the internet, or even that distance has the same meaning: socio-economic status can make a considerable difference.

Our data from the Global South indicate that, when it comes to technology, different types of migrants experience different challenges, which reflect issues of access and affordability that may differ radically from the experiences reported in the literature focusing on the Global North or even from the experiences of our middle-class (e)migrants and their families. What has been called the digital divide was very evident in the experiences of our African participants. While those interviewed generally shared positive experiences of their use of technology in maintaining relationships at a distance, there were also some stark realities: the less-resourced migrants might use mobile phones, but in most cases these were not smartphones with access to multiple applications but basic (often old) phones with limited features.

One of the most significant consequences of not having a smartphone is that one cannot use relatively cheap communication apps, such as WhatsApp: 'I use direct calling, of which is very expensive. I'm supposed to buy like a smartphone for my family ... Even myself, so I can call using WhatsApp, which is cheaper. But I can't afford to do that. Even I'm failing to buy for myself because of the finances that I'm getting; it's just for food, rent and supporting my family ... other things ... These are things that I can't access them' (Gift, Malawian migrant). WhatsApp was by far the most popular application because of the immediacy of the kind of communication that it offers, as well as its relatively low use of data and concurrent costs. However, even for those participants who possessed a smartphone, buying data was a financial challenge, because in situations of great socio-economic deprivation, where necessities such as food and rent are more urgent, buying data or airtime becomes a luxury.

Furthermore, in many of the geographical settings where people who participated in our study lived or worked, poor network quality and infrastructure limited people's access to the internet and its benefits: 'So far, I don't have any access. As long as I go and maybe if I borrow a phone from someone then I use it. But so far, I don't have any access to the phone … To internet … so I am all alone here. I don't talk much to them' (Charles, DRC refugee). This applied to both the migrants and families at home. It is an ironic twist that this lack of internet access often forces people to make direct phone calls, which are much more expensive, even though recent international research on migration shows that international phone calls have become considerably cheaper since the 1990s, improving the possibility and frequency of phone calls for migrant families (see, for example, Vertovec 2004). However, as Steven Vertovec (2004) points out, there is still an uneven distribution of telecommunications infrastructure; in low-income countries such infrastructure is often marginal, so that their citizens are at a disadvantage. This implies that it is important not to overlook the extreme economic deprivation in many of the countries that were part of our research, where even the least expensive calls are still expensive in the context of these countries' average incomes. Ray (DRC refugee) said: 'In Congo DRC, the telecommunication is very expensive for the country; calling Congo for one minute, it'll cost you about R15 [US$0.82]; you have a minute. So, when WhatsApp came it was a much better way because it is much cheaper. You can call them using voice calls for such a long time.' These sentiments were echoed by George (Malawian migrant), 'Yeah, because direct call is expensive, yeah, its R5 [US$0.29] a minute, so that is expensive.'

Another striking difference between our findings (possibly excluding some of the Kenyan migrants and their families, and middle-class migrants) and those of prior studies in the Global North is that for our least-resourced participants mobile phones are the only technological tools available, while more affluent migrants have access to other options, including smartphones, laptops and applications such as Skype, to stay connected to family members, as is evident in the experiences of the out-migrants. Even where technology is available, ICT use requires digital competence and literacy. In this regard, the challenges of limited digital citizenship, particularly for older people, have been described by Loretta Baldassar and Raelene Wilding (2020). We found that older people generally struggled more with technology, irrespective of socio-economic differences. For elderly participants in rural areas, the picture was even bleaker, as their level of digital literacy was very low. For all the older participants, the difficulty was compounded by physical challenges that older people may face, such as diminished vision and hearing, as well as increasing difficulty with the fine motor skills required to use technology, as has been pointed out by Leslie Swartz and Maria C. Marchetti-Mercer (2019). In the final analysis, all the migrants and their families in our samples relied heavily on technology to maintain relationships with their loved ones, but their access to technology, suitable devices and adequate infrastructure, as well as the financial means to maintain ICT use, differed greatly.

Another aspect of our findings that is important is the different experiences and understandings of distance in the migrant and transnational families in our samples. Kathy Burrell speaks of the 'recalcitrance of distance' – this implies that the distances that migrants have to manage are what she calls 'asymmetrically governed spaces' (2017, 813). She adds that 'not all people in all places can access the mobility aids that technology keeps delivering', and 'the asymmetries of power at play in migration movements are inequalities which are physically endured' (2017, 813). Those who leave South Africa for other continents are the most geographically distant from their loved ones, while those from the rural areas of South Africa who move to urban areas such as Gauteng have the shortest distance to travel. However, 'distance' is relative: depending on their circumstances, people experience it differently. One factor is the capacity to travel – what we might call 'mobility capital'. Capacity to travel depends on whether you are affluent or poor, on the resources available, and on constraints imposed by state border regimes, visa requirements and, more recently, restrictions relating to Covid-19. Thus 'distance' is socially constructed from individual and collective relationships and experiences (Baldassar, Wilding and Baldock 2007). The challenges described by rural migrants upon entering an urban environment, and the difficulties they face in visiting their families in rural areas, are similar to the constraints mentioned by migrants leaving South Africa for other continents. The level of cultural alienation and the financial and logistical difficulties related to travel seem very similar, despite the fact that rural people often moved no more than 200 kilometres away from their original home rather than thousands of kilometres. Similarly, when their older parents describe why visiting their children in Gauteng is not easy, they lament the physical difficulties they would face in taking public transport: 'It is difficult to go and visit other family members who live far because I have a problem with my legs and also a problem with having to carry my grandson on my back. My legs are very troublesome as I cannot walk for a long period of time' (Mmabatho, Giyani). This finding supports Swartz and Marchetti-Mercer's (2019) argument that distance is less problematic for bodies considered 'normal'. However, that distance is a very real, practical issue for those living in bodies that need more direct physical care and assistance (see also Marchetti-Mercer and Swartz 2020). Consequently, 'technology' and 'distance' should not be seen as unambiguous terms: what they mean to each individual depends on who that person is and where that person comes from or goes to.

Another area of difference in the general migration experience is how transnational families from different backgrounds experience their family members' decision to migrate. This process refers to Baldassar's (2007b, 2015) notion of a 'licence to leave', which she sees as an important factor in migrants' ultimate experience of migration. For migrants from disadvantaged socio-economic backgrounds, their 'stay-behind' families' approval of the decision to migrate was often linked to the perceived economic advantages of the migration for the family left behind. By contrast, for more privileged middle-class migrants, the potential advantage (professional advancement and personal fulfilment) was perceived to be mainly on the side of those who were leaving. Those staying behind did not see the move as having particular advantages for them, as financial remittances were not common, and so they often experienced their family members' migration as a severe interpersonal challenge and personal sacrifice, despite rationalisations to the contrary: 'I knew his decision was for the best, you know, as hard as it is for us, it was for the best' (Lauren, mother of an emigrant to a non-African country). However, although in less-resourced communities there was also a sense that migration would be an interpersonal challenge, the potential gain of financial survival was prioritised.

In most of our African samples (including the rural–urban migrant sample but excluding our particular Kenyan sample), there was strong evidence of financial obligations in the form of remittances, as well as of goods and 'social remittances' (including sharing knowledge about new technologies and digital skills). In the Kenyans' case, money was sent back occasionally, mainly in emergencies or for special occasions, but families in Kenya did not rely on remittances for their financial survival. The role of social remittances in transnational families is well researched (see Boccagni and Decimo 2013; Levitt 1998; Levitt and Lamba-Nieves 2011), in relation to new technologies (see Suksomboon 2008) as well as the emotional meaning of sending goods rather than money (see Burrell 2017). Among the middle-class international migrants, sometimes migrant children would pay for travel costs for parents to visit them, but there was no strong evidence of financial obligation. Instead, across all samples of migrants in and into South Africa and their families, there was evidence of migration and transnational family life as a significant motivation to increase digital literacy skills and knowledge about ICTs, although this motivation was, as we have shown, affected by access and capacity issues.

The notion of a licence to leave is linked to expectations of an obligation to return (Baldassar 2007b, 2023). In general, migrant families found it easier to support migrations that were expected to end with the return of the migrants to their country of origin or their home. However, in the samples in our study, there was in many instances a sense that migration was permanent. For the DRC refugees, there is little or no possibility of return. The Zimbabwean migrants also seemed more established in South Africa, despite the undeniable challenges they faced, and few mentioned returning to Zimbabwe. This is in contrast to many in the Malawian sample, who shared the hope of returning once they had saved sufficient money, a hope deepened by the strong sense of alienation that Malawian migrants experience in South Africa.

Many rural–urban migrants left their children behind with their parents. This was also evident among the Zimbabwean and Malawian migrants. This phenomenon undoubtedly has an impact on the parent–child relationship, as the unhappy memories of Tendai (son of a Zimbabwean migrant) underscored when he said that he 'grew up without a father', adding that this meant his mother was left 'playing both parts', and he was left to rely on his own resources in finding his identity: 'So I had to grow up here alone without a father without guidance ... so I had to be a man and find myself out.' In emigrating middle-class nuclear families, the children migrated with their parents, but members of the family who stayed behind mourned the implications for their relationship with their grandchildren: 'It's very sad to say, but it is. They don't really know me' (Lesley, mother of an emigrant to a non-African country). Such a separation between parents and children or grandchildren required more money, time and effort to devise ways to use the technology to communicate effectively, especially with younger children.

Some participants mentioned that technology is an improvement on older ways of communicating, such as letter writing: 'Previously, I'm reminded of the days I went into high school, if you wanted to get in touch your parents, you went to the post office, and you did the telegram, Daddy send this. But today, you don't need to travel anywhere' (Masai, Kenya). Philani (emigrant to a non-African country) described the long wait for a letter: 'I used to write to my mother ... get a letter every two months and she would get a letter every three months ... so yeah, I mean now it's in your pocket – you can instantly communicate, so ja, [it] definitely shorten[s] the gap.' Nevertheless, some older participants did miss writing and receiving letters.

We noted several similarities in the impact of migration on the larger family system. All the migrants in our sample across the spectrum experienced the migration of their loved ones as an interpersonal challenge. Some articulated this strongly: 'Broken family ... we are a broken family ... A family should ... stay together under one roof' (Tendai, Zimbabwe). The level of grief about what life might have been like without migration, as well as the potential advantages inherent in the migration process, differed considerably. Responses to the migration and its outcome were shaped by normative understandings of ideal family life, and are somewhat difficult to interpret in the absence of data on the impact of choices by comparable families not to pursue migration. It would not be true to claim that all the families we engaged with could be described, as Tendai puts it, as 'broken', but the sense of loss was acutely felt even in the presence of ongoing efforts to keep the family together emotionally.

All the participants in the different samples used some form of technology to keep in touch with distant family members. The difference seemed to lie in the type of technology they used and their access to that technology. WhatsApp was the most popular choice because of its affordability as well as its features, especially the option of a video call, which was very popular with both migrants and families who stayed behind. The ability and need to be able to 'see' one's loved ones was a strong theme that ran across the data: 'When I want to see my grandmother's face because I could hear she was sick. She was not feeling well, so I wanted to see her face; I wanted to see that she's okay. I wanted her to see my face; I wanted to assure her that it's me' (Bongani, Zimbabwean migrant). The significance of visibility – of being able to see each other through video calls – was generally experienced as facilitating a greater sense of co-presence than audio calls alone, a finding supported in the broader literature (see, for example, Baldassar et al. 2016). However, the inherent limitations of technology in providing real physical presence are also very prominent: 'Getting a hug from someone that you love, it makes you feel [more] at home than just seeing him or her on the screen' (Thando, Zimbabwe), and this also supports findings elsewhere in the broader literature (see, for example, Merla, Kilkey and Baldassar 2020).

Social media were also employed by participants, but again there were different experiences. For refugees from the DRC, Facebook was useful because it sometimes enabled them to trace lost family members in the DRC. This reflects other research that has been carried out in refugee populations (see, for example, Bacigalupe and Cámara 2012; Alencar, Kondova and Ribbens 2019). In some instances, migrants experienced social media platforms as potentially intrusive, as they did not want to reveal a more lavish lifestyle, in case family members left behind saw this and added to the migrants' sense of guilt: 'I cannot be posting pictures like that because they'll think I'm living large and I'm not looking after [them] ... So there's things that I don't really show them or tell them that I'm doing' (Shmiso, Zimbabwean migrant). Middle-class migrant families (again, people with access to the most technological resources) mentioned using Facebook as a positive experience, and as a useful tool to keep abreast of the many activities of family members living abroad or at home.

A sense of complementarity between technology and visits was also evident, as frequent communication made it easier when family members eventually met up, because the relationship had been maintained: 'It will be as if I am with her ... Yes, it is like you are continuing from yesterday. It's like we were together yesterday and now we are together again' (Innocentia, Zimbabwe). Similarly, Feye (Kenyan migrant) commented: 'They've been talking on the phone, they've been talking through WhatsApp communication, video call and so it brings that bond together ... And so that barrier has been broken. So I do find that that does help a lot so that you know by the time we land in ... there, it's easy to relate with everyone.' Other research has shown that online communication often intensifies before and after visits, as people put in extra effort in preparation for visits and also after them (Baldassar 2023; Baldassar et al. 2016; Wilding 2007). Visits were generally experienced as important: 'I think physical visits like ... they are mandatory. We need to see ... that physical ... there's nothing that can replace physical visits. No matter how much technology we have, we still have to be on the ground and yeah see eye to eye' (Kwando, Zimbabwean migrant). But visits often required overcoming many challenges.

A common theme is that all families tend to hide information from each other in order to protect each other or not cause unnecessary concern, thereby supporting a finding by Baldassar (2007b). The use of technology makes this a possibility. One of the Kenyan participants, a mother, wanted to 'see' her daughter to ascertain the state of her health:

> And then we are able to see one another, we are able to face-to-face. We are able to face-talk. I don't know whether it is face … We are able to see her, we are able to see whether she is actually … like the other day I was talking to her and I realised that she has lost weight. So I'm able to see her and I'm able to see her gestures and her verbal communication and I learn a lot and I get a lot of information. (Mary, Kenya)

The topic of silence in migrant families (Sampaio 2020), and the meaning that we can attribute to those silences, form an important area to consider and study, as silence is potentially multi-layered – it can be both a means of mutual protection and a source of alienation (De Haene et al. 2018). In thinking about how families communicate, we also need to think about what they do not say and when they do not say it.

As mentioned in many of the chapters in this book, older people, more than their younger counterparts, tend to struggle with the technology (although educational or economic disadvantages also had an impact on some of the younger migrants). This form of the digital divide was evident across all the samples. The difference probably lies more in how that lack of competence is addressed – in other words, who assists older people to become more familiar with the technology. Middle-class adult children could afford to buy technology for their parents: 'We brought my parents as well as his parents each an iPad, so to make it easier to be able to Skype, and my parents have really gotten into the whole technology and getting in touch and stuff' (Mary, emigrant, non-African destination).

In low-income communities, even buying a smartphone for one's family members was unthinkable: 'I'm supposed to buy like a smartphone for my family, maybe one or two ... One of the two members. For example, like my father or mother. Or one of the sisters or brothers, including my wife so that ... But I can't afford to do that' (Gift, Malawian migrant).

There was also strong evidence of providing care to one's loved ones through the use of technology, although this differed in form: 'It has made people to still be able to keep in touch and get the care despite being far away ... if it was in the past not be able to talk often, so now things have changed and the care is better because of technology' (Evelyn, Kenya). Among low-income migrants, care was often material or financial, but psychological care and moral support were given in families even where there was not much reliance on economic support. There were also instances of migrants without enough income, who were not able to provide financial support but who provided spiritual and emotional support through prayer or just a shoulder (even if it was a digital one) to cry on: 'If I am going through a bad day, and I have someone to tell even through my phone, and that someone comforts me, I would call that support. But maybe because I need the actual shoulder to cry on and it's not here, the actual shoulder I have is my phone' (Innocentia, Zimbabwe).

CONCLUSION

The samples in the studies discussed in this book revealed significant diversity in access to the technological and mobility resources that are critical in supporting transnational family lives. But the experiences of the participants also suggest that most families, whatever their means, are strongly motivated to use whatever resources they have at their disposal to fulfil their familial obligations and to participate in family life across distance. In one of the earliest accounts of the role of technology in transnational family life, Wilding (2006) suggests that the very capacity for increased communication afforded by ICTs appears to have given rise to renewed expectations and obligations in transnational family relationships (see also Baldassar 2007b). Our research suggests that most families attempt to provide the support that is needed with whatever resources they can access. This raises interesting questions about whether the increased accessibility of technological connectivity has increased the sense of family obligation, and whether it results in different ways of 'doing family'.

As with any study, there were omissions and constraints. The Covid-19 pandemic both accelerated our own use of ICTs as a research team and drew into sharp focus the importance of technological communication in a world under threat. Our sample sizes were small and often accessed through existing networks – we cannot claim to be able to generalise about any other groups with whom we interacted. We are also aware that our study is an exploratory one for Africa – we have yet to see how the issues we have raised evolve as Africa's migration and data landscapes are enlarged. We have not yet examined the role of specific forms of technology or their roles in family rituals, although this is an emerging issue in the study of families, migration and ICTs (Ahlin 2023; Toumi 2023). Our study focused very closely on family relationships between migrants from specific countries and their families back home, so we have not explored the emerging phenomenon of hybrid family formation – where, for example, migrants from other African countries form families with South Africans (Pineteh 2015) – as we might have liked to, although some of our participants had formed such families. We have also not directly explored broader social discourses about migration and families, discourses that may profoundly affect family experiences, such as, for example, discussions in Zimbabwe about what have been termed 'diaspora orphans' – a term used (sometimes in a judgemental and pejorative way) for children left behind as their parents seek opportunities elsewhere (Kufakurinani, Pasura and McGregor 2014). Another issue only implicitly considered in this book, but hinted at strongly by our Malawian participants, is the fact that while access to data and the internet allows new forms of family relationships, it may also expose already vulnerable groups to increased surveillance, which may not always be benign. The role of data and data access in contributing to vulnerability thus also needs consideration (Munoriyarwa and Mare 2022).

Overall, migration and transnational families within Africa remain underexplored – the recently published *Handbook of Transnational Families around the World*, edited by Javiera Cienfuegos, Rosa Brandhorst and Deborah Fahy Bryceson (2023), has some excellent chapters on African migrants in the Global North but not a single chapter focusing on African migrants within Africa. Given the number and variety of migration patterns within Africa (see Chapter 1), we see our book as a small first step to filling a major gap. But much more work remains to be done.

REFERENCES

Ahlin, Tanja. 2023. *Calling Family: Digital Technologies and the Making of Transnational Care Collectives*. New Brunswick, NJ: Rutgers University Press.

Alencar, Amanda, Katerina Kondova and Wannes Ribbens. 2019. 'The Smartphone as a Lifeline: An Exploration of Refugees' Use of Mobile Communication Technologies during Their Flight'. *Media, Culture and Society* 4, no. 6: 828–844. https://doi.org/10.1177/0163443718813486.

Bacigalupe, Gonzalo and Maria Cámara. 2012. 'Transnational Families and Social Technologies: Reassessing Immigration Psychology'. *Journal of Ethnic and Migration Studies* 38, no. 9: 1425–1438. https://doi.org/10.1080/1369183X.2012.698211.

Baldassar, Loretta. 2007a. 'Transnational Families and Aged Care: The Mobility of Care and the Migrancy of Ageing'. *Journal of Ethnic and Migration Studies* 33, no. 2: 275–297. https://doi.org/10.1080/13691830601154252.

Baldassar, Loretta. 2007b. 'Transnational Families and the Provision of Moral and Emotional Support: The Relationship between Truth and Distance'. *Identities* 14, no. 4: 385–409. https://doi.org/10.1080/10702890701578423.

Baldassar, Loretta. 2008. 'Missing Kin and Longing to Be Together: Emotions and the Construction of Co-presence in Transnational Relationships'. *Journal of Intercultural Studies* 29, no. 3 (Special Issue: Transnational Families – Emotions and Belonging): 247–266. https://doi.org/10.1080/07256860802169196.

Baldassar, Loretta. 2015. 'Guilty Feelings and the Guilt Trip: Emotions and Motivation in Migration and Transnational Caregiving'. *Emotion, Space and Society* 16: 81–89. https://doi.org/10.1016/j.emospa.2014.09.003.

Baldassar, Loretta. 2016. 'De-demonizing Distance in Mobile Family Lives: Co-presence, Care Circulation and Polymedia as Vibrant Matter'. *Global Networks* 16, no. 2: 145–163. https://doi.org/10.1111/glob.12109.

Baldassar, Loretta. 2023. 'Migrant Visits over Time: Ethnographic Returning and the Technological Turn'. *Global Networks* 23, no. 1: 160–173. https://doi.org/10.1111/glob.12393.

Baldassar, Loretta, Mihaela Nedelcu, Laura Merla and Raelene Wilding. 2016. 'ICT-Based Co-presence in Transnational Families and Communities: Challenging the Premise of Face-to-Face Proximity in Sustaining Relationships'. *Global Networks* 16, no. 2: 133–144. https://doi.org/10.1111/glob.12108.

Baldassar, Loretta and Raelene Wilding. 2020. 'Migration, Aging, and Digital Kinning: The Role of Distant Care Support Networks in Experiences of Aging Well'. *The Gerontologist* 60, no. 2: 313–321. https://doi.org/10.1093/geront/gnz156.

Baldassar, Loretta, Raelene Wilding and Cora Baldock. 2007. 'Long-Distance Care-Giving, Transnational Families and the Provision of Aged Care'. In *Family Caregiving for Older Disabled People: Relational and Institutional Issues*, edited by Isabella Paoletti, 201–228. New York: Nova Science.

Boccagni, Paolo and Francesca Decimo. 2013. 'Mapping Social Remittances'. *Migration Letters* 10, no. 1: 1–10. https://doi.org/10.33182/ml.v10i1.106.

Burrell, Kathy. 2017. 'The Recalcitrance of Distance: Exploring the Infrastructures of Sending in Migrants' Lives'. *Mobilities* 12, no. 6: 813–826. https://doi.org/10.1080/17450101.2016.1225799.

Cairncross, Frances. 2002. 'The Death of Distance: How the Communications Revolution Is Changing Our Lives; Distance Isn't What It Used to Be'. *RSA Journal (Royal Society for Arts, Manufactures and Commerce)* 149, no. 5502: 40–42. https://www.jstor.org/stable/41380436.

Cienfuegos, Javiera, Rosa Brandhorst and Deborah Fahy Bryceson, eds. 2023. *Handbook of Transnational Families around the World*. Handbooks of Sociology and Social Research Series. Cham: Springer.

De Haene, Lucia, Cécile Rousseau, Ruth Kevers, Nele Deruddere and Peter Rober. 2018. 'Stories of Trauma in Family Therapy with Refugees: Supporting Safe Relational Spaces of Narration and Silence'. *Clinical Child Psychology and Psychiatry* 23, no. 2: 258–278. https://doi.org/10.1177/1359104518756717.

Falicov, Celia J. 2005. 'Emotional Transnationalism and Family Identities'. *Family Process* 44, no. 4: 399–406. https://doi.org/10.1111/j.1545-5300.2005.00068.x.

Horst, Heather A. 2006. 'The Blessings and Burdens of Communication: Cell Phones in Jamaican Transnational Social Fields'. *Global Networks* 6, no. 2: 143–159. https://doi.org/10.1111/j.1471-0374.2006.00138.x.

Kufakurinani, Ushehwedu, Dominic Pasura and JoAnn McGregor. 2014. 'Transnational Parenting and the Emergence of "Diaspora Orphans" in Zimbabwe'. *African Diaspora* 7, no. 1: 114–138. https://doi.org/10.1163/18725465-00701006.

Levitt, Peggy. 1998. 'Social Remittances: Migration Driven Local-Level Forms of Cultural Diffusion'. *International Migration Review* 32, no. 4: 926–948. https://doi.org/10.1177/019791839803200404.

Levitt, Peggy and Deepak Lamba-Nieves. 2011. 'Social Remittances Revisited'. *Journal of Ethnic and Migration Studies* 37, no. 1: 1–22. https://doi.org/10.1080/1369183X.2011.521361.

Madianou, Mirca. 2016. 'Ambient Co-presence: Transnational Family Practices in Polymedia Environments'. *Global Networks* 16, no. 2: 183–201. https://doi.org/10.1111/glob.12105.

Marchetti-Mercer, Maria C. 2012a. 'Is It Just about the Crime? A Psychological Perspective on South African Emigration'. *South African Journal of Psychology* 42, no. 2: 243–254. http://hdl.handle.net/2263/19278.

Marchetti-Mercer, Maria C. 2012b. 'Those Easily Forgotten: The Impact of Emigration on Those Left Behind'. *Family Process* 51, no. 3: 373–383. https://doi.org/10.1111/j.1545-5300.2012.01407.x.

Marchetti-Mercer, Maria C. 2016. '"If You Uproot a Tree You Leave a Big Hole Behind": Systemic Interconnectedness in Emigration and Family Life'. *Contemporary Family Therapy* 38, no. 3: 339–352. https://doi.org/10.1007/s10591-016-9386-6.

Marchetti-Mercer, Maria C. 2017. '"The Screen Has Such Sharp Edges to Hug": The Relational Consequences of Emigration in Transnational South African Emigrant Families'. *Transnational Social Work* 7, no. 1: 73–89. https://doi.org/10.1080/21931674.2016.1277650.

Marchetti-Mercer, Maria C. and Leslie Swartz. 2020. 'Familiarity and Separation in the Use of Communication Technologies in South African Migrant Families'. *Journal of Family Issues* 41, no. 10: 1859–1884. https://doi.org/10.1177/0192513X19894367.

Merla, Laura, Majella Kilkey and Loretta Baldassar. 2020. 'Examining Transnational Care Circulation Trajectories within Immobilizing Regimes of Migration: Implications for Proximate Care'. *Journal of Family Research* 32, no. 3: 514–536. https://doi.org/10.20377/jfr-351.

Munoriyarwa, Allen and Admire Mare. 2022. *Digital Surveillance in Southern Africa: Policies, Politics and Practices*. Cham: Springer. https://link.springer.com/book/10.1007/978-3-031-16636-5.

Pineteh, Ernest A. 2015. '"The Challenges of Living Here and There": Conflicting Narratives of Intermarriage between Cameroonian Migrants and South Africans in Johannesburg'. *African and Black Diaspora: An International Journal* 8, no. 1: 71–85. https://doi.org/10.1080/17528631.2014.966958.

Sampaio, Dora. 2020. 'Caring by Silence: How (Un)documented Brazilian Migrants Enact Silence as a Care Practice for Aging Parents'. *Journal of Intergenerational Relationships* 18, no. 3: 281–300. https://doi.org/10.1080/15350770.2020.1787038.

Suksomboon, Panitee. 2008. 'Remittances and "Social Remittances": Their Impact on Livelihoods of Thai Women in the Netherlands and Non-migrants in Thailand'. *Gender, Technology and Development* 12, no. 3: 461–482. https://doi.org/10.1177/097185240901200309.

Swartz, Leslie and Maria C. Marchetti-Mercer. 2019. 'Migration, Technology and Care: What Happens to the Body?' *Disability and Society* 34, no. 3: 407–420. https://doi.org/10.1080/09687599.2018.1519409.

Toumi, Ikram. 2023. '"A Wedding through a Piece of Glass": Transnational Tunisian Family Communication as Driver of ICT Adoption'. *Media, Culture and Society* 45, no. 1: 142–156. https://doi.org/10.1177/01634437221099616.

Vertovec, Steven. 2004. 'Cheap Calls: The Social Glue of Migrant Transnationalism'. *Global Networks* 4, no. 2: 219–224. https://doi.org/10.1111/J.1471-0374.2004.00088.X.

Wilding, Raelene. 2006. '"Virtual" Intimacies? Families Communicating across Transnational Contexts'. *Global Networks* 6, no. 2: 125–142. https://doi.org/10.1111/j.1471-0374.2006.00137.x.

Wilding, Raelene. 2007. 'Transnational Ethnographies and Anthropological Imaginings of Migrancy'. *Journal of Ethnic and Migration Studies* 33, no. 2: 331–348. https://doi.org/10.1080/13691830601154310.

10

Looking Ahead: Paradox, Criticality and a Way Forward

Daniella Rafaely, Maria C. Marchetti-Mercer, Leslie Swartz and Loretta Baldassar

The task we set ourselves and described in this book was a vast one. We chose to study the experiences of several sets of participants under the umbrella term 'transnational families'. They inhabit a range of countries and have diverse socio-economic statuses, regional and age identities, races, genders and ethnicities, and a score of other factors and characteristics. We acknowledge that all of these terms are in themselves contested and politically loaded, as Jonathan Jansen and Cyrill Walters (2020) point out, which added to the complexity of the undertaking. The task and field were so vast that we could capture only limited aspects of the range of embodied lived realities of the many participants who gener-ously shared their experiences and thoughts with us. As we collected and analysed our data, the impossibility of doing their experiences full justice became more and more apparent. We persevered, nevertheless, and have presented here a collection that represents a small part of what we encountered, itself only a partial mirror of the many unwitnessed lives endured and celebrated day by day, by migrants conducting their lives in a South African context, and those who have chosen to leave, and by their families both in South Africa and in their countries of origin.

What emerges most clearly from this kaleidoscope of lived experience is paradox. The fundamental paradox is one of ambiguous loss and gain that characterises the phenomenon of migration for those who leave, and those who remain behind, but there are many other paradoxes at the heart of the migratory experience. We want to reflect a little on these, as a way of articulating the precarious space within which we can begin to rethink migrants in, into and out of South Africa.

Paradox is the home of the migrant. Migrants are born into a home, a country, a culture and a place but choose or, in many cases, are forced to leave in order to seek economic opportunities, safety or other benefits. The migrant is therefore displaced, yet this displacement and unbelonging may be what keeps the migrant's family in place and belonging. Many of the migrants whom we interviewed while writing this book expressed ambivalent or explicitly conflicting emotions, including resignation and sadness, but they also displayed dignity and understanding, as they reflected on a self-negating and simultaneously enabling process that enhances their survival and that of others, and at the same time challenges the ties that unite them.

Paradox was evident also in the matter of distance, a fundamentally economic rather than geographical experience. Distance was felt in terms of resources, rather than kilometres, with many out-migrants to places such as New Zealand and Australia experiencing their South African families as more accessible to them than families in relatively nearby Giyani were to the rural migrants living in Johannesburg. Refugees from the Democratic Republic of Congo (DRC) shared with us the expectation that they could never return home – there is an unbridgeable distance between their present and their past. In migration, distance should thus be measured as access and connection, rather than simply as geographical space. Space is commonly thought of as absolute and easy to measure – but our participants taught us how relative the experience of space can be.

In practical terms, economic constraints precluded many migrants from gaining access to smartphones, the technology that enables inexpensive communication with family far away, even in other countries. A smartphone with VOIPs (voice over internet protocols) such as WhatsApp or Facebook supports inexpensive connection, but *obtaining* a smartphone and data requires a degree of economic privilege. Our research suggested that income and communication costs were inversely related, thereby supporting the findings of Matolwandile M. Mtotywa et al. (2022). Ironically, well-resourced people have more access to inexpensive or free modes of communication than those who lack resources. We found that the most profoundly economically disadvantaged participants were those who were forced to spend their hard-earned money on expensive international telephone calls, if they wanted to maintain contact with their families at home, because of the inaccessibility of smartphones, data and functioning internet networks. Inexpensive communication presupposes expensive devices, and many of the economic migrants, in particular, saw family connection and care as a luxury that was often eclipsed by the most immediate and pressing need to survive. Many of our participants were forced to choose on a daily basis between communication and sending money back home to family. They were in the devastating position of having to sacrifice ways of articulating their love and care to their families in order to enact their love and care through economic caretaking responsibilities. Children of migrant parents expressed the difficulty of recognising that it was only possible to sustain their physical well-being through the absence of articulated communications of care, to see that care was being enacted through silence and absence.

Another example of this was found in the barber shop in Johannesburg (Chapter 7), where a key way for migrants from the DRC to communicate with family back home was to share resources with others, including transient and infrequent contacts. In this case, the creation of a new family-like support network in South Africa enabled access to digital kinning (Baldassar, Wilding and Worrell 2020) with family back home. Maintenance of the family of origin and communication with them was made possible only through the creation of a 'new family' in the destination country; conversely, the creation of the new family was necessitated by the absence of the family of origin. In general, the configurations of care among these DRC migrants were often a product of the need to re-create a sense of belonging and home not available to them in the country to which they had migrated, because of prejudice and exclusion in South Africa, and because they were unlikely ever to return to the DRC. Yet simultaneously, these new substitute families were themselves a resource in the maintenance of the family back home (when there was any contact with family in the DRC). While the need for new families was itself a product of migration, it was also an important solution to some of the problems of migration.

Many participants mentioned examples of the complexity of communicating care via digital technology. Participants described how silence performs its own narrative in these moments, and how the absence of communication is often a way of showing care. Migrants who struggle financially, emotionally, physically and socially often seek to protect their families from their experience, and protect themselves from disappointment, guilt and loss (Baldassar 2007). Silence is a way of attending to the obligation and expectation that is the migrant's burden, and it is deployed in moments when the stark reality may be unbearable for family back home to witness (Sampaio 2020). In this way, through silence, migrants communicate love. And, through silence, their families provide support when the details and difficulties of daily life at home are smoothed over in conversation, and connection rests more on imagined forms of co-presence (Baldassar 2008), rather than the untidy glue of intimacy that is a product of shared realities.

Another ambiguity revealed by the participants was the paradox of presence. Many studies of technology and transnational migration have explored the conditions by which different types of co-presence are achieved (Baldassar 2008; Madianou and Miller 2013a). Can presence be achieved through language? Written text? The spoken word? Mutual gaze? Virtual and proxy forms of embodiment? We were curious about the contested nature and meaning of presence for our participants.

In many cases, migrants spoke of the joy of visits back home, and of how difficult it was not to see family in person for years at a time. For them, technology was often used as a bridge between visits, a simulacrum of presence that stood in for the 'real thing' (Baldassar 2023). In some cases, especially for better-resourced individuals, presence was achieved through a co-construction of activities via video calls, which include eye contact, spoken conversation, and co-ordination of tasks and rituals (see Madianou 2016; Madianou and Miller 2013a, 2013b). Many of the participants described the establishment of a family WhatsApp group and daily check-ins as a form of co-presence in which they participated in the activities of family life while being physically distant from that family, as Baldassar et al. (2016) also found. This was not always possible, and sometimes it was not enough. The children of migrant parents were saddened by the absence of physical presence (as the presence of love and care), and parents who lived far away from their children, especially in the case of Zimbabwean migrants, spoke of the pain of not being physically close to their children, despite the fact that their economic labour enabled these children's well-being and survival. In a sense, their economic labour was a form of love that was nevertheless experienced by parents and children alike as a poor substitute for embodied presence.

The nature of presence is complex, subjective, personal and transient. Some tasks cannot be achieved in the absence of embodied presence. Physically caring for elderly parents or young infants, providing a shoulder to cry on or a hand to hold are acts that require bodies, and there are many moments in which digital and virtual forms of co-presence fall short. Presence, too, is negotiated and in many ways relies on threshold economic conditions that facilitate in-person or digital intimacy. Digital co-presence is interdependent with the material conditions of economic, political, spatio-temporal and social contexts (Madianou and Miller 2013a, 2013b) – these, more than anything, became a focal point for the issues of digital access and digital justice around which our findings cohered, and whose intersections form the basis of the lived realities of African migrants in, into and from South Africa.

Through the often-heartfelt reflections and reporting of our research team, many of whom identify with or belong to the groups they researched, we have attempted to untangle some of the complexities, in particular the ambivalence, inherent in the migrant experience (Bakewell 2008; Boccagni and Kivisto 2019). The recognition of paradox guided the co-construction of meaning-making and interpretation in our data and findings, and paradox functions as a liminal space within which the African migrant experience may be theorised and conceptualised more fully. Simultaneously, in a way that extends the existing literature, this complex and contested terrain provided fertile ground for the anchoring of commonalities regarding digital access and digital justice.

As social scientists from different professional backgrounds, we came into this research with an interest in family relationships and patterns of care among migrant families. Through this process, we have acknowledged the profound intersections of political, social, economic, ecological and geographical forces that are so deeply constitutive of the intimacy that weaves together families and their patterns of care. Thus, while our research began with the aim of studying migrant families, we came to recognise the enormous impact of the structural forces within which these family arrangements are played out. A critical study of migration must account for the economic conditions constitutive of the migrant experience and for the possibilities of care and presence in migrant families. It must also, however, study the political forces that preclude so many individuals from being able to perform their familial responsibilities competently in their countries of origin, and that make migration the only way to sustain the family unit. A critical study of migration must also examine the social conditions in which migration is enacted, through which migrants re-create small communities of belonging, share resources and maintain their past through their (re-)creation of a present. It must look squarely at the xenophobia, hatred, suspicion and rage to which migrants are vulnerable on a daily basis. It must acknowledge the longing for home that accompanies migrants and is a hallmark of their experience. We must also continue to study the psychology of migration, the struggle for identity, the trauma of displacement, but within rather than against these larger forces. We must examine all of these, and more, as mutually constituting the migrant experience and the experience of the families who stay behind.

Migration is a complex and multifaceted process. Clearly, more deeply interdisciplinary work is urgently needed to bridge the multiple intersecting tensions and ambiguities of the migration experience and to privilege the voices of migrants (Eriksson 2020) without erasing the conditions of their emergence (Brettell and Hollifield 2020), and to map the detail and complexity of their lived experiences onto the larger structural forces that shape and are shaped by them (De Haas 2021).

Finally, we must acknowledge the Africanness of the experiences of our participants, the way that the continent and its colonial history have imposed lingering inequities that shape the present-day concerns of daily life (Fechner 2022; Mushonga and Dzingirai 2022). We need to look not only, or not simply, at colonialism, but also at the interlocking issues of inequities in wealth, tribalism, evolution, war, resources, and other historical and contextual factors that have shaped the continent, its national borders, and its ethnicities and regions. The stories in this book highlight the depth of difference between migrants and their families within and between countries, some of the drivers of their migration, commonalities in and discrepancies between their experiences, and the losses and the challenges they face. Countries produce economic refugees, political exiles, foreign-national students, and many other forms of migrants and their associated practices and identities. The differences between migrants of different countries, between the migrants inside South Africa, and between those coming into South Africa and those leaving South Africa are stark and are representative of racialised and nationalised identities and their underlying socio-economic histories and conditions, as described by Inocent Moyo and Sabelo J. Ndlovu-Gatsheni (2022).

As noted above, what emerges most eloquently from our data, given our focus on information communication technologies (ICTs) and their use by migrants and their families, is the matter of what Richard Heeks (2022) describes as digital access and digital justice. Again, paradoxes are expressed profoundly in the context of these unequal divides. Digital access, which is slowly becoming a fundamental need and right, a product of what some term the Fourth Industrial Revolution, is interdependent with, and limited and bounded by, access to different kinds of resources, which are themselves contested and unevenly distributed in South Africa. Digital justice, the restitution of data-driven inequities, must become a matter of action in developing countries that seek to increase accessibility for, and opportunities to, all citizens and inhabitants. The significance of these emerging concerns of a technologised, 'digital by default' global society was highlighted profoundly in our study, suggesting that these are in fact new markers and measures of equitability in South Africa.

At the same time, we must critically interrogate the meaning of technology-driven communication in patterns of transnational care. Technology provides meaningful advantages in enacting family obligations across space and time, but it also brings to the fore the limitations of certain forms of presence and the possibilities of silence. It is exhilarating to imagine that technology can allow us to bridge the physical spaces between our embodied selves; nevertheless, the alienation and ambivalence expressed by many migrants about the use of technology suggest an impersonal aspect, indeed a ruthlessness, about technology that is not always apprehended in relation to embodiment, physical contact and proximity. Technology can serve as a form of presence, but what are the conditions that best safeguard and deliver this presence? What is potentially lost in the constant possibility of communication? And what is erased in the performance of a kind of connection that is measured in data and currency? What is potentially gained through online communication that is perhaps more difficult to share in person? For many participants in our research, the intimacy that is a by-product of embodied co-presence is often forgone and replaced with idealised versions of reality, creating an absence at the heart of the digital connection. And, yet, all participants appreciated the opportunity to be co-present that the technology afforded them when physical proximity was unattainable.

These and other concerns must inform further studies of migration, in particular of the Global South, and we must be cognisant of the experiences that are indigenous to the African continent and to African migrants in, into and from South Africa.

REFERENCES

Bakewell, Oliver. 2008. ' "Keeping Them in Their Place": The Ambivalent Relationship between Development and Migration in Africa'. *Third World Quarterly* 29, no. 7: 1341–1358. https://doi.org/10.1080/01436590802386492.

Baldassar, Loretta. 2007. 'Transnational Families and the Provision of Moral and Emotional Support: The Relationship between Truth and Distance'. *Identities* 14, no. 4: 385–409. https://doi.org/10.1080/10702890701578423.

Baldassar, Loretta. 2008. 'Missing Kin and Longing to Be Together: Emotions and the Construction of Co-presence in Transnational Relationships'. *Journal of Intercultural Studies* 29, no. 3 (Special Issue: Transnational Families – Emotions and Belonging): 247–266. https://doi.org/10.1080/07256860802169196.

Baldassar, Loretta. 2023. 'Migrant Visits over Time: Ethnographic Returning and the Technological Turn'. *Global Networks* 23, no. 1: 160–173. https://doi.org/10.1111/glob.12393.

Baldassar, Loretta, Mihaela Nedelcu, Laura Merla and Raelene Wilding. 2016. 'ICT-Based Co-presence in Transnational Families and Communities: Challenging the Premise of Face-to-Face Proximity in Sustaining Relationships'. *Global Networks* 16, no. 2: 133–144. https://doi.org/10.1111/glob.12108.

Baldassar, Loretta, Raelene Wilding and Shane Worrell. 2020. 'Elderly Migrants, Digital Kinning and Digital Home Making across Time and Distance'. In *Ways of Home Making in Care for Later Life,* edited by Bernike Pasveer, Oddgeir Synnes and Ingunn Moser, 41–63. London: Springer Nature.

Boccagni, Paolo and Peter Kivisto. 2019. 'Introduction: Ambivalence and the Social Processes of Immigrant Inclusion'. *International Journal of Comparative Sociology* 60, nos 1–2: 3–13. https://doi.org/10.1177/0020715219835886.

Brettell, Caroline B. and James F. Hollifield, eds. 2020. *Migration Theory: Talking across Disciplines.* Oxford: Routledge.

De Haas, Hein. 2021. 'A Theory of Migration: The Aspirations–Capabilities Framework'. *Comparative Migration Studies* 9, no. 8. https://doi.org/10.1186/s40878-020-00210-4.

Eriksson, Erik. 2020. 'The Naked Truth about Migrants' Views: User Involvement as Radical Knowledge Production'. *Nordic Social Work Research* 10, no. 4: 302–316. https://doi.org/10.1080/2156857X.2018.1547786.

Fechner, Heiner. 2022. 'Legal Segmentation and Early Colonialism in Sub-Saharan Africa: Informality and the Colonial Exploitative Legal Employment Standard'. *International Labour Review* 161, no. 4: 615–634. https://doi.org/10.1111/ilr.12350.

Heeks, Richard. 2022. 'Digital Inequality beyond the Digital Divide: Conceptualizing Adverse Digital Incorporation in the Global South'. *Information Technology for Development* 28, no. 4: 688–704. https://doi.org/10.1080/02681102.2022.2068492.

Jansen, Jonathan and Cyrill Walters, eds. 2020. *Fault Lines: A Primer on Race, Science and Society.* Stellenbosch: SUN Press. https://doi.org/doi:10.18820/9781928480495.

Madianou, Mirca. 2016. 'Ambient Co-presence: Transnational Family Practices in Polymedia Environments'. *Global Networks* 16, no. 2: 183–201. https://doi.org/10.1111/glob.12105.

Madianou, Mirca and Daniel Miller. 2013a. *Migration and New Media: Transnational Families and Polymedia*. London: Routledge.

Madianou, Mirca and Daniel Miller. 2013b. 'Polymedia: Towards a New Theory of Digital Media in Interpersonal Communication'. *International Journal of Cultural Studies* 16, no. 2: 169–187. https://doi.org/10.1177/1367877912452486.

Moyo, Inocent and Sabelo J. Ndlovu-Gatsheni, eds. 2022. *The Paradox of Planetary Human Entanglements: Challenges of Living Together*. London: Routledge. https://doi.org/10.4324/9781003319580.

Mtotywa, Matolwandile M., Smilo P. Manqele, Modjadji A. Seabi, Nontando Mthethwa and Mankodi Moitse. 2022. 'Barriers to Effectively Leveraging Opportunities within the Fourth Industrial Revolution in South Africa'. *African Journal of Development Studies* 2022, no. si2 (1 May): 213–236. https://doi.org/10.31920/2634-3649/2022/sin1a10.

Mushonga, Rufaro H. and Vupenyu Dzingirai. 2022. '"Becoming a Somebody": Mobility, Patronage and Reconfiguration of Transactional Sexual Relationships in Postcolonial Africa'. *Anthropology Southern Africa* 45, no. 1: 1–15. https://doi.org/10.1080/23323256.2021.1978851.

Sampaio, Dora. 2020. 'Caring by Silence: How (Un)documented Brazilian Migrants Enact Silence as a Care Practice for Aging Parents'. *Journal of Intergenerational Relationships* 18, no. 3: 281–300. https://doi.org/10.1080/15350770.2020.1787038.

CONTRIBUTORS

Loretta Baldassar is professor of anthropology and sociology and director of the Social Ageing (SAGE) Futures Lab at Edith Cowan University, Perth, Western Australia. Loretta has published extensively in the field of migration, focusing especially on the role of ICTs in maintaining relationships of care in transnational families. She is vice-president of the International Sociological Association Migration Research Committee and a regional editor for the journal *Global Networks*. She is one of Australia's leading social scientists and an internationally recognised leader in migration and diversity studies. In 2020, 2021 and 2022 she was named Australian Research Field Leader in Migration Studies (Social Sciences) and in 2021 she was also named Research Field Leader in Ethnic and Cultural Studies (Humanities, Arts and Literature).

Thembelihle Coka completed a Master's degree in research psychology in the Department of Psychology, University of the Witwatersrand, in 2021. She works for a non-governmental organisation in Johannesburg as a bursary support officer.

Glory Kabaghe worked at the MAC-Communicable Diseases Action Centre at the College of Medicine in Blantyre, Malawi, at the time of the research. She holds a Master of Science degree in community health nursing and is passionate about community health programme implementation and research to help promote the health and well-being of vulnerable populations in various communities.

Sonto Madonsela acted as manager of this project as part of her National Research Foundation internship in the Department of Psychology at the University of the Witwatersrand. She is currently a PhD candidate in the Department of Paediatrics and Child Health at the same university. Her Master's dissertation, 'Mobile Health Services for Adolescent Mental Health', examined factors that act as barriers to as well as facilitators for the implementation and use of mental health services in lower-middle-income countries. Her other interests include health equity, access to care, and social determinants of health. She works as a research assistant in the School of Human and Community Development.

Lactricia Maja completed her Master's degree in research psychology in the Department of Psychology, University of the Witwatersrand, in 2021. She worked at the Aurum Institute in Parktown, Johannesburg, and also served as a junior researcher for DSI-HSRC. She is currently busy with her PhD in public health at the University of Cape Town.

Maria C. Marchetti-Mercer is an Italian-born clinical psychologist and family therapist who emigrated to South Africa as a child. She was the head of the Psychology Department at the University of Pretoria for ten years before moving to the University of the Witwatersrand in 2012, where she served as the head of the School of Human and Community Development for five years. She is now a professor in the Department of Psychology at the University of the Witwatersrand. She is a C1-rated National Research Foundation scientist and her current area of research is the impact of emigration on South African families. She is a fellow of the Oxford Symposium of School-Based Family Counselling and a member of their Refugee and Migrant team. In 2008, she received an award from the Institute for School-Based Family Counselling and the University of San Francisco Center for Child and Family Development for outstanding international contributions to school-based family counselling. She has recently received the Order of the Star of Italy from the Italian government in recognition of her academic work.

Risuna Mathebula is originally from Giyani in Limpopo and moved to Soweto as a young child. She completed her Master's degree in community-based counselling psychology in the Department of Psychology, University of the Witwatersrand, in 2022. She is currently working as a counselling psychologist at Westville Girls High School in Durban.

Siko Moyo is originally from Bulawayo in Zimbabwe, and still has family living there. He came South Africa to pursue his studies and has completed his Master's degree in community-based counselling psychology in the Department of Psychology, University of the Witwatersrand, in 2022. He is now pursuing his PhD studies at the same university.

Esther Price was a clinical psychologist and lecturer in the Department of Psychology, University of the Witwatersrand, at the time of the writing of this book. She lived in Malawi for several years. She now works with FVB Psychologists in Mississauga, Ontario, in Canada. Her work includes research on bullying and peer victimisation, as well as trauma and post-traumatic stress.

Daniella Rafaely is a lecturer in the Department of Psychology at the University of the Witwatersrand. She uses an ethnomethodological and discursive approach to the study of social order, social categories and common-sense knowledge. Her research focuses on a range of settings in order to examine the methods by which morality is reproduced as a social institution in everyday interactions.

Leslie Swartz is a clinical psychologist and professor in the Department of Psychology at Stellenbosch University. He holds a PhD in psychology from the University of Cape Town and a PhD in English from Stellenbosch University. He has published widely in the fields of mental health and disability studies, and is actively involved in developing academic writing skills in Africa. He has received a number of awards for his work, including the Academy of Science of South Africa Gold Medal for Science-for-Society. He is an A-rated National Research Foundation scientist. He was founding editor-in-chief of the *African Journal of Disability* and is currently editor-in-chief of the *South African Journal of Science* and of the *Scandinavian Journal of Disability Research*. His most recent book, *How I Lost My Mother* (2021, Wits University Press), deals with care issues in the southern African context. His family immigrated to South Africa from Zimbabwe (then Rhodesia) when he was a child.

Ajwang' Warria was a senior lecturer in the Department of Social Work at the University of the Witwatersrand at the time of the research project documented in this book, and moved to the University of Calgary, in Canada, in 2022. She is originally from Kenya and lived in South Africa from 2002 to 2022. Her research has focused mainly on migration, child protection and intervention research.

INDEX

Printed and bound by CPI Group (UK) Ltd, Croydon, CR0 4YY

13/04/2025

14656582-0007